PRAISE FOR
BRANDED

"A sexy hero, a sassy heroine, and a compelling story line, *Branded* is all that and more—I loved it!"
—Lorelei James, *New York Times* bestselling author of *Unwound*

"Secrets, sins, and spurs—Laura Wright's Cavanaugh brothers will brand your heart!"
—Skye Jordan, *New York Times* bestselling author of *Reckless*

"Saddle up for a sexy and thrilling ride! Laura Wright's cowboys are sinfully hot."
—Elisabeth Naughton, *New York Times* bestselling author of *Stolen Chances*

"Deadly secrets, explosive sex, four brothers in a fight over a sprawling Texas ranch. . . . Ms. Wright has penned ⌐al page-turner."
—Kaki Warner, bestselling author of *Behind His Blue Eyes*

⌐r a sexy, intensely emotional ride with cow-ys that put the 'wild' in Wild West. Laura Wright never disappoints!"
—Alexandra Ivy, *New York Times* bestselling author of *Hunt the Darkness*

continued . . .

D0448436

Also by Laura Wright

Mark of the Vampire Series

Eternal Hunger
Eternal Kiss
Eternal Blood
(A Penguin Special)
Eternal Captive
Eternal Beast
Eternal Beauty
(A Penguin Special)
Eternal Demon
Eternal Sin

BRANDED

THE CAVANAUGH BROTHERS

Laura Wright

A SIGNET ECLIPSE BOOK

SIGNET ECLIPSE
Published by the Penguin Group
Penguin Group (USA) LLC, 375 Hudson Street,
New York, New York 10014

USA | Canada | UK | Ireland | Australia | New Zealand | India | South Africa | China
penguin.com
A Penguin Random House Company

First published by Signet Eclipse, an imprint of New American Library,
a division of Penguin Group (USA) LLC

First Printing, June 2014

Copyright © Laura Wright, 2014

SIGNET ECLIPSE and logo are trademarks of Penguin Group (USA) LLC.

ISBN 978-0-451-46487-3

Printed in the United States of America
10 9 8 7 6 5 4 3 2

To you, my readers.
Save a horse and ride a cowboy.

Diary of Cassandra Cavanaugh

Dear Diary,

Today it took five dollars to get the cowboys to look the other way when Mac and I saddled up one of Daddy's prize cow horses. They're so darn mean and greedy. And it's my birthday too! Thirteen years old, people! So, you know, shouldn't I at least get a discount from them boys or something? Jeez. Mac came through, though. She always does. She gave them a piece of her mind, and lots of curse words, too. But they wouldn't budge, so she flipped them her middle finger, paid them off, and told me happy birthday.

She's so funny and crazy.

Mac's been wanting to give Mrs. Lincoln a spin forever. Well, ever since the gray mare came to the Triple C, anyway. Between you and me, I think Mrs. L's a little too much horse for Mac to handle. But o'course Mac doesn't think so. She's as hardheaded as they come. She says what she wants and does what she wants, and she ain't afraid of anything.

I wish I could be like that.

I wish I could be tough.

Mac and me rode out to the Hidey Hole o'course. We had lunch and swam a little bit; then we sunbathed. I'm a total sun worshipper. I wish it were sunshine all day and night and never dark. I don't like the dark. Mac wanted to just wear our underwear and bras while we lay out, but I said no way. The Hidey Hole was always top secret, real hidden down in the gulch, but lately I've been getting the feeling someone might know about it. And I was right!

Not an hour and a half into our fun, my oldest brother, Deacon, found us. He was in a mood, too. He's seventeen and pretty much has his own life. He hates having to come look for me. 'Course, so do James and Cole. But when Mama says move, we all move. Anyway, Deac barked at me to get home and get ready for my birthday party. I told him I'd come along soon. The thing wasn't for another five hours, for goodness' sake! But he wouldn't have any of that. He was in a real snit. Bossy as hell. Which, o'course pissed Mac off to no end. She gave it to him good. She sounded like the cowboys when they're working cattle. Definitely R rated! And Deacon hates it. He thinks Mac is a bad influence.

I don't know if I'm right or wrong, but lately, I

get the feeling that Mac might have a crush on Deac. Not that she doesn't tell him to take a hike in her colorful way and all, but lately, when she does it, her cheeks go all red. And her blue eyes get all shiny like gemstones. She also plays with her hair, wraps it around her finger into a long brown snake. I don't think she knows she's doing it.

Maybe I should tell her?

Ugh, I dunno.

I don't want her to be mad at me. She's my best friend, but she's also like my sister. And my family is like her family. All she's got at home is her pops, and he ain't nothing to sing songs about in the parenting department, if you know what I mean.

Maybe I can go roundabout with it? Talk about all the girls who call our house wanting to speak to Deacon during dinnertime and see how Mac reacts? Yeah, that sounds good. I'll know if she's jealous or not. But, Lord, what do I do if she is?

I'll write again tomorrow and let you know what happens. Wish me luck!

Cass

One

The glass doors slid open and Deacon Cavanaugh walked out onto the roof of his thirty-story office building. Sunlight blazed down, comingling with the saunalike air to form a potent cocktail of sweat and irritation. The heat of a Texas summer seemed to hit the moment the sky faded from black to gray, and by seven a.m. it was a living thing.

"I've rescheduled your meetings for the rest of the week, sir."

Falling into step beside him, his executive assistant, Sheridan O'Neil, handed off his briefcase, iPad, and business smartphone to the helicopter pilot.

"Good," Deacon told her, heading for the black chopper, the platinum *Cavanaugh Group* painted on the side winking in the shocking light of the sun. "And Angus Breyer?"

"I have no confirmation at this time," she said. Which was code for there was a potential problem, Deacon mused. His assistant was nothing if not meticulously thorough.

Deacon stopped and turned to regard her. Petite, dressed impeccably, sleek auburn hair pulled back in a perfect bun to reveal a stunningly pretty face, Sheridan O'Neil made many of the men in his office forget their names when she walked by. But it was her brains, her guts, her instincts, and her refusal to take any shit that made Deacon respect her. In fact, it had made him hire her right out of business school. When he'd interviewed her, the ink on her diploma had barely dried. But despite her inexperience, her unabashed confidence in proclaiming that she wanted to be him in ten years hit his gut with a *hell yes, this is the one I should hire*. Forget ten years. Deacon was betting she'd achieve her goal in seven.

"What's the problem, Sheridan?" he asked her.

She released a breath. "I attempted to move Mr. Breyer to next week, but he's refused. As you requested, I told no one where you're going or why." Her steely gray gaze grew thoughtful. "Sir, if you would just let me explain to the clients—"

"No."

"Sir."

Deacon's voice turned to ice. "I'll be back on Friday by five, Sheridan."

She nodded. "Of course, sir."

She followed him toward the waiting chopper.

"Should I ask Ms. Monroe if she's free to accompany you on Friday?"

Only the mildest strain of interest moved through him at the mention of Pamela Monroe. Dallas's hottest fashion designer had been his go-to for functions lately. She was beautiful, cultured, and uncomplicated. But in the past few months, he'd been starting to question her loyalty as certain members of the press had begun showing up whenever they went out.

"Not yet," he said.

"Mr. Breyer is bringing his . . . date—" Sheridan stumbled. "And he's more comfortable when you bring one as well."

A slash of a grin hit Deacon's mouth. "What did you wish to call the woman, Sheridan?"

She lifted her chin, her gaze steady. "His daughter, sir."

Deacon chuckled. His assistant could always be counted on for the truth. "I'll let you know in the next few days if I require Pamela."

He stepped into the chopper and nodded at the company's pilot. "I'm taking her, Ty. Bell's been instructed to deliver another if you need it."

The pilot gave him a quick salute. "Very good, sir."

"Mr. Cavanaugh?"

Deacon turned and lifted an eyebrow at his assistant, who was now just outside the chopper's door. "What is it, Sheridan?"

Her normally severe gaze softened imperceptibly. "I'm sorry about your father."

Deacon waited for a whisper of grief to move through him, but there was nothing. "Thank you, Sheridan."

After a quick nod, she turned and headed for the glass doors. Deacon placed his headphones on, stabbed at the starter button, and checked his gauges. Overhead, the rotor blades began to turn.

He'd been to River Black nearly once a month over the past six years. In the first two, he'd attempted to buy the Triple C from his father. When that hadn't worked, he'd tried blackmailing the man. But still Everett Cavanaugh wouldn't sell to him. The idea of buying up land in and around the ranch soon followed. Deacon thought that if he couldn't take down the Triple C through ownership and subsequent neglect and/or bulldozing the property to the ground, then he'd do it the old-fashioned way.

Competition.

His ranch would offer lower prices to the cattle buyers, better wages and benefits to the hands, and the best soil, grass, and grain for the healthiest cattle around. Only problem was, the place wasn't near being done. Even with all the overtime he was paying, his ranch still wasn't going to be up and running for at least a year.

Revenge would have to wait.

Or so he'd thought.

"Tower, this is Deacon Cavanaugh. The *Long Horn* is cleared for departure. Confirm, over."

"Roger that, *Long Horn*. You are clear. Have a good flight, sir."

"Copy, Tower."

As the engine hummed beneath him, Deacon pulled up on the collective and rose swiftly into the air. For ten years, he'd dreamed of seeing the Triple C Ranch destroyed. And now, with his father's death, he would finally have his goal realized.

Gripping the stick, he sent the chopper forward, leaving the glass and metal world of Cavanaugh Towers for the unpredictable, rural beauty of the childhood home he planned to destroy.

Mac thundered across the earth on Gypsy, the black overo gelding who didn't much enjoy working cows but lived for speed. Especially when a mare was snorting at his heels.

"Is the tractor already there?" Mac called over her shoulder to Blue.

Her second in command, best friend, and the one cowboy on the ranch who seemed to share her brain in how things should be run brought his red roan, Barbarella, up beside her.

"Should be," he said, his dusty white Stetson casting a shadow over half his Hollywood-handsome face.

"Any idea how long she's been stuck?" Mac called as the hot wind lashed over her skin.

"Overnight, most like."

"How deep?"

"With the amount of rain we got last night, I can't imagine it's more than a couple feet."

In all the years she'd been doing this ride and rescue, she'd prayed the cow would still be breathing by the time she got there. Never had she prayed for a speedy excavation. Slow and steady was the way to keep an animal calm and intact, but there wasn't a shitload of time.

"Of all the days for this to happen," she called over the wind.

Blue turned and flashed her a broad grin, his striking eyes matching the perfect, summer-blue sky. "Ranch life don't stop for a funeral, Mac. Not even for Everett's."

Just the mention of Everett Cavanaugh, her mentor, friend, savior, and damn, Cass's father, made Mac's gut twist painfully. He was gone. From the ranch and from her life. Shoot, they were all without a patriarch now, the Triple C's future in the hands of lawyers. God only knew what that would mean for her and for Blue. For everyone in River Black who loved the Triple C, who called it home, and all those who counted on it for their livelihood.

"Giddyap, Gyps!" she called, giving her horse a kick as she spotted the watering hole in the distance.

She had just two hours to get the cow freed and get herself to the church. And somewhere in there, a shower needed to be had. She wasn't showing up to Everett's funeral stinking to high heaven; that was certain.

With Blue just a fox length behind her, Mac raced toward the hole and the groaning cow. When she got there and reined in her horse next to the promised tractor, she tipped her hat back and eyed the situation. The freshly dug trench was deep and lined with a wood ramp. Frank had done a damn fine job, she thought. And he'd done it fast. Maybe the cowboy had been looking at his watch, too.

She nodded her approval to the muddy eighteen-year-old hand as Blue's horse snorted and jerked her head from the abrupt change of pace. "Leaving us the best part, eh, Frank," she said, slipping from the saddle with a grin.

The cowboy lifted his head and flashed her some straight, white teeth. "I know you appreciate working the hind end, foreman."

"Better than actually being the hind end, Frank," Mac shot back before slipping on her gloves and walking into the thick, black muck.

"She got you there, cowboy." Blue chuckled as

he grabbed the strap from the cab of the tractor and tossed it to Mac.

"Get up on the Kioti, Frank," Mac called to the cowboy. "This poor girl's looking panicky, and we got a funeral to go to. I'd at least like to change my boots before I head to the church."

As Frank climbed up onto the tractor, Blue and Mac worked with the cargo strap, sliding it down the cow's back to her rump. While Mac held it in place, whispering encouragement to the cow, Blue attached both sides of the strap to the tractor.

"All right," Mac called. "Go slow and gentle, Frank. She's not all that deep, but even so, the suction's going to put a lot of pressure on her legs."

As Blue moved around the cow's rear, Mac joined him. When Frank started the tractor forward, the two of them pushed. A deep wail sounded from the cow, followed by a sucking sound as she tried to pull her feet out of the muck.

"Come on, girl," Mac uttered, leaning in, digging her boots in further, using her shoulder to push the cow's hind end.

Blue grunted beside her. "Give it a little more gas, Frank!" he called out. His eyes connected with Mac's. "On three, Mac, okay?"

She nodded. "Let's do it."

"One. Two. Push fucking hard."

With every ounce of strength she had in her, Mac pushed against heavily muscled cow flesh.

Her skin tightened around her muscles, and her breath rushed out of her lungs. She clamped her eyes shut and gritted her teeth, hoping that would give her just a little extra power. It seemed like hours, but truly it was only seconds before the sucking sounds of hooves pulling from mud rent the air. Hot damn! The cow found her purchase, and groaning, she clambered onto the wood boards. Maybe the old gal darted away too fast and Mac wasn't expecting it. Or maybe Mac's boots were just too deeply embedded in the mud. Or, shit, maybe she was thinking about how she'd never do this with Everett again, this life and death moment that both of them loved so damn much it had bonded them forever.

Whatever the reason, when the cow lurched forward, so did Mac. Knees and palms hitting the wet black earth in a resounding splat.

"She's out!" Frank called from the cab.

"No shit!" Mac called back, laughing in spite of herself, in spite of the thoughts about Everett.

Eyes bright with amusement, Blue extended a muddy hand, and Mac took it and pulled herself up.

"Good thing you have time for a shower," he said, chuckling.

Mac lifted an eyebrow at his clothes caked in mud and sticking to his tall, lean-muscled frame. "Not you. You're all set. Say, why don't you head over to the church right now?"

"Come on, Mac," he drawled, wiping his hands on his jeans as he started out of the mud hole. "I can't go like this."

Mac followed him. "What do you mean? You look downright perfect to me."

"Shit, woman." Standing on high, dry ground now, Blue took off his Stetson, revealing his short black hair. "You know I need a different hat. This one's way too dirty for church."

Mac broke out into another bout of laughter. It felt good to be joking after some hard-won labor. It felt right in this setting, on this day in particular. Everett would approve. Nothing he liked better than the sound of laughter riding on the wind.

Overhead, another sound broke through their laughter and stole their attention. And it wasn't one Everett would think kindly on.

Frank glanced up from tending to the exhausted cow and shaded his eyes. "What the hell's that?"

Mac tilted her face to the sky and the gleaming black helicopter with a name she recognized painted on the side in fancy silver lettering. Instantly, her pulse sped up and her damned heart sank into her shit-caked boots.

"That'd be trouble," she said in a quiet voice.

"With a capital C," Blue agreed, his eyes following the movement of the chopper, too. "Looks like the eldest Cavanaugh has come home to bury his daddy."

"And bury us right along with it," Mac added dryly.

"You think?" Blue asked.

"Hell, yes." As the chopper moved on, heading toward the sizable ranch land Deacon Cavanaugh had bought a few years back, Mac's gaze slid back to Blue. "He's been trying to get his hands on the Triple C since he walked out its gate ten years ago. I'm guessing he thinks this is his big chance."

"But he's got all that property now," Blue observed. "More land than we got here. A house being framed up, the whole thing fenced in for cattle." He shrugged. "Maybe he's over wanting to run the Triple C."

Mac smiled grimly. "I don't think he ever wanted to run this place, Blue."

That had the cowboy looking confused and curious. "Then what? Why would he work so hard and offer so much money for something he didn't want?"

Mac shook her head, dug the tip of her boot into the dirt, into the land she loved. "I don't know. I'm not sure about his reasons. I just know they ain't pure. I tried talking to Everett about it a few times, 'bout why Deacon was pushing him so hard, being such a slick-ass bastard—trying to take over the very home he and James and Cole had all run from as soon as they were able. But he brushed me off, said all his boys had been changed in the head after

Cass was taken, and they weren't thinking right." Mac chewed her lip, shook her head. That explanation had never made sense to her, but she didn't push it. Everett had gone through hell, and if he didn't want to talk about it, that had to be respected.

'Course, that didn't mean she hadn't tried to work it out in her head a few times.

"I always wondered if it was just Deacon's way of doing business," she continued. "How he makes his money. Buying and selling off pieces of other people's dreams and sweat." Her eyes lifted to meet Blue's. "But he could do that anywhere. Why the Triple C?"

Blue was silent for a moment. Granted, the cowboy knew some of the history with Deacon, his father, and the ranch, because Mac had filled him in when the former had started his war with Everett six years ago. But Blue didn't know the particulars of the loss the Cavanaugh boys had endured before they'd left home. He didn't know about the day Cass had been taken or the night Sheriff Hunter had come to their door with the news that her body had been found. He didn't know that her killer was never caught, or about the morning they all sat in the very same church Everett Cavanaugh would be eulogized in today, over a beautiful white casket, their lives changed forever.

But Mac knew. And hells bells, she'd shared that unending grief along with them. Her best friend gone before she'd seen her fourteenth birthday. It wasn't right. For none of them. But neither was taking that grief out on people. Especially family. Especially a man as goodhearted as Everett.

"So you think this is Deacon's big chance?" Blue asked her, his face a mask of seriousness now. "You think he's gonna get his hands on the Triple C?"

"Not if I can help it," Mac uttered tightly.

She watched the helicopter shrink to the size of a dime and then finally disappear behind the mountain. She didn't know what Everett's will was going to say, who he'd left the Triple C to. But she did know that whoever it was, they'd have her standing over them, watching every move they made. Making sure that this land she'd come to love so damn much was taken care of properly.

"Let's drive this cow home to her friends, boys," she called out. Determination coursing through her, she walked over to Gypsy and shoved her boot in the stirrup. "Let's do the job we've been hired on to do, then go pay our last respects to our boss, our friend, and hand-to-God, one of the best men I've ever known, Everett Cavanaugh."

Two

Deacon exited the *Long Horn* and strode across the lawn to the long, metal garage that housed his cars. He was pleased to see that in the six weeks since he'd last been on the property, much had been done to the house and barns. All three were framed in, and as he was flying over, he'd seen fencing around the entire property. Next he'd have his guys get on a foreman's house, working pens, guest cottages, a pool area, and maybe a landing strip. If they kept up this pace, in nine months he'd be spending his weekends in River Black.

He tossed his bags into the back of the custom charcoal Dodge Ram Laramie he'd instructed his staff to have readied and waiting outside. It had been a few months since he'd been behind the wheel of the diesel engine and those stellar three hundred and fifty horses, and damn, he was looking forward to it. No matter how citified he'd become in the past ten years, in his heart and guts, he was one hundred percent country boy.

He slipped the key into the ignition, felt and heard the engine roar to life all around him, then hit the gas. Dust and gravel kicked up behind him as he peeled away, leaving his new, uncomplicated property for the lush, spiteful ranch he'd once called home. The ranch he'd loved, then feared, then despised, then ran from, then tried to take control of. Shit, could this be it? Could the place of death and pain and cruelty finally be leveled to the ground?

The air rushing into the Ram's cabin was sweet and always so achingly familiar. It filled Deacon's nostrils, entered his lungs, and wrapped around his guts, squeezing the hell out of him. That was the thing about River Black—no, about the Triple C. Beauty was plentiful and endearing, but it masked the secret evil that lay beneath all too well and all too easily. Surrounded by spring-fed lakes, rugged mountain crags, and lush, expansive rolling grasslands, the Triple C Ranch sighed with contentment and prospered—even under the weight of a twelve-year-old unsolved abduction and murder and its terrible aftermath.

The dense memory of his little sister, Cass, assaulted him as he passed through the wrought-iron front gates of the Cavanaugh Cattle Company. Granted, the forever-thirteen-year-old girl was always near to his cold heart, her free and gentle spirit propelling him forward, reminding him of the vengeance he sought and the salvation he would soon find. The grand property spread out before him on both sides of the drive. Time had been kind to the Triple C. Fresh paint glistened on the well-kept fencing, the miles of grassland looked thick and fertile, and every structure he passed, or spied in the distance, appeared well appointed and well kept.

His lip lifted in a sneer. How the hell could something that had seen a devastation like Cass's death, then witnessed the subsequent cruelty by two grieving parents who believed their three remaining children to be responsible, blossom over the years? Shouldn't it be rotting out like a Halloween pumpkin come spring? Maybe his mother had been right. Maybe her words to him in the months following Cass's death all those years ago were true. Maybe he and James and Cole had been the true blight on this landscape, and now that they were gone, it could flourish.

Well, he'd see soon enough if that were the case.

About a mile in, Deacon passed the barns, both painted cherry red, both expanded to accommodate big equipment and at least two dozen horses. Farther down, over the grand stretch of fertile pastureland, near the creek, he could just make out the bunkhouse and a decent-sized guest cottage. The hundred-thousand-acre property and forty thousand heads of cattle had to be worth upward of thirteen million, and over the years, Deacon had made one offer after another to his father, near to doubling that sum. But the old man had refused. No doubt, Everett Cavanaugh had known in his sour gut what his eldest child had planned.

Another mile in, Deacon spotted a few cows on the north ridge. They looked peaceful, mouths full of green, no idea their lives were about to change in just a few hours with the reading of a will. It was going to be interesting to see if Everett had left even a blade of grass to Deacon. Not that it mattered, of course. Even if the entire ranch were given to James and Cole, Deacon knew his brothers wanted nothing to do with the place. Both of them were so far removed from River Black now, and from the home that had become a living hell after their sister was taken, Deacon hadn't been certain either one of them was coming. Not until he'd gotten a call from James a few days ago.

As he headed over the rise, the sprawling family ranch house burst into view. Even though Deacon had been to River Black nearly every month for the past six years, he was never welcome on the property, and he looked on it now with fresh eyes. The exterior had been changed to dark gray

stone, and the porch had been redone, but everything else looked exactly the same. Even down to
the hanging baskets of red geraniums his mother
had always had strung across the beams and those
two ancient handmade rocking chairs sitting side
by side out front. It was like stepping back in time,
and Deacon felt his gut clench with pain, then ex-
pand with a strange adolescent warmth. That
house called to him like a lover. A hateful, spiteful
lover with her arms outstretched. He knew her
body well and was more attracted to it than any of
the chrome and glass dwellings he worked and
lived in now. It was a damn shame.

He hit the brakes, stopping the truck a few
hundred yards from the front door. His gaze traveled the landscape, catching on a pair of horses
and their riders coming up over the hill toward
the barn. He wondered momentarily if he knew
either rider. If maybe the cowboy on the left was
James or Cole. But as the pair drew nearer, then
pulled up sharp near the hitching post on the far
side of the barn, Deacon's body stilled. He didn't
know the man in the white Stetson, but he sure as
hell knew the woman. He hadn't seen her for a
year or so, and even then it had been just a quick
pass by in town. But forgetting Mackenzie Byrd,
the foreman of the Triple C, his sister's best friend,
and one of the biggest pains in his teenage ass,
wasn't possible.

Deacon's eyes moved over her. Dressed in a green tank top, blue jeans, and chaps, she was a far cry from the scrawny kid with mud in her hair and the devil in her large blue eyes. The kid who used to give him a verbal beating every time he tried to steer Cass away from that too-tight friendship.

She slid down from her horse and granted Deacon a perfect view of her very fine ass. No, this wasn't a girl. This was a full-grown woman. Tall, tanned, and tight, her lean muscles earned working on the land. Movement to her right drew Deacon's eye, and he observed the broad-shouldered cowboy she was with. Grinning, the man leaned in, his hand finding Mac's shoulder, his fingers dipping dangerously close to the curve of her right breast, and said something near her ear. Whatever it was, it made Mackenzie laugh, her pink, always-wicked mouth kicking up at the corners. Deacon continued to watch the pair, wondering who the man was. No. Wondering who the man was to Mackenzie.

Crossed arms suddenly dropped onto the ledge of his open window, and a gravelly voice he knew all too well broke through the soft sound of the breeze. "Well, well, look what the *Forbes* list dragged in."

Deacon turned and gave the grizzled old cowboy and barn manager a once-over. Same black

Stetson, same deep, wide grin, and skin the color and texture of leather. "Good to see you, Sam."

The shit-eating grin curved upward even further, making the man's brown eyes flash. "Didn't know if you'd be showing up for the funeral, Deac."

A whisper of something dangerously close to grief moved through Deacon, but he shoved it away. "Come on, now. I wouldn't miss it for the world."

"Hope we're talking about paying respects here."

"No one expects respect out of me, Sam. You know that."

The old man's bright eyes dimmed and he clucked his tongue. "Don't like that kinda talk, boy. Don't like it at all."

Deacon laughed, but the sound was hollow as hell. "How you doing, Sam? Gettin' on all right?"

The question seemed to pull the aging cowboy out of his momentary irritation and into a subject he appreciated discussing. "Everything on this old body aches like a sonofabitch."

"Maybe it's time to pack it in and move to the coast, sit on the beach and watch the waves?" Deacon said, then waited a moment, knowing what was coming next.

"Beach and waves?" Sam's disgruntled snort echoed inside the truck. "Shoot." He unfolded himself from the window. "Don't be talking nonsense to me, boy. I'll die in the saddle and you know it."

Deacon nodded, his smile genuine. "Yup. I know it."

"Just like your daddy," he added.

That whisper of grief was back, and this time it threatened to settle inside of him. "That where he died? His butt in the saddle?"

"That's right."

"How romantic."

Tired brown eyes flared with heat. "Don't be a shit, Deac."

"Too late for that, Sam," he tossed back.

"You and Everett had your issues, but he's gone now. Show some respect for the dead or I swear I'll tan your hide. I don't care how old you are."

Deacon released a weighty breath. Wasn't the time or the place to tell one of his father's oldest friends that he hadn't had respect for Everett when he was alive, and he sure as hell wasn't having it for him now, no matter what was whispering through him or what tricks his gut was playing. His attention drifted back to the barn down the way and to the couple who were tying up their horses.

"You ignoring me now, boy?" Sam piped in.

"No. Just observin' things."

He could practically feel Sam's gaze shift toward the barn.

"Things?" the old man drawled. "Or Mac?"

Mac. The name ran across his skin like a feather. "Mac?" he asked, deadpan. "You don't mean Mackenzie Byrd?"

" 'Course I do."

Deacon made like he was squinting. "You sure?"

Sam paused, confused. "What you mean?"

"You sure that's a girl in them jeans and tank top?"

"What the Sam Hill you talking about?" Sam cried. " 'Course that's a girl!"

Deacon shook his head, fighting a grin. It had always been so damn easy to mess with Sam. "Can't tell from here."

"Shit, boy," the old man spluttered. "I'm fixin' to give you a smack upside the head. I can tell that's a girl, and I got cataracts. In fact, I'm pretty sure I could tell that was Mac from space. She's got a figure a man don't forget or look past, if you know what I mean."

He did. He glanced back at Sam and felt the pull of familiarity and home course through him once again. It was a strangely comfortable feeling. One he'd have to watch and keep in check in the days ahead. "You're talking like a dirty old man— you know that?"

"Naw," Sam returned. "Just a man. A man who can still notice a pretty gal."

Deacon turned back to the barn. Pretty didn't

come close to describing how Mackenzie Byrd had turned out. She was more along the lines of "stunning" or "fucking drop-dead gorgeous" if you asked him. But no one had, and he wasn't about to state that fact out loud. Hell, he really shouldn't be thinking it at all.

"She a good foreman?" Deacon asked.

"Best I ever seen," Sam replied. "And you know I seen a few." He sighed. "The girl is tough, smart, and she loves this land. Almost more than Everett did. Takes care of it like it's her lifeblood."

Well, that was damn unfortunate. Despite her wild, pain-in-the-neck ways before Cass's death, Mackenzie had been the one calm in the storm—shit, more like Noah's second coming—afterward. She'd offered herself up as sister and friend to each of them. Trying to get them to talk, to rely on her for comfort. Cole had wanted to, but both James and Deacon thought it was best not to bring her into the secret and shameful hell they were in.

"Where's she livin'?" Deacon asked the cowboy. "Up at the foreman's quarters?"

"Was," Sam answered. "Until a few hours ago, anyway."

That brought Deacon's head around. "What do you mean?"

The cowboy was leaning on the truck now. "She gave it over to your brother. Thought James would want to be near the horses with his work an' all."

Deacon's brow lifted. "James is here?"

The old man nodded. "Got in this mornin'. So all we need is Cole, and the family's back together."

Deacon snorted. "So, where's Mac staying, then? The river cottage?"

"Why you so interested in her?"

"Just curious, is all."

It was Sam's turn to snort. "Yeah, I believe that."

"She with that cowboy?"

"Blue Perez? Nope. Just good friends."

Deacon nodded.

Sam narrowed his eyes, shook his head, even wagged a finger. "Don't be settin' your sights there, Deac. She may've had a crush on you back when she was a girl, but she's a woman now. A ranch foreman. She ain't interested in slicked-back hair, silk ties, French restaurants, or men who run from the very thing she holds most dear."

Heat coiled inside of Deacon, and he asked through tightly gritted teeth, "And what is that?"

"The Triple C Ranch," Sam said without a second's hesitation.

Eyes narrowed, Deacon turned back to watch Mac and the cowboy lead their horses into the barn. He wasn't interested in her. Not in the way Sam was implying. Sure, he thought she was a beautiful woman. But hell, there were a million of those running around. He had one reason for being here, and it had nothing to do with romancing the Triple C's foreman.

"So, where you staying then, boy?" Sam asked him. "That house on your land finished yet?"

"Nope. I'll be bunking up at the main house, I think. Maybe my old room. If it hasn't been turned into a smoker or a sewin' circle or something."

"There's a decent hotel in town," Sam suggested quickly. "That might be a better idea—"

"Don't think so," Deacon cut him off. "Want to be around the family, like you said."

Sam's voice went dangerously soft. "Don't make no trouble here, Deac. I know what you do in the city. How you earn your billions, breakin' up companies and sellin' 'em to the highest bidder. And I know how you play around with all those beautiful, plastic fillies. Don't bring that 'round here. Don't take what doesn't belong to you. Pigs get fat, boy, but hogs get slaughtered."

Deacon turned and lifted one dark eyebrow. "Is that last bit going on Everett's tombstone?"

"Watch yourself," Sam nearly growled. "Goddammit, Deacon. What happened is in the past. Times change. People move on. Everyone's forgotten—"

"No." The humor in Deacon's tone turned to ice. "Not everyone."

Sam's lips thinned. "Well, they should." He let out a heavy breath. "Cass ain't coming back. Everett's gone now, too. I say we all start up fresh and clean."

Deacon didn't answer. What burned inside him, what had burned inside of him for ten long years, wasn't something Sam could ever understand or respect. And truly, it didn't matter. "Service in an hour?" he said.

Sam nodded, his expression grim. "In town. You driving this rig in, or do you want one of the mares saddled for you?" He grinned halfheartedly. "Maybe you've forgotten how to ride, living in the city."

"Like I said, Sam, I haven't forgotten anything." Deacon's gaze returned to the house as his hand palmed the gearshift. "I'll see you at the church."

He didn't wait for a reply. Just thrust the truck into gear and took off.

Mac stood over Everett's casket in the stiflingly hot church on Main and Fifth wearing the charcoal-gray linen dress and black heels she'd bought on the Internet the night her mentor and friend had passed away. Droplets of sweat snaked down her shoulders to her back, making her shift uncomfortably. Behind her, pretty much all two hundred and twenty inhabitants of the small ranching community were assembled, fans at the ready, expressions appropriately grim as they paid their respects to the man who was both their friend and the one who had given many of them a livelihood.

Mac put her hand on the closed casket and released the air she was holding in her lungs—the air she'd seemed to have been holding for three days now. God knew, Everett wasn't a saint, but he'd been so good to her. Hired her on when she barely knew shit about cattle. Promoted her when she learned. And gave her the home and family she'd always coveted when her father passed on.

She eased her hand from the wood. Despite the heat, her palm felt ice-cold and prickly, like she'd lost circulation, and she fisted it at her side as she turned around. Seated in the first pew, Blue and his mom, Elena, who'd been the Triple C's housekeeper for more than ten years, gave Mac a gentle, encouraging smile. She was about to head for the spot between them when her attention was diverted by a tall, good-looking man who had just entered the church. He was glancing around, no doubt searching for his kin in the crowd. Standing somewhere between the casket and the congregation, Mac just stared at him, her heart squeezing painfully in her chest. He'd changed in the ten years since he'd been gone. He'd grown taller certainly, and his body was thick with muscle, but his white blond hair was now cut close to the skull, and he had tattoos peeking out from both the collar and the cuffs of his white shirt. He barely resembled the ragtag cowboy he'd once been. But one thing about Cole Cavanaugh hadn't changed. Those black eyes. Those deep, soulful, penetrating black eyes were still a perfect match to his twin sister's, and just looking at them made Mac's breath catch in her throat and her eyes well with tears.

She'd felt it over the years, the aching loss of her best friend, but it had always seemed removed from her heart somehow. Maybe because the Cavanaugh brothers were no longer around—especially *this* Cavanaugh brother. But now, seeing Cass's eyes in his, Mac felt the pain afresh. She tore her gaze from Cole and made a beeline to her seat in between Blue and his mother. The instant she sat down, the Triple C's housekeeper placed a hand over hers and squeezed. Mac turned and gave the woman a tearful smile.

Elena Perez was a beautiful woman, somewhere around her midfifties, with short jet-black hair and brown eyes that flashed with mischief when she was happy. But it was her warm and caring nature that drew Mac to her, made her feel she could strip off her hard-ass ranch foreman armor and allow herself to be vulnerable once in a while.

Elena may've been hired as a housekeeper and cook, but she was truly a master of all things. She could do anything she set her mind to: cooking and cleaning, sewing, fixing fences, fixing squabbles, doctoring. And all the while, leaving the comforting scent of lemons and barbecue sauce in her wake.

Mac had once thought that Elena would've been the perfect wife for her father—or maybe it was more that Mac had wanted Elena for a mother. But Travis Byrd had been too blind or too chickenshit or too consumed with getting drunk to ask the beautiful housekeeper out on a date.

"You all right, Mac, honey?" Elena asked, leaning in, her expression rife with concern. "You look torn up."

"Just sad," Mac whispered back. "And funerals are the one place cryin's not frowned upon."

Once again, Elena squeezed her hand. It was such a warm, capable hand. "It's just you never cry."

That almost made Mac smile. It was how all of River Black saw her. Impassive, tough. But, boy, she'd cried plenty in her twenty-five years, especially when she found out Cass had died. But a female ranch foreman didn't give in to tears or a soft heart outside her bedroom if she wanted the respect of her cowboys.

"I saw Cole," she whispered. "That's all."

There was a quick, sharp intake of breath from Elena. "Aww, baby girl. I know that must be hard."

Hard didn't even begin to cover it. "He looks so much like her."

"'Spect so. They being twins and all." She lowered her voice even further. "I've seen all them photo albums. That family has powerful genes. Hell, when I saw James a few minutes ago, I thought he was the spittin' image of Everett at that age."

Once again, Mac's heart squeezed. "Where's he sitting?" She'd seen James that morning, offered up her place near the barn, expecting he would probably feel more comfortable being so near the horses with what he did for a living.

"He's in the back, by himself," Elena whispered as several people moved past the casket. "You should've heard some of the hens going on about him when we first got here. You'd think they'd never seen him on television."

That made Mac smile a little. "James was always the flower who attracted all the honeybees. And now that he's a famous horse whisperer, it's probably gotten worse."

"Never seen eyes that color in my life," Elena remarked. "Like them pictures of the ocean on postcards from far off places like Bali or Tahiti."

"Those were his mom's eyes," Mac said, with another lurch of her heart. Seemed it was truly the day of mourning.

Elena continued on as if Mac hadn't said a word. "Only one I haven't seen is Deacon."

A droplet of sweat serpentined down Mac's temple to her cheekbone and jaw.

"Maybe he's not coming," Elena whispered. "Wouldn't miss him after all the crap he's pulled these past few years . . ." Her voice trailed off for a second, then, "Going after the ranch any darn way he could."

The scent of too many floral arraignments pushed into Mac's nostrils. "He's coming. I saw his million-dollar helicopter fly overhead when Blue and I were rescuing the cow earlier."

Elena's eyes widened. "Well, let's hope he behaves himself."

"If he doesn't, he'll have me to deal with," Mac said.

"Don't I know it." Elena smiled warmly at her. "Ranch foreman."

Mac smiled back.

"I wonder if he's got that fancy model girlfriend with him. I always enjoy seeing city folk taking in the country. Complaining about all the meat we eat and manure on their Manolo Blahniks."

Mac gave her a strange look. "How do you know about that? The shoes, I mean."

"Sex and the City," Elena whispered with a shrug. "It's on at night, and I watch it when I can't sleep. From what I've seen in the papers, Deacon's girlfriend looks just like that Samantha."

Reverend McCarron emerged from his private prayer room then and started for his pulpit. The young man who Mac remembered from high school as being one of the biggest bullies around now held a dutifully somber expression. *Deacon's girlfriend.* Lord, those were two words she hadn't heard in a while. Back in the day, her teenage self had hated them somethin' fierce. Back when she'd actually thought Deacon Cavanaugh was the one for her. But those days and adolescent fantasies were long gone. Tucked away in the back of her brain along with the wanting to die her hair pink and being a contestant on *The Price Is Right.* Now, the man with the gleaming black chopper was nothing but a ruthless billionaire who thought he could buy whatever he wanted, even if it wasn't for sale.

"The Lord is righteous in all His ways and kind in all His deeds," Wayne McCarron began, his voice as close to godlike as she'd ever heard him. *"The Lord is near to all who call upon Him, to all who call upon Him in truth. He will fulfill the desires of those who fear Him; He will also hear their cry and will save them. The Lord keeps all who love Him, but all the wicked He will destroy."*

Except for the rustle of a handheld fan or two, the church was still, listening, remembering.

"That was Psalm 145:17–21," Wayne said, then looked out at the congregation and smiled gently.

Odds were, this was the biggest crowd he'd ever had in his three years at the pulpit, and he was wondering how he could manage to keep them, bring them back every Sunday. "Thank you all for coming," he continued. "Everett Cavanaugh was a good man, a good friend and a hard worker. We honor him today and give his soul over to the Lord."

The heat in the church was starting to get to Mac. The fabric of her dress was now completely fused to her skin, and she was feeling slightly light-headed from all the emotion and anxiety over what the future would hold. She wondered if Deacon *was* here, if he'd driven one of his fancy cars into town and was sitting in the back row with James and Cole. She wanted to look. Wanted to take a quick glance over her shoulder and check. She wanted to see what might be lurking in those green eyes of his. Those eyes that had always pinned her and Cass where they stood, then quickly narrowed in suspicion. Grief? Possibility? Was he thinking about Everett at all? Or was the reading of the will afterward his main concern?

"Everett's one thought was this town," Reverend McCarron continued, "keeping us going, keeping us prosperous."

And if she did manage to catch his eye, would she see any of the young man he used to be before he left? Before he and his brothers took off for parts unknown?

Her heart started to pound dramatically inside her chest, and she reached over and grabbed Blue's hand. It was big and dry and familiar, and it instantly made her feel grounded and safe. That was how it was with Blue. Kind of like how it had been with Cass. Best friends, family without the blood, a shoulder to lean on.

"You okay?" he whispered, leaning in. "Your hand feels like ice, and it's a hundred degrees in here."

"I'm fine," she whispered back.

"You look like a damn ghost."

She shook her head. It was all she could do. Even with Blue's hand in hers, her mouth was getting drier by the second, and her breathing had turned shallow. Lord, she needed some air. Something cold to drink and maybe a hard run on Gypsy later. Between Everett and her memories of Cass, the Cavanaughs being home, and Deacon's certain plotting, she had a strange and unwelcome desire to stand up and run out of the church. But she stayed where she was. The cowboys would never let her forget it if she had a panic attack or some other fluttery reaction to what they liked to refer to as *Female Feelin's*. Even if those feelings stemmed from Everett's death.

"Everett's legacy, the Triple C, has brought such prosperity and such peace to this town," the reverend continued. "We will be forever grateful to him." Wayne offered them all his most sympathetic smile. "Everyone in this sanctuary has been helped by the kind heart and generous spirit of Everett Cavanaugh."

"No," came a cold, masculine voice from the back of the church. "Not everyone."

It was a voice Mac knew—knew so deeply within herself that it shocked her heart like a defibrillator, and she dropped Blue's hand. Even after ten years of living without that voice, it still remained crystal clear in her mind.

Around her, the room buzzed with soft, irritated chatter. *Who was that talking out of turn? Interrupting the service? Deacon? That Deacon Cavanaugh?* The prodigal son who had done his level best to buy, blackmail, or bully his way into gaining control of the Triple C?

Yes, Mac wanted to hiss at them. *The very same.*

A slow burn of anger intermingled with the anxiety his voice had created within her. *Good God. The man has no shame.* No matter what had happened in the past between him and Everett, what grievances he held locked up in that soon-to-be stone heart of his, the man he'd once called father deserved this time, deserved to have his friends and work colleagues tell his stories and honor his life. Because for Mac, and for most of the people in River Black, Everett had been nothing but a blessing.

Beside her, Elena leaned in and whispered, "With an attitude as plentiful as his bank account."

Mac turned and glanced over her shoulder. The movement was completely involuntary and was perhaps her grandest mistake ever. She should've kept her eyes forward on the very pious, yet confused, Reverend McCarron. But the draw was too powerful. The moment her gaze hit its mark, the air inside her lungs promptly vanished, along with her heartbeat. She felt the past rush up on one side of her and the longing she'd held captive inside her heart—the longing she'd truly believed was dead and buried—rush up on the other. She'd seen him on the cover of rag mags in the supermarket checkout and a few times in town—from afar, mind you—over the past few years. But those quick glances didn't prepare her for what lived and breathed and took up residence inside the archway of the chapel door.

A cold, calculated expression playing about his rough, chiseled features, Deacon Cavanaugh was six feet four inches of terrifying alpha male, wrapped up in jade-green eyes, thick black hair, and a custom-made, finely tailored navy-blue suit. He fairly oozed money, ire, and obsessive power, and Mac knew that even if she'd wanted to turn away from him in that moment, her body wouldn't allow it.

A lump formed in her throat and she tried to swallow it down with a silent curse. What the hell was this? This heat and anxiety barreling through her. Couldn't be attraction. Hell no. She was done with all that. Had been for years. Must be something akin to pissed off. After all, the suit had just interrupted a goddamn funeral.

Her eyes followed him as he moved down the aisle toward the front of the church. Control and dominance clung to his every movement, making the crowd stare—making Mac's heart beat a violent tattoo inside her ribs. What the hell was he doing?

When he reached the pulpit, he fairly towered over Reverend Wayne, who looked put out by the interruption but was clearly far too intimidated by the man to stand his ground. With a nervous nod, he backed up several feet and stood there with his hands stacked on his gut.

Deacon turned and looked out over the crowd, his eyes as cold as the precious stones they resembled. He knew most of them were aware he'd bought up a sizable piece of land outside town, not to mention that he'd tried like hell to acquire the Triple C before that. And it didn't seem to concern him at all.

"Everett Cavanaugh was good to this town,"

he said in a deep, controlled voice. "No question about it. His success shows in every building, every business, and every home. But his failures were just as impactful. And like his successes, they shouldn't go unobserved."

Beside Mac, Elena gave a tiny gasp. The rest of the room, however, fell silent and still. Clearly captivated by Deacon Cavanaugh's audacity. Even the members of the congregation with fans held them aloft and immobile.

"A town can be built on the destruction of others," he said, his voice near to ice now. "But that kind of foundation ain't strong. It won't last. It can't. I won't allow it."

Without warning, his eyes dropped to the front row, hitting Mac with a dark, quizzical look, which turned her insides lava. *Will you be the one who gets in my way now?* he seemed to be asking.

Damn right, she wanted to shout back at him. But she had no voice. No goddamn voice. Staring up at him, she felt as if she were completely alone—on the bench and inside the church. She felt like a prisoner to his stare and that if he wanted to take something from her, not only would she let him, but she might just be inclined to fall to her knees when she handed it over.

After a few long seconds, he pulled his gaze from hers and settled it back on the crowd again. As Mac regained her mind and chastised herself for shrinking under the weight of that intense look, Deacon continued with his backward eulogizing, undaunted.

"Today you bury Everett Cavanaugh," he said tersely. "Tomorrow I bury everything he's ever worked for."

The words—the threat—pierced the hot, thick air of the church and reverberated off the walls. Where moments ago, the crowd had remained in their seats, riveted, held captive, now they were surging to their feet, hands wringing, fingers pointing, loud, angry words strewn together into some pretty vile threats of their own.

Mac didn't move. She just sat there among the chaos, staring at Deacon, stunned by his calm, cool, unfettered attitude. From behind the pulpit, he touched the brim of his Stetson in an attempt to pretend he was some kind of gentleman, then moved on, down the aisle and out of the church. Leaving the townsfolk of River Black, Texas, to their gnashing of teeth and bitter I-told-you-sos.

Three

"Go to three million. But if he so much as hesitates, end the meeting." Phone to his ear, Deacon entered the house and headed for the living room. He needed a drink and that will read ASAP. "I want the property, Avery, but I want it at that price. When I break it up, I want to triple my investment." He heard a car pulling up outside. Damn, whoever it was had left the church about the same time as he had. "I've got to go. Let me know when you have something."

Deacon had barely ended the call when the front door opened and James strolled in, his expression as unreadable as ever. He did however have his suit jacket off, his white shirtsleeves rolled up, and his top two buttons undone.

Normally, Deacon would've read that as a sign the guy in front of him was ready to do battle, but with James it was hard to tell. His eyes and his expression were utterly impassive.

Everyone knew the middle Cavanaugh brother was a man of few words, kept things locked up nice and tight. Only gave his true self to the wild things he attempted to tame. But only a fool would think those traits were a sign of weakness, and Deacon waited for the inevitable shit storm he was certain was coming.

Settling himself on the arm of a leather chair, James raised one light brown eyebrow at Deacon. "And the point of that was?"

His tone was as calm as his manner. He would've made a damn fine lawyer, if only he hadn't found those horses first.

With an easy shrug, Deacon returned, "I thought it was only fair to give 'em a heads-up."

James nodded. "Full disclosure kinda thing?"

"Exactly."

"I don't believe you, Deac. I think you wanted to wave your asshole flag in front of the entire town." His brow lowered over his ocean-blue eyes. "I believe you wanted everyone in that room to know just how much you despised Everett Cavanaugh."

Deacon's lips thinned. "You didn't expect me to pretend to be sorry he's gone, now did you?"

James shook his head. "No. I wouldn't ask that of any of us. But was it really necessary to share your plans for not only his home, but a ranch that sustains many of the folks—"

The front door burst open, cutting James off. And this time a pissed-off tornado entered. Eyes black as a starless night, expression unabashedly fierce, Cole stalked into the living room. He too had ditched his jacket, and was now wearing just a black T-shirt and jeans. With his closely cropped blond hair and sleeves of ink running down both arms, Deacon's little brother was a complete badass. He'd been that way, or maybe had starting leaning that way, after Sheriff Hunter had told them all he was closing the investigation into Cass's death—that the man they'd searched for all those months on a tip from the girl's best friend didn't exist, that they'd been chasing the desperate imaginings of a grieving girl while the real killer got away. Shit, that news had marked them all, but Cole had turned to fighting both above and underground—wearing his rage on his skin and expressing his anger with his fists.

Looking every bit the champion UFC fighter that he was, Cole narrowed his eyes at Deacon, then casually flipped him off. "At his fucking funeral? Are you drunk or just out of your mind?"

Deacon regarded his youngest brother with cool eyes. "Haven't had a thing. But I wouldn't mind a cold one." He turned to James, lifted his brow. "J?"

"You serious?" James asked.

"Yep." Though he continued to stare at James,

he spoke to the inked-up man standing near the TV. "Hey, Cole, go get us a couple of beers, okay?"

James's eyes flashed with just the tiniest bit of humor.

"What?" Cole said, irritated.

"Yeah, Cole," James said, deadpan. "I think there're a few Coronas on the bottom shelf."

Cole looked from one brother to the other, pissed and confused; then realization dawned, and he flipped off the both of them. "Fuck you. And fuck you. I ain't your little brother no more."

"Come on, boy," Deacon said with an amused drawl. "You'll always be that. No matter how many tattoos you get or how many teeth you knock out."

"What I mean to say is I don't fetch and carry anymore," Cole spat out.

Both Deacon and James stopped talking and just turned to look at him. It was like ten years hadn't come and gone. They were in their house, playing around, picking on Cole. And back then, Cole always caved.

Thirty seconds later, the inked-up fighter, who truly could kick both their asses into next week—*and* at the same time—groaned. "Fine. I see nothing's changed 'round here."

As Cole disappeared into the kitchen, Deacon chuckled and James grinned back at him. Some shit did stay the same, like the bond—no matter how tenuous it seemed—between brothers, and maybe that was good to know. Maybe that was something to hold on to as Deacon moved forward with his plans.

Thirty seconds later Cole reappeared with three sweating bottles. "No Corona. Sam Adams." He shoved one into Deacon's hand first, then James's. "If you don't like it, you can kiss my ass."

"I'm good," Deacon said. "How 'bout you, James?"

The man's nearly aqua eyes were shuttered as he stared at his beer.

"What?" Cole said with only halfhearted irritation now. "Not cold enough for you, J?"

James glanced up. "I think this is Everett's."

For a moment, no one said anything. Just processed where they were and why—maybe for the first time, really. Within Deacon, a battle raged. Good and evil, right and wrong, vengeance and acceptance. And hell, then there were the memories he was being bombarded with every second he was inside this house. Not just the back-and-forth, talking-smack shit he'd just enjoyed for a fucking millisecond with his brothers, but with the sights and sounds and smells he'd once loved so much.

Ah, Cass. Why'd you have to leave us, girl? Leave us all so wrecked . . .

His jaw tight, Deacon raised his bottle. "A toast." To Everett? No. No, he couldn't do that.

"To Cass," he said finally.

Both his brothers stared at him, unblinking.

"Damn, Deac," James said, then brought the beer to his lips and took a healthy swallow.

Cole, on the other hand, looked ready to explode. His face was white and those eyes of his were shark-black. He placed his bottle on the coffee table very carefully. Then he eyed Deacon again. "You want to toast Cass?" He laughed bitterly. "Christ, Deacon. After what you did? After you made that spectacle in the very church we said good-bye to her in?"

"Shit," James muttered before taking another swallow of his beer.

Deacon's heart ripped another inch inside his chest. He hadn't even considered that. Didn't want to consider that.

Cole continued. "And what makes you think you can even make a decision like that—taking down the Triple C, destroying the Triple C, whatever you mean to do—without my say-so, or James's?"

Deacon's eyes slid to his middle brother. He lifted an eyebrow. "You want this place, J?"

James didn't answer, but his aqua eyes were heavy with disgust.

Deacon turned back to Cole. "What about you, Champ? You want to live here? Maybe turn the barn we had so much fun in after Cass got taken into a weight room or something? Switch out the bullwhips and the branding irons for a treadmill and a weight bench?"

"Fuck you, Deacon," Cole uttered.

"Or better yet, make it your summer home. You know, where you return for solace and reflection after you get your face bashed in?"

Cole's nostrils flared. "I don't get my face bashed in. You're thinking of the other guy."

"Enough with the hissy fits," James cut in, placing his finished beer on the table beside the two nearly full bottles. "From both of you."

Deacon heaved a breath. "Listen. I say we just make this easy. If the ranch comes to us, I'll buy you both out. All you have to do is name your price."

"We don't need your money, Deac," James said evenly. "But I'm sure you already know that."

He did. Despite leaving the ranch at an early age, each of the Cavanaugh brothers had managed to not only find success in his chosen field but amass a sizable fortune.

"Then what do you want?" Deacon asked them. "Because I know it ain't the Triple C. You two hate this place as much as I do. Christ, maybe you hate it more."

James shook his head. "I don't know if I hate it enough to bulldoze it to the ground and put an entire town out of work."

"I'm not going to let that happen," Deacon assured them. "I have a ranch of my own to care for not twenty minutes from here. Barns and housing going up as we speak. I'm gonna need as many folks as need jobs. And I'll treat 'em all better, pay 'em better." Lifting his chin, he sniffed. "Shoot, I give 'em one year on my land before they forget the name Everett Cavanaugh altogether."

"Jesus, Deacon." The muscles in James's jaw looked tight enough to snap. "Listen to yourself."

Deacon looked from one man to the other. "What?"

"You are so fucking arrogant," Cole practically snarled. "But then again, you always were."

"No," Deacon corrected indignantly. "That wasn't arrogance, little brother. Not back then anyway. That was raw, hopeful, desperate, livin'-on-a-prayer confidence. But things change, don't they?" His eyes moved between the two of them. "After Cass was buried without no one payin' the price and Everett turned his back on us, and on Mama's prime directive of making us pay for her baby girl's death, this place destroyed every good, worthy, upstanding thing in me—and in the two of you." Nostrils flaring, he dared them. "Tell me I'm wrong. Tell me I'm full of shit for wanting to put an end to this place and all the misery that came with it, and I'll walk away."

For the first time in a long time, James's expression hardened, his eyes, too. He opened his mouth, ready to say something.

But he never got the chance.

Again the front door flew open, and again, a pissed-off force of nature entered. But this time, it was the one Deacon worried about more than any of the others. This one had never listened to him without arguing, never backed down without a fight. This one didn't mind getting dirty—she enjoyed it. Especially when she believed in the cause.

"Deacon Cavanaugh!" Her battle cry rent the air, sending all the male eyes flying to the doorway.

Standing there, hip cocked, in her gray dress and her black heels, those midnight-blue eyes fixed on him, Mackenzie Byrd looked like she wanted to rip his head from his body and feed it to the squirrels. Better yet, use it as a receptacle for nuts come winter.

"You are one coldhearted bastard!" she said, stepping into the room.

Deacon tracked her movement. He barely remembered how she'd looked as a kid. Lots of mud, scraped knees, big eyes. But her attitude—that had stuck with him. She'd been all fireworks and fits. Now, however, he had both to contend with. Beautiful woman and ferocious hellcat.

"Mac," Cole began as she walked up to Deacon, her chin cocked and her eyes tossing off sparks. "I'm real sorry about this."

She shook her head. "Don't. This wasn't your doin'."

"Have something to get off your chest, Mackenzie?" Deacon asked, noticing just how tall she'd become. She was nearly eye to eye with him in those heels.

"I'm trying hard to understand you, Deacon." Her eyes moved over his face. "I'm trying to understand why you'd come to a funeral and act that way." She put a hand up. "Forget for a moment that the man lying in the casket is your daddy."

Deacon frowned. He wouldn't forget that. Ever.

"Why would you choose to express yourself and your anger that way?" she demanded.

"We all wanted to know the answer to that question," Cole ground out.

"Is that right?" Mackenzie said, glancing over her shoulder. "And did you get an answer?"

Cole shook his head. "Nope."

She turned back to Deacon. "So?" She put her hands on her hips and gave him a hard, impatient stare.

Not unlike his connection with his brothers, there was a flicker of need inside of Deacon to connect with Mac, too. The house, this land, all that had been in the good times, it was right powerful. But he wasn't here to reminisce or release the demons inside himself. Shit, he needed those demons. They'd made him rich. And they'd get him the Triple C.

"I don't owe you an explanation, Mackenzie," he said in a tone that he usually reserved for the Cavanaugh Group boardroom.

Her eyes narrowed. "Oh, come on. Don't go all corporate dickhead on me, Deacon Cavanaugh. I helped Cole here pull thorns out of your naked ass that time you fell in a briar patch."

His lips twitched. "That was James."

"Oh, right," Mackenzie agreed, nodding. "You were the one who pissed yer pants when your brothers zapped you with a cattle prod."

Both Cole and James chuckled softly and Deacon's nostrils flared. "Are you done?"

"Not by a long shot." She moved an inch closer. He could smell her perfume. Something flowery. Not at all what he'd expect from a foreman.

"What the hell's happened to you?" she asked, her tone a little less aggressive than it was a moment ago. "I mean, you were never the friendliest kitten in the box when we were young, but you weren't ruthless or heartless. Or shit, pointless."

He looked down his nose at her. "You know exactly what happened to me, Mac. 'Cause it happened to you, too, and to those two hyenas on the couch over there."

She went pale instantly. And after licking her lips and clearing her throat, she uttered softly, "Cass."

"That's right."

The answer moved over her, maybe even inside her, and she straightened her shoulders. "Are you telling me that these past six years you've been trying to buy, steal, and bully your way to taking over this ranch because of Cass?" The pissed-off tone was back, and her eyes were flashing blue fire. And hell, that rich flowery scent—lilacs, maybe?—was pushing its way into his nostrils. "You stood up before a group of mourners and told them that their life, their work, the business that sustains this town, was gonna be destroyed because of Cass?" She laughed bitterly. "That's insulting to her memory. And it makes no sense."

Deacon bristled. "It doesn't need to." *Not to you, Mackenzie Byrd.*

"This was Cass's home, Deacon. Where she ate and slept and played and loved you and Cole and James. She wouldn't want this." Her brow lifted. "So, either you're being a heartless asshole or there's something else going on here."

Without hesitation, he said, "I'm a heartless asshole, Mackenzie."

Her face scrunched up, like she was mad or sad or both. "Why'd you leave the Triple C ten years ago, Deacon?" She turned from him a little wildly and looked at Cole and James. "Why'd any of you go?"

The room fell still and silent.

"And why did none of you come back?" She chewed her lip as she stared at each of them in turn, a hitch in her voice. "I know it was hard with Cass leaving us. And never finding out who was responsible." She inhaled deeply. "I wish to God I'd pushed her for more on that guy she believed . . ." She shook her head, then found Deacon's gaze again, imploring him. "But this destructive plan of yours can't be just because of Cass."

"Mac?"

The new male voice coming from the hallway brought Deacon's head around. He wasn't sure if he appreciated the interruption or was annoyed by it.

The cowboy stood there. The one Mackenzie had been riding with earlier. Sam had said his name was Blue. Blue Perez. He wasn't as tall as the Cavanaugh brothers, maybe just a hair under six feet. But he had muscle. The kind of muscle that could drive cattle all day, then knock out a couple drunk bastards who were hitting on his woman later that night. Deacon wondered if Mackenzie was that woman.

"Your boyfriend's here," Deacon said in a voice he hardly recognized. Deep and slightly fractured.

Mackenzie didn't answer him. She went over and put a hand on the man's shoulder. The cowboy spared no time for Deacon or his brothers. His full attention was on Mac.

"You all right?" he asked. He was soft on her. That much was certain.

"Fine," she told him. "Just family squabbles."

The word pierced through Deacon, and he was about to set things straight. Let the blue-eyed cowboy know that Mackenzie was no relation of his. But before he could say a word, two more people dropped in to their little party.

"Afternoon, y'all."

The woman who greeted them far too merrily for the occasion was somewhere in her fifties, dressed in a dark gray suit and a pair of fancy jeweled-up cowboy boots. Her face was virtually unlined, but her hair was nearly all gray and swept off her face in a loose bun at the nape of her neck.

"Name's Beatrice Carver," she said, heading for an unoccupied chair like she knew the lay of the land and was far more comfortable in it than any of the Cavanaughs or their hired hands. "I'm

Everett's attorney," she announced, then moved the two beer bottles down to one end of the coffee table and dropped her briefcase. "I suggest we all take a seat. We have a will to go over."

While everyone else sat, Mac stood beside the unlit fireplace, fiddling with a small birdcage on the mantel. It had a miniature bull inside that moved when you tipped it forward or back, and she remembered Cass had had it in her room long ago. She sighed. She hated this so much. Standing there, listening to Everett's lawyer pass out his possessions like she was Santa Claus and it was goddamn Christmas morning.

Her gaze traveled the room. Gathered, were the Cavanaugh family, immediate staff, and Everett's closest friends, Sam and Booker. In the past fifteen minutes, the lawyer had bequeathed most of Everett's personal items to those two friends, given each member of the staff a sizable bonus, and Mac three of her favorite horses, including Gypsy, as well as a home at the Triple C for as long as she wanted it, a raise in salary, and the very best gift of all because it truly came from the heart: the remainder of Cass's belongings.

She felt Cole's eyes on her, and she turned to look at him. He was smiling. It was a sad smile surely, but one she understood, and she returned it wholeheartedly. A silent promise between the two of them that one day very soon, they'd meet up in the attic, go through those boxes together, and Mac would let him have whatever he wanted of his twin sister's. After all, she and Cole were the two who had loved her the best, known her best. It was only right that they should share what was left of her life.

"Now," Ms. Carver began, flipping through her papers. "We conclude with the Triple C Ranch, otherwise known as the Cavanaugh Cattle Company."

Cole ripped his gaze from Mac then and pinned it on the lawyer. Shoot. Him and everyone else. It was like the air had been sucked out of the room with that announcement, and all the attention and energy was focused on the woman with the stern expression and bedazzled cowboy boots. Mac just knew Deacon was sitting there beside a very pensive James, waiting, salivating, ready to get his hands on the Triple C. Do whatever irrevocable harm his damaged mind, and maybe his damaged heart, had planned.

Why wouldn't he tell her what this was about? Mac just knew in her guts that his six-year battle against Everett and the Triple C was so much bigger than the memory of Cass or a fight with his daddy or Deacon just lookin' to make more money. This was personal, involved all three of them boys, and she was determined to find out what it was.

"The ranch," Ms. Carver read, "its properties, including the main house, cottages, bunkhouse, et cetera, as well as all livestock and equipment, is to be divided equally between my four children."

Mac froze. Her face scrunched up, she turned to look at the woman, unsure of what her ears had just brought to her brain. Had Ms. Carver just said *four* children?

"There's been a mistake," Deacon said, his voice dangerously soft as he bore a hole into the lawyer's graying head with his piercing stare.

"That's right," Cole agreed tightly, his nostrils flaring. "There aren't four, ma'am. Not anymore."

Ms. Carver glanced up from her paperwork, her expression controlled. "It's not my place to make sense of what the deceased has bequeathed, or to whom. I am merely here to read the will as it was written." Without waiting for a response, she continued. "Once again, the ranch, its properties, including the main house, cottages, bunkhouse, et cetera, as well as all livestock and equipment, is to be divided between my four children: Deacon Cavanaugh, James Cavanaugh, Cole Cavanaugh and"—she paused, cleared her throat—"Blue Cavanaugh."

The air that had been pulled from the room a moment ago suddenly rushed back in and formed a goddamn cyclone. A few people gasped. One cursed. A couple were talking back and forth in harsh whispers. But Mac, she just stood there, staring, openmouthed, at the wall behind where the lawyer was seated.

Blue?

Oh my God, Blue.

It wasn't possible. Everett would never have . . . Maybe he considered Blue his son? Someone who was like a son to him?

Her breath was being held captive inside her chest. This couldn't be. She turned to witness one shocked expression after the next. But the only face she truly wanted to see was her closest friend, her partner. And when her eyes found him, her heart started to bleed.

Blue looked so young sitting there on the couch, his hands balled into fists, his mouth pulled into a thin line, his jaw set. And his eyes—those Texas-summer-blue eyes—sliding questioningly toward his mother.

Four

Rage swirled inside of Deacon, but outside he resembled cold, hard stone as he sat across from Ms. Carver, his gaze pinned to the top of her head. Her words were impossible and unacceptable. Clearly there was an error, a misunderstanding, perhaps, and it needed to be rectified before another moment passed.

"Ms. Carver," Deacon said, his tone even and calm. "Obviously, there's been a mistake."

Her gaze remained on the paper in front of her. "There's no mistake."

Deacon's nostrils flared with irritation. "This is Blue Perez, Ms. Carver. Not Cavanaugh. He's no relation. Everett may have thought of him as a son, but—"

"Everett claimed him, Mr. Cavanaugh," the woman interrupted.

This time, her eyes lifted and connected with his. They were razor sharp and unapologetic. They were also prepared. Once upon a time, Deacon mused dryly, she'd been as confused as the rest of them. But not anymore. At some point, she'd had this conversation with Everett. Maybe even asked the same questions.

A slow, sickly burn began to move through Deacon's gut. It was a physical reaction he recognized but had experienced only a handful of times over the course of his career.

The possibility of failure.

"Claimed him?" Cole repeated, on his feet now. "What the hell does that mean?"

"It means—" Ms. Carver began tightly. But before she could finish her thought, she was cut off by a woman's cries.

"No! Stop this! Please."

Deacon shifted his gaze to the older, dark-haired woman seated alone on the leather ottoman. He remembered her. She'd come in with Everett's lawyer. Her face was a mask of despair, and her brown eyes were shining with tears. But she wasn't looking at Ms. Carver as she spoke. She was looking at Blue.

"Don't do this," she begged. "Please don't do this."

"Ma'am," Ms. Carver began. But she was once again cut off.

"Mom." Blue sat forward on one of the couches, looking agitated as hell. "What's going on?"

Mom. Deacon's eyes narrowed. So, this was the cowboy's mother, and the Triple C's housekeeper.

"Please," Mrs. Perez implored Ms. Carver, her pained, impassioned gaze trained on the lawyer now.

"I'm sorry," Ms. Carver said. "It's the law."

Mrs. Perez put her face in her hands and whimpered. "I told him not to do this. That it would ruin so much, so many."

The confusion, heat, and rage inside Deacon burst as understanding, and acceptance of one kind dawned. "Unfortunately, my father rarely cared if his loved ones got hurt."

The eyes of most everyone in the room turned to regard him. But Deacon's attention was focused solely on Ms. Carver. "Before I decide if I'm going to challenge this will or not," he began, "I'm going to need a DNA test."

The woman's lips thinned. "It's already been done, of course, but I'll order another."

"No," Deacon said. "I'll order it." It would be executed by his people, not Everett's.

"Fine," Ms. Carver said quickly.

"That was easy."

She gave a small shrug. "He knew this would happen. And he knew you'd be the one to demand it, Mr. Cavanaugh."

"Did he, now?"

She nodded.

"That arrogant bastard," Cole ground out.

Deacon turned to see James regarding him. The man's way-too-handsome face was a mask of calm disinterest. But Deacon knew better. Could tell by the nearly imperceptible flicker of his hard jaw that James was both shocked and furious.

"So it seems Dad kept a secret from us," Deacon said, his eyes shifting to the broad-shouldered cowboy seated on the couch across from him. "And by the looks of it, though he could be faking it, a secret from Blue here as well. Behold, ya'll, the fourth Cavanaugh brother."

Mac walked across the lawn in the heels she hadn't had a chance to change out of yet. The day was starting its slow descent into evening, and a gorgeous breeze ruffled the leaves of the nearby trees and the grassy hillock a few yards away. The hillock Blue stood on, legs spread, back to the house he might just be able to stake a claim to if he wanted.

Ten minutes ago, chaos had erupted within the Triple C's overly warm living room after Deacon had called Blue the fourth Cavanaugh brother. Everyone had started asking questions, arguing shit, making a timeline in their minds. And Elena? Poor mortified, devastated Elena just sat there with her head in her hands, crying. Mac had gone to her, straightaway. But Blue? He didn't say a damn thing. Just stood up and walked out.

At the bottom of the incline, Mac stopped and yanked off her heels, tucked them under one arm. The cool grass beneath her feet came as a quick and wonderful relief, and she took off, sprinted up the rise toward her friend.

"Taking in the view, cowboy?" she asked slightly breathlessly, coming to stand beside him.

He didn't take his eyes off the burgeoning sunset. "Come to laugh at me, foreman?"

Mac's heart squeezed at the bitter sound in his voice. "Shit, Blue. Never." She bumped him with her hip. "Don't be an idiot."

"I'm no idiot, darlin'," he said blackly. "I might be a bastard, but I'm no idiot."

Mac flinched. Blue had always been one of the most relaxed, take-things-as-they-come people she'd ever known. He rarely got ruffled. Never took things to heart. But she could see by looking at him, listening to him, that he was hurtin'. That what had gone down in Everett's living room had not only shocked him, but had cut him deep.

She slipped her arm through his and pressed herself against him. "Could this actually be true?"

He shook his head. "No idea."

"Could Everett be pulling some prank? Or worse, trying to get back at the brothers for taking

off? Or Deacon for these last six years of attempt-
ing to buy the C out from under him?" Even as
she said it, she didn't believe it. No matter what
Everett's faults were, he wouldn't use Blue like
that. "You never mentioned your dad to me. What
do you know about him?"

"Just that he was never in the picture. My mom
told me they split up before she even had me."

"And you never asked anything else? Wanted
to see him?"

His jaw tightened. "I asked."

Oh, Lord. And Elena had what? Deflected? Or
flat-out lied? Is that what he was saying? Shit. Mac
released a breath. This couldn't be happening. That
was not the Elena Perez she knew—had known for
nearly ten years. That woman was a saint, not a
sinner. That woman baked pies and fixed the cowboys' bloody hands and sunburns. That woman
loved her son more than anything in the world.

"Did you have any feeling about this?" she
pressed Blue gently. "That Everett might be . . . ?"
Damn, she could barely say it. "Your daddy?"

"Shit, Mac." He turned to look at her then. Pain
glittered in those incredible sky-blue eyes. "Why
would I?"

She shrugged. "I don't know. He was really
good to you."

"He was good to you, too."

True, but it was different. She'd been Cass's

best friend practically since birth. "It's just so impossible sounding. Elena . . . Everett and Elena."

Blue growled softly.

"How long you think they were taking up with each other? You know, *if* they were . . ."

"I'm twenty-two, Mac," he ground out. "You do the math."

"Oh my God, he was still married to Lea—"

"Stop," he broke in, real fire in his tone now. He cursed. "Maybe it's not true. Maybe there was a mistake with the test."

She wanted to agree with him. God, she wanted to. For the sake of his feelings and their friendship. But she was really starting to believe that this could be true.

"I saw your mom's face," she said softly. "Heard what she said . . ."

"Try what she didn't say," Blue put in. "Fuck!" Tears pricked his eyes, and he swiped them away quickly. "How could she lie to me, Mac? My whole life?"

"I don't know. Why do people do what they do?" She reached for his hand, laced her fingers with his. "Maybe she didn't want to hurt you, embarrass you."

"Too late for that."

The ice in his tone made her gut ache. "It's probably why she and Everett didn't get together after Lea died."

Blue's eyes widened in horror. "You think that's why Lea had the breakdown? Why she was put in the mental hospital?"

"No," Mac assured him. "God, no, Blue. That happened because of Cass's death."

Lea Cavanaugh had never been an overtly happy woman, but she'd had a kind, generous heart. From Mac's perspective, she'd loved her kids more than anything and seemed to go out of her way to make 'em happy, make each event in their lives somethin' special. Cass had told Mac more than a few times that after having three boys, her mama had been so excited about having a little girl she'd had the nursery painted pink and ready to go six months in advance.

It's funny how life can change on a dime. How one horrific event can cancel out all the good, all the memories, cut ties and sever deeply woven relationships. The day Cass was taken—the day that dime flipped over and landed on tails—she'd been at the movies with her brothers. Halfway through, she'd gotten up to go to the bathroom and had never come back. A few days later, when they brought her body home, Lea Cavanaugh broke—inside and out. And from what Mac had heard, she never healed. Mac hadn't seen things firsthand, as she was grieving herself and Everett just hadn't wanted visitors around. But she'd see them in town, all five of 'em, looking like they were barely existing.

Six months later, the case was cold. A few months after that, Everett put Lea in a hospital, where she passed away not eight weeks later. Poor Deacon, James, and Cole. They left River Black days after her funeral without a word to anyone. Seemed as though everybody just wanted to forget and move on.

Blue made a sound, a sound so close to a moan it brought Mac's head around. "I wonder if she knew," he said. "Lea. I wonder if Everett told her."

"Oh, Blue . . ." Mac began.

"I'm not staying here."

"What?" Panic claimed her suddenly.

"You heard me."

"That's bullshit," she said back. The idea of not having Blue in her life turned her insides out. He was like family. Closest thing she had. "You're not going anywhere."

"I can't, Mac."

"This is your home. Now, more than ever."

His gaze found hers, and under the warm, Creamsicle light of the late-afternoon sun, he said with deep conviction, "I'm not fighting those boys over their ranch—their home."

Passion and fear overtook the panic, fueling her blood. "Yes, you are, and you'd better."

Blue's eyes filled with confusion, pain. "Mac . . ."

"You heard Deacon at the service today. What he said in front of everyone in this town." The breeze whipped her hair around her face, cooling her skin. But her blood remained hot. "You know what he plans to do to this place and to everyone who needs it. Everyone who relies on it to survive." She laughed bitterly. "I have no idea what James and Cole are thinking, what they want, but they have lives outside of River Black. Odds are they're planning on going back to them. You and me, we belong here. You can take over."

"You're not thinking—" he began in warning.

"You *have* to stay," she implored him. "You have to help me. Fight with me."

"Come on, Mac. Shit." His eyes softened, and he reached out, brushed a strand of hair away from her face. It wasn't a romantic gesture, but a tender one. A brotherly one. "You know I'd do anything for you, but this . . ." He shook his head.

"You belong here, Blue," Mac said, continuing the fight. "You and the family you might have someday. I know that's what you want. And a Cavanaugh should carry on here. Keep building, keep growing. Not destroying."

"Cavanaugh," he muttered, looking away.

She grabbed his arm, forced him to look at her. "That's right. Blue Cavanaugh. Everett's son."

"Son," he repeated. "Son. Goddamn. My daddy?

Shit, Mac, if this is really true . . ." His eyes implored her. "It's not fair. I never got to know him like that. Be recognized as a son to him."

She smiled sadly. "You just were."

Those incredible blue eyes went soft.

"Now, what are you going to do about it?" Mac shrugged. "Walk away? Or help save what we've called home for longer than we can remember? Save Everett's legacy?"

With a weighty breath, Blue dropped one arm around her and turned to look out over the land. "He was a damn coward."

Mac's stomach clenched. "Maybe." She didn't want to think about that. Or what else Everett might have hidden from them all. She had a ranch to save. "But there's one thing I know for certain."

"What's that?" Blue asked.

She let her head fall onto his broad shoulder. "You're not."

Five

Deacon leaned against the porch railing and watched Mackenzie with the cowboy. Watched her head fall to his shoulder and remain there as Blue's arm snaked around her waist. They looked like a postcard for River Black, Texas. The attractive, young couple on their ranch, the fertile landscape, the waning sun, all spread out promisingly before them. For a brief moment, Deacon wondered if his parents, back in the early days of their courtship and marriage, had stood on the same hill and surveyed their new land. If they'd had grand hopes for their future. Or if Everett Cavanaugh had already stepped out on his wife, maybe even spied a beautiful young woman in town named Elena Perez.

His father's affair didn't anger him exactly. It did make him curious, though. When? Where? How long? Was there anyone else? And were there any other brothers or sisters running around he should know about? That last bit made his gut tense. There was a part of him, which had a tendency to take over, that wanted nothing whatsoever to do with his family. He loved his brothers—it wasn't that—but they represented a time in his life that had nearly destroyed him. And every time he looked at them, it came back, all hot and ready to squeeze the blood from his heart. Or what remained of that sorry muscle, anyway. He knew Cole and James probably felt the same. He knew it was why they'd all gone their separate ways and barely kept in touch.

But this new development, it had shifted something inside of him. Did he want Blue to get his spurs into the Triple C? Hell no. But he did want to know the truth.

Deacon pulled out his cell phone and punched in some numbers. His eyes still pinned to the pair on the hillside, he spoke in a deadly calm voice when a man answered. "Evening, Billy."

"Mr. Cavanaugh." The PI on the other end of the line was quick to inquire, "What can I do for you, sir?"

"I need everything you can find on a Blue Perez. River Black, Texas. Early twenties, I believe. Mother's name is Elena Perez."

"And the father?"

"Undetermined. That's the second thing I need."

"Yes, sir?"

"DNA testing. Best you can find. I want them here."

"Of course." There was a furious tapping of fingers on a keyboard, then, "I should have this for you in a few days."

"Tomorrow," Deacon said, then ended the call.

Mackenzie had broken away from the cowboy, who remained staring out at the sunset—or maybe what he thought he was about to inherit—and was walking back toward the house, her shoes dangling from the fingers on her right hand. The late-afternoon sun blazed red and pink behind her, making strands of her dark hair flash copper as it whipped in the wind. Her hips swayed in her gray dress as she walked, and her long legs and bare feet had his mind conjuring up country songs he hadn't heard or thought about in ages.

It was damn unfortunate how beautiful she'd become. Granted, he was pretty exceptional at resisting the things that were bad for him. But in that moment, he wasn't sure how he'd react if Mackenzie Byrd put her head on his shoulder like she had the cowboy's. Wasn't sure if his arm would steal around her waist, too, or if he'd pull her close to his side and brush his lips over the curve of her right ear.

He frowned. Thoughts like that were dangerous. This was Mac he was talking about. The foreman of the Triple C. Cass's best friend. Blue Perez's . . . undetermined. She was annoying, muddy little Mac. Sure, she'd grown, in all sorts of ways he couldn't help but notice. But she was, and would always be, troublesome. And he didn't have time for troublesome.

A yard or two before she hit the bottom stair of the porch, she looked up and spotted him. Her expression tightened instantly, and even in the shadowed light, Deacon noticed how stormy her blue eyes had turned. She was pissed. As usual. But this time, he wasn't exactly sure who she was pissed at.

"Giving my new baby brother a little comfort, darlin'?" he called out.

"'Course. That's how friendship works," she returned, her tone as thunderous as her gaze. She moved up the steps and around the porch railing to face him. "All right, Deacon. Let's have it. What are you going to do?"

He inhaled deeply, glanced at the driveway and his truck parked there. "I haven't decided. Get to bed early, or maybe head into town for some supper."

"Dammit, that's not what I'm talking about and you know it. I'm sure you're concocting a plan as we stand here. How to get Blue off the Cavanaugh ticket."

He turned back and regarded her. "He's not on the ticket yet, sweetheart."

"You don't believe it?" she said incredulously.

"What I believe is that science is unbiased," he said. "Except when you pay it not to be."

Her eyes widened to the size of silver dollars. "Are you accusing Blue òr . . . or Everett of a bull-shit DNA test? Blue didn't even know he'd been tested."

"Exactly," Deacon said, pushing away from the railing. "This time around, everyone will know."

"This time around . . . Christ, you've already made the call, haven't you?"

"Someone'll be here by tomorrow."

Dark brows lifted over stunning blue eyes. "That quick? That easy?" She snorted. "Have someone who handles this type of problem on staff, do you?" She leaned in and whispered, "Maybe you need to start wearing protection, darlin'."

She was close. Too damn close. He could smell that perfume again, and something else, too. The heat off her skin or the shampoo she used.

"You haven't changed, Mackenzie Byrd," he growled softly.

She drew back, a serious expression moving over her face. "No, I haven't. I'm still the girl from River Black who loves this ranch, remembers good times here, remembers her best friend. I'm still that girl who lives for the land, loves a good

horse underneath her, loves causing some trouble."
She locked eyes with him, and her voice softened.
"I'm the country girl who's saying to you—don't
do this, Deacon."

His eyes dropped to her mouth. "Do what?"

"Destroy the Triple C."

He watched the movement of her lips as she
spoke. Had a strange, hypnotizing way about it.
"Did your boyfriend ask you come over here and
beg me to abandon my plans? Walk away?"

She snorted. "Please. I only beg if chocolate's
involved."

His eyes flipped up.

"And," she added, "Blue's not my boyfriend."

Deacon's lips twitched. "You might want to tell
him that."

"I don't have to. He knows. I know. We have an
understanding."

Deacon grinned at her now. "You don't know
how guys think, Mackenzie."

She shrugged. "Maybe not, but I know Blue.
And he knows me. We're family, Deac." Her eyes
lost their momentary playfulness, and she was
back to rain and thunderclaps. "Don't walk into
this life, these relationships, thinking you know
anything."

"I know when a man wants to get a woman
into bed," he countered.

"Yeah. I'm sure you do." She turned toward the

door and grabbed the handle of the screen. She yanked it back and was about to head inside when the sound of ripping fabric rent the air. Stopping in her tracks, she glanced over her shoulder. "Dammit." The back of her dress near her left thigh was caught on a nail.

"Back up before it rips clean off you," Deacon said, heading her way. When he got there, he dropped to one knee. She didn't move, and he said again, in a darker tone this time, "Do as I say, Mackenzie."

She gave an impatient sound, but finally moved back a few inches until her thigh was flush against Deacon's palm.

"Hold still now," he ordered, awareness snaking through him. *Nice. Goddamn. Legs.* He eased the fabric off the nail that was embedded in the wood of the screen door, then smoothed her skirt. "All better," he ground out.

Quick as a jackrabbit, she moved away from him, from his proximity, from his touch. After that, a man might be inclined to think a woman wasn't into him—was maybe even disgusted by him. But what Deacon saw when he lifted his head to find her staring down at him, her eyes connecting instantly, made his insides flex and burn. As always with Mackenzie, there was determination in those blue depths and free will and strength. So much damn strength. But on that day, on his family's porch, inside that circle of three formidable attributes was passion. Clear and hot. Not for a cause, mind. But for him.

The look disappeared in an instant, and she said nothing as she turned away and walked into the house.

Holy shit, Deacon thought, coming to his feet. She was attracted to him. Not the child's crush he always knew she'd had on him—the one she'd used a colossal attitude to hide behind—but a woman's desire.

With that curious and possibly problematic development on his mind, he returned to the railing and to the enemy who remained on the top of the hill: Blue Perez Cavanaugh.

The house was quiet when Mac descended the stairs, her stomach grumbling. After all that had happened during the day, the last thing in the world she felt like doing was eating. But now that everyone was either gone or tucked away in their rooms, she wanted a word with Elena.

She was still stunned by what Deacon had said in the church and what Everett had placed in his will, and she needed to get the woman's take on things. Plus, she was worried about her, too.

Twenty different scents rushed her nostrils as she entered the extralarge eat-in kitchen. Though no one sat around it, the supper table was already cluttered with food. Except for Thanksgiving and Christmas, Mac had never seen anything like it. Elena must've started cooking the moment the lawyer had left and not stopped since. A presumption that proved correct as Mac looked over to see Elena rush from stove to refrigerator, her ancient blue checkered apron fastened over her fancy black mourning dress.

Mac took a seat at the table, her eyes moving over every favorite dish of every person who lived on the Triple C property. This was Elena's amends, her hope for forgiveness. Mac's heart pinched with sympathy.

"Come sit down, Ellie," Mac said in a gentle voice. "You look worn-out."

Elena stopped and looked at her. Her eyes were red-rimmed from crying, and she was chewing at the inside of her cheek.

"I'm fine, gal," she said, turning away, bending down and grabbing a large mixing bowl from the cabinet. "I'm fixin' to start some bread pudding. I heard that was Cole's favorite when he was young."

Oh, dear, Mac thought bleakly. Did Elena really think Cole was coming to supper? Or Deacon or James or Blue? When she'd checked on Gypsy earlier, Sam had told her that Cole and James were at the bunkhouse, and she had no idea where Deacon was. Probably on the horn to his lawyers, trying to find some loophole in the will as he waited for his DNA expert to arrive. And Blue. Mac's heart sank. Blue had taken off on Barbarella somewhere. She was pretty sure he wasn't coming anywhere near the house tonight.

"Forget the pudding, Ellie," Mac said gently. "It's just gonna be you and me. Come sit down."

Her back to Mac, the woman fiddled around with a bowl and wooden spoon. "I'm not hungry."

"Yeah, me neither." She pushed a few delicious-looking dishes to the side. "So how 'bout you drink with me, then?"

Elena stilled, the bowl and spoon poised in her hands. "Oh, Mac," she whispered.

"I know, Ellie. I know. Come on over here."

This time when the housekeeper turned around, her eyes were filled with tears and her dry lips were pressed together tightly. She placed the bowl and spoon on the counter, then opened one of the cupboards and grabbed a bottle of tequila and two glasses. Her shoulders limp, she came over to the table and pulled out the chair across from Mac.

"Good girl," Mac said, breaking into a melancholy grin. "Lord, if there's ever a night for it, it's tonight."

Elena didn't answer. Her eyes drawn and sad,

she poured Mac two fingers of tequila, then two for herself.

Mac held up her glass. "To a shitty day." Then she shrugged lightly. "And to being alive."

It took a moment, but finally Elena followed suit. "To Everett," she whispered on a shaky breath.

Mac paused, the rim of her glass pressed to her lips. Her eyes moved over the woman, really studying her. Maybe for the first time all day. This devastation wasn't just Elena mourning the fact that her secret had been revealed. This was a deep, painful ache that came from loving someone hard and long, someone who was gone and never coming back, and it made everything much more complicated.

When Elena downed her shot, Mac followed, then grabbed the bottle and poured them both another round.

"Oh, my Blue," Elena uttered sadly. "He hates me, doesn't he, honey?"

"He's angry," Mac said, placing the bottle back on the table and picking up her glass. "He has a right to be."

Elena took her glass and pounded the thing back, hissing with the second round of lovely, painful heat. "I didn't want to hurt him," she said. "I didn't want him to ever know."

The alcohol's soothing heat spread through

Mac's chest and made her sink back into the chair. "The not knowing is what hurt him, Ellie."

The woman's eyes filled with fresh tears.

On a sigh, Mac reached out and took her hand. "Listen. I'm not one to cast stones. Shit. Way too many coming back my way, but why?" Her words sounded slightly slurred, but not enough to make her stop drinking.

"I loved him, honey."

Mac shook her head as she poured them both a third. "But he was married."

"Doesn't stop the love."

"It should."

Elena didn't say anything, just stared at the glass of tequila in front of her.

"When did you meet him?" Mac started in a soft voice. "Where? Was it here in River Black?"

"It wasn't in River Black. That's all I'm sayin'."

"Did he lie to you?" Mac asked, blinking to clear her vision.

"Stop, Mac, okay?"

"Not tell you about his family?"

"I said stop."

"Because I know you, Ellie. You wouldn't do this, break up a family—"

"Mac!"

Mac's eyes cut to the older woman's. Tears were streaming down her cheeks, but she brought the glass to her lips and drank. When she'd drained the thing, she dropped it on the table. It fell on its side and rolled back and forth.

"My history and my life with Everett is my own business," she said with more passion than Mac had ever heard from her. "Understand?"

Did she understand? Hell no. She didn't understand one thing that had gone down today. But pushing and barking for an explanation wasn't the answer. Not now. Not while Elena's grief was so raw and fresh.

"All right, Ellie," Mac said pouring them both another round. "But Blue has a right to know that history when he's ready."

"When he's ready," she whispered, taking up her glass. "When we're both ready."

It was all that was said, and for the next hour, they drank in compatible silence.

Diary of Cassandra Cavanaugh

January 30, 2002

Dear Diary,

Today Cole told me that he wished I was never born. Well, not never, he said, just not the same day and time he was. He said he doesn't mind that we have the same eyes or the same rocket ship—looking birthmark on our bellies, but he thinks I get all the attention 'cause I'm a girl. He thinks that Mama didn't want another boy after Deac and James, and that she accepted him only because he came in a pretty pink package with me. I told him I thought he was crazy. But he wouldn't budge. He thinks she's always hugging and kissing on me more. I told him maybe he should take a bath, that he always smells like the cows, and Mama doesn't like cows.

He started to cry after I said it. Then he told me I'm the worst sister ever.

Maybe I was being mean, but I can't help it. It's just hard sometimes. Three of them and one of me. I mean, I know I got Mac, but she doesn't

*live here. The boys just all want to hang out
together and sometimes I feel like I don't belong.
Like they wouldn't even notice if I was gone.*

I wish someone would notice me.

I'm going to go watch TV.

*Bye for now,
Cass*

Six

The bunkhouse located between the creek and the stables had been a dusty dorm room for cowboys once upon a time, but things had changed. Over the last few years, a girl had moved in, and subsequently moved the boys out to new, larger ranch hand quarters near the big lake. Granted, the girl was the Triple C's foreman, so there was a good amount of rustic still going on inside. But the place was light and airy and clean, and James was real appreciative that Mac had forced his hand on taking the place. Truthfully, he'd tried every which way to let her know he'd be fine in the loft apartment in the barn, but she wouldn't hear of it. Said he needed to be near the horses while he was there. She was something, that woman. As kind and thoughtful as she was tough.

James pushed open the screen door and headed out of the bunkhouse, down the steps and into the still, breezeless night. Over near the creek, under the light of a nearly full moon, he spied a heavy grain sack hanging by a few ropes that were wrapped around a thick branch on a nearby tree. Performing some fancy footwork while delivering several death blows to the sack's gut, Cole didn't notice his approach until James was right up on him.

"So, who you imagining this is?" James asked.

Wearing only a pair of gray sweat shorts, the rest of him covered in a sheen of sweat and aggression, Cole bobbed and weaved and tore into the sack several more times before he answered. "No one. Anyone."

James nodded. "Right."

"I have a match coming up, that's all," Cole said, giving the dejected-looking sack a roundhouse kick. "I need to be in top form. Which means training, even if we're stuck here."

"You don't have to be stuck here."

Cole stopped abruptly, then reached out and grabbed the bag to steady it. Breathing heavy, he turned and regarded James. "What the hell does that mean?"

Those black eyes narrowed and flashed with heat, and James knew that sometimes all it took was that look for one of his brother's opponents to raise the white flag in the ring.

"Do you want any part of this place, little brother?" James asked.

"Fuck no," Cole grumbled, then amended with

a sigh, "Shit, I don't know. Even when I'm away from here, it's still with me. Clings to me like a disease I can't cure. Maybe Deacon's right. Maybe there's only one way to finally have a little peace."

"Destroying the Triple C," James said evenly.

"Why not?" Cole turned and punched the bag again and sent it flying. "What's left here but death and bad memories?"

James wasn't sure of that himself, but he couldn't help saying her name. "There were a lot of good memories, too. And there's Cass."

"Don't." His lip curling back, Cole pointed at James, his eyes—a perfect match to his twin's—now ice-cold obsidian. "Don't bring her into this. You and Mac talking like this. I don't know what's going on with Deacon. But this decision to keep the Triple C alive has nothing to do with her. She's been gone a lifetime."

Releasing a weighty breath, James leaned back against a nearby tree. "Yet she's still here. All over this place. Never given the justice she was due." His gaze darted around, from the cottage to the creek to the stars overhead. "I feel it. I feel her."

"That job of yours," Cole began in a dark voice, "whisperin' to horses and whatnot . . ."

"Yeah?"

"Well, I think it's made you soft."

James just watched him, completely unruffled by the accusation. "You think so?"

Cole nodded, sniffed. "Either that or it's all the Shakespeare you read."

James laughed softly. "I'm just made different, little brother." His head cocked to one side. "Did you know the memory in a horse, good or bad, remains inside of them, inside their guts, inside their movements and reactions to everything and everyone around them? It doesn't go away. They don't deal with it. They may forgive or move on, but in my experience, they're emotionally broken for good."

His face shining with sweat, Cole studied him. "We talking about horses, or we talking about you?"

James shrugged lightly, knowing his eyes had just gone blank. "Horses."

Cole nodded, unconvinced. "You feel whole again, J?"

James didn't answer.

"Yeah, me neither." Chuckling, Cole shook his head. "So, if I go, if I sign away my share of this godforsaken place, what then?"

"If you sign it over to Deac, the Triple C is as good as destroyed."

"And what if I sign my share over to Blue?"

The question surprised James, though it probably shouldn't have. This was Cole, through and through. Shit stirrer extraordinaire. He gave the fighter a slow grin. "You mean our new brother?"

Cole nodded, his eyes flashing with dark humor.

"Well, I guess that'd be a real nice gesture on your part."

"Right?" Cole agreed, his lips twitching. "Real brotherly."

"Problem is, you'll never actually get to see it happen 'cause Deac will remove your larynx and your right hand before you can agree or sign."

Cole burst out laughing. "Come on, J. You know what I do for a living, right?"

Grinning broadly, James nodded. All talk of the past and all the pain that rode its back now momentarily pushed aside. "I do. But you remember Deacon pissed off, don't you?"

"Shit," Cole muttered, turning to face the grain bag. For the next twenty seconds, he beat the living hell out of the thing, tearing into the side so deep and long that the grain spilled out in a dusty brown waterfall.

"Ha! There's the answer to your question, big brother," he said, drawing back, breathing hard.

"What question's that?" James asked.

Cole turned and grinned at him, his black eyes flashing, his face heavy with sweat. "Who I'm imagining this is."

"Are you still in River Black, Mr. Cavanaugh?"

"Yes," Deacon said tightly, unconcerned with

the surprised expression on his lawyer's face, which was coming to him live via FaceTime on his smartphone. "You received the will, Ken?"

"About an hour ago," the man confirmed with a nod.

"What can you tell me?"

Conducting business on a pale blue quilted bed-spread atop a lumpy mattress was not Deacon's way, but he wasn't about to leave the house. His house. No matter how uncomfortable the situation inside it became. He wasn't about to give Blue any advantages. If the cowboy did come back tonight, there would be no staking claims, no carrying out plans—not without Deacon knowing about it.

"All three partners have gone over it," Ken said, his brow creased. "And I'll do it once more. But it appears solid and, I believe, difficult to challenge. If the language provided for distribution was to Everett's 'children' or 'descendants' without using the names, then we'd have a better shot. But it mentions a distribution by name."

It wasn't as though Deacon hadn't expected this answer; he was just hoping that the minds he paid more than seven hundred dollars an hour to be simultaneously brilliant and devious had come up with a way to break, bend, or melt down iron-clad.

"I have a DNA expert coming tomorrow," Deacon said. "If the newest addition to our family doesn't share our DNA, what then? Can the entire will be thrown out? Would James, Cole, and I be the sole recipients of the property?"

"Because he is named Blue Cavanaugh and not Perez, yes, I believe we'd have something." He paused for a moment, his brow furrowed. Then he said, "Perhaps using the idea that somehow Everett was defrauded into thinking that Blue was his offspring."

Yes. Deacon liked that. The first step would be the DNA test, of course. And if Blue wasn't a Cavanaugh, Deacon would pursue the legal route. But if he was, Deacon was going to have to approach his plan from a different angle. Already he had his PI looking into Blue's background. He would see what that turned up. And then there was the remote possibility that maybe Blue didn't want the ranch. That maybe he'd rather get himself a million-dollar payday and a one-way trip on the Cavanaugh jet anywhere he liked.

Deacon glanced up, narrowed his gaze on the door. Someone was outside his room. Or some*thing*. Shit, the way it was stumbling around, stomping down the hall, it could be one of his father's prize bulls.

He turned back to his lawyer. "Use a very fine-toothed comb with that final read-through, Ken. I'll contact you tomorrow."

"Yes, sir."

After disconnecting, Deacon placed his phone on the side table and got off the bed. Whatever was going on out in the hall, he was pretty sure it had to do with his neighbor. He hadn't seen Mackenzie since she'd left him on the porch. Since she'd stared down at him with hot eyes. It was a look he'd been trying to erase from his mind ever since.

He opened his door and stepped out into the hall. No one was there, and for a second he wondered if maybe she'd just been passing through on her way downstairs. But then he heard her. A few doors down, barking at someone inside her room.

"Goddamn you, Blue!" she called out in a strange combination of a hiss and shout.

Blue? Deacon mused darkly, instantly on the move. Was the cowboy back and in Mac's room? And why was she so pissed?

"You!" she continued, her voice echoing down the hall. "This whole thing . . . You're acting like a . . . bullshit."

Deacon stopped outside her open door, frowned when he saw that she was talking on her cell phone. Talking and trying to unzip the back of her dress at the same time.

"You know I'm so worried," she rambled on loudly, her words slurred.

Well, well. She'd been drinking.

"I'm worried, Blue. Don't you get that? Worried. You'd better call me back, cowboy. No, you'd better be up and out at dawn or maybe I'll fire you." She pulled at her zipper, managed to get it halfway down her back before it refused to go any farther. She released it with a frustrated curse. "Ah, hell. I wouldn't fire you, Blue. You know that, right? I love you."

Crossing his arms over his chest, Deacon leaned against the doorjamb, his frown downgrading to a scowl. Why was she saying that? *Like* that. All fearful and passionate. Friends didn't talk like that. Not any of the people he called friends, at any rate.

"I love you," she said again, then punched the end button on her cell and threw the thing on the bed. She stared at it, and in a soft voice, whispered, "And I can't lose another person I love."

Dammit. For a moment, Deacon contemplated walking away and pretending he hadn't seen or heard a thing. That would've been the right move, the smart move. He didn't need to engage with a drunk woman who was grieving the man he despised and crying out for the cowboy who could threaten his plans for vengeance. But then she turned and caught sight of him.

She didn't even startle, which was a big clue to how drunk she probably was. She did however narrow her eyes, and her upper lip lifted into a sneer. "What do you want, Deacon?" she muttered irritably.

"I heard you yelling all the way down the hall," he said. "How's a man supposed to get any sleep with all that racket?"

She snorted. "If I see a man I'll ask him."

Deacon grinned. "You all right, darlin'?"

"As if you care," she said, pointing at him, her cheeks flushed.

"I care, Mackenzie."

She snorted again, then started working her zipper again. "You are a mean upstart."

"Yup."

"Greedy, too."

"Sometimes."

"Don't patronize me, Deacon Cavanaugh."

"Not trying to." Shit, if she did manage to get that zipper down and started undressing in front of him, things were going to get problematic. He wasn't a dickhead, but he wasn't much of a gentleman either. She was a beautiful woman, and he couldn't say he wasn't curious.

"You shattered this day," she said, yanking and pulling. "Wasn't your day, Deacon. Not every day is your day."

If she tugged on that thing any harder, it was going to rip in two. He pushed away from the wall and stepped into the room. "Come on, Mac. I'm responsible for only one of the scandals today. And, frankly, I'm thinking it's not the worst of the lot."

"Your plan to destroy us all is the ultimate of worsts," she slurred, turning to look at him. She narrowed her eyes. "Wait a minute. I didn't invite you in here."

"Your door was open."

"Still not an invitation."

"All right. Say the word and I'll leave."

Her eyes widened, hopeful. "The ranch? You'll leave the ranch?"

He laughed. "No."

She scowled. "Well, then, you might as well stay. Witness what you've come to destroy. What you've wrought." Her voice dropped to a whisper. "And maybe what Everett wrought a little bit, too."

Her eyes filled with tears on that last bit, and Deacon sighed. Damn woman. Damn Everett. "You been drinking, darlin'?"

"No."

He went to her and took her by the shoulders. "Just a little bit?"

Her head dropped back and she looked up at him. "Maybe."

"Whether you believe it or not, I'm not looking to destroy you, Mackenzie." Her cheeks were flushed, and the color made her eyes so brilliantly blue it was like staring at the sky around noon on a perfect spring day. "Beautiful works of art should never be destroyed."

Deacon realized what he'd said one second after it was out of his mouth. *Where the hell did that come from*? he mentally growled. Not from any rational or reasonable place he knew of. Shit, that was Hallmark card, romantic bullshit territory. He didn't deliver that kind of slop to women.

He released his hold on her, ignoring the heat and tension building in his chest.

Mac didn't move. She was still staring at him, pursing her full, pink lips. "Don't you try to sweet-talk me, Deacon Cavanaugh. Unlike those bean-poles with fake tits and faker smiles that you go out with, I know you." She pointed at his face. "I know the country boy you were and the heartless man you've become. I know everything."

No, Deacon thought. She didn't know everything. If she had, she might never have taken Everett up on his offer to work at the Triple C. And clearly, she'd needed that job. It was a conscious choice he and Cole and James had made long ago. To keep the truth from her. Losing Cass and dealing with a drunk for a father had been more than enough for her to handle. She hadn't needed to take on their pain and humiliation along with it.

"Why do you pick women like that, Deac?" She

verbally stumbled on, reaching behind her back and once again working her zipper. "You came from real. Why wouldn't you want real?"

His lips twitched. "Sounds like you've been spying on me, Mackenzie."

She cocked her head, trying to get a better angle on the willful little bit of metal. "Don't have to. You're all over the rags in town. Every time I buy a tub of ice cream, there you are."

His brow lifted. "A *tub* of ice cream?"

She glared at him. "You got a problem with that?"

"Nope." He laughed. "No problem."

"Good answer," she growled softly as she continued to pull on that zipper.

That damn zipper.

"Need a hand, Mackenzie?" he asked.

"I have two." And she brought both out from behind her back to show him.

"They don't seem to be working all that well."

She ignored him and kept at it for the next thirty seconds. Then she let out a frustrated groan and dropped her hands to her sides. "I think it's stuck."

"You think?" he said, chuckling.

"Shut up."

He reached for her waist and turned her around. She gasped.

"Drinking alone isn't a good idea," he whispered near her ear. "You should've waited for me."

She sighed tiredly. "I got tired of waiting for you, Deacon."

The words were spoken softly, but Deacon heard them clear as day. His gut tightened as his fingers went to her dress, wrapped around the zipper, and eased the tiny piece of metal out of the fabric it was caught on. Mackenzie Byrd wasn't some female from the city who wanted a few nights of uncomplicated fun. She was real and familiar, and smelled like sunshine. She was his past. Or a part of it, anyway. She belonged to a different time, and no matter how grown up she was or how his body might be reacting to her hot stares and cool attitude, he didn't want any part of that time.

He stared at her back. The smooth, tan skin and the clasp of her pale blue bra. His mouth watered, and his nostrils widened to take in that warm, sunshiny scent. Even with the warnings his mind had just conjured, the urge to slip his hands inside the flared material of her dress, feel the heat of her skin against his palms, was nearly debilitating.

"I wasn't alone," she whispered.

Deacon's fingers flexed. "What?"

She turned around, held her dress up with both hands, and lifted her dark blue gaze to his. Once again, heat and confusion battled within their depths. "I wasn't drinking alone. I was with Elena."

Deacon's jaw tightened, and rational thought returned in a quick, jarring manner. The woman his father had been allegedly having an affair with for years—the woman who had borne Everett's child, then kept it a secret. The woman Everett had no doubt turned to when he should've been helping his wife with her grief and protecting his sons from the terrifying effects of that grief.

Her eyes still hazy from all the alcohol she'd consumed, Mackenzie looked at him, studied him, like she was trying to read his mind. "Does it make you crazy not to have control all the time?"

His brows came together in a frown. "I always have control, Mackenzie," he said, not sure where she was going with that line of questioning. "Even when it might not appear that way."

Her cheeks flushed, and the confusion disappeared from her eyes. "You don't now."

"Why do you say that?"

Without warning, she reached up, fisted the collar of his shirt in her hands, and pulled his face down to hers. Her lips captured his in a hungry, almost angry way that made the breath leave his body, then rush back in at a hundred miles per hour. *Holy shit! What the hell?* She groaned against him, lapped at him with her tongue, then nipped at his bottom lip with her teeth as her hands ran up his jaw and neck, then into his hair.

Fuck! This was insane. Dangerous. But Christ, she tasted good. *Felt* good. Deacon had his hands around her waist in seconds, the pads of his fingers pressing into the small of her back until he had her flush against his body. Hot damn, she fit. Perfectly. He groaned and kissed her deeper. At some point, he thought he heard her mutter the words, "No control," into his mouth, but he wasn't sure. Hell, he hardly cared. She was grinding her body against his, fisting his hair, making sounds that were causing his mind to melt and his dick to beg for release from the prison of his zipper.

He needed to stop this, end this stupidity before it got out of hand. Before she got the wrong idea. Or he did. But in that moment, his mind and his body just didn't give a fuck. About anything. He'd never had this kind of reaction to a woman. Ever. Never felt like he wanted to slow things down and speed them up all at the same time. Never felt like he was going to explode, come, just from a round of goddamn necking.

With a growl of need, he took her mouth hard, tasting her, lifting her up and heading for the bed. Instantly, she wrapped her legs around his waist, and Deacon felt the heat—the wet heat—of her sex through both cotton and denim. Christ, he wanted her. Would've taken her right there in one of the Triple C's flowery guest rooms. Stripped her bare, licked her up and down, then slid inside that warm, wet heat if the shrill ring of her cell phone hadn't stopped him.

It was like a damn ice bath over both their heads. *Ring. Ring.* She unwrapped her legs from his waist. *Ring.* Her feet hit the floor. Fuck, Deacon cursed silently. He released her, didn't even get to look in her eyes before he did.

Mackenzie was off, diving onto the bed for the phone.

"Blue? Blue, is that you?" she said, her words sounding a lot clearer than they had before. "Where the hell are you?"

Jaw tight, nostrils flared in frustration, Deacon just stood there, staring at her, feeling like a huge asshole. How the hell could he have made such a stupid mistake? With both of them being impaired? She was drunk and emotional. And he was curious and horny. Christ, he still was. He needed to get out of the room. Needed to get a football field between them.

Her eyes lifted as she talked, catching his gaze. They were stormy blue and passion filled, and they made his gut clench and the erection behind his zipper grow impossibly harder. Mother of God, what had he done?

He gave her a cool smile. "Night, Mackenzie. Keep it down, all right?"

He didn't wait for a response. Just turned and walked out. Left the heat and the scent of sunshine and a past he wanted nothing to do with behind.

"Sleeping under the stars?" Mac repeated, her tone a little sharp as her body fought its way back from complete and total erotic desperation.

Stupid tequila.

Stupid woman.

Her eyes locked on the door. Deacon had just left, and she was doing everything possible to try to remember how to breathe. Her chest felt tight, her skin felt hot, and every square inch between her trembling thighs was wet. She closed her eyes and swallowed. If Blue hadn't called, she was pretty sure she'd be hitting the sheets right now with the man who wanted to destroy her home and her job.

"What's wrong with you?" Blue asked over the line, though he was the one who sounded utterly bereft. "You're out of breath. Are you sick?"

"I'm fine." Just unbelievably stupid.

"You sure?" he asked. "Your message was nuts. I could barely understand it."

She was never drinking tequila again. "It's been a long day." *And it's going to be an even longer night if I can't calm the hell down.* She rolled her eyes at the thought.

"You need some sleep, Mac. Shit, we all do. I'll talk to you tomorrow, okay?"

What was wrong with her? She was sitting here, chastising herself for grabbing Deacon Cavanaugh by the collar and kissing him like it was the most normal and natural thing in the world when her friend was going through something ten times more disturbing. "Hey, wait. Blue?"

"Yeah?"

"You gotta know . . ."

"What?'

"That I'm here for you. Always."

He was silent for a moment; then he said, "I appreciate that. But first I need to decide where it is I actually am, you know?"

"Sure. Yeah." She wanted to push again, tell him he belonged here, always would, that Elena loved him and he should at least listen to what she had to say before he did anything rash or went off half-cocked. But that's not why she'd called him up tonight. She'd wanted to know if he was okay. Safe. Now that she knew, she could let him think and stew in peace.

"Say howdy to the stars for me?" she said. "Especially the Big Dipper."

"You got it." She could practically hear him smile through the receiver.

"And take the day off tomorrow," she continued.

"Mac—"

"That's not coming from me," she said quickly. "That's an order from your foreman, cowboy."

"Yes, ma'am."

She smiled. "Night, Blue."

"Night, Mac."

The wash of calm that moved over her when she hit the end button was a stark contrast to the hot frenzy of emotion and feeling and hunger she'd felt when she'd answered the phone a short time ago. But that's how it was. Blue made her feel grounded and safe. While Deacon Cavanaugh, it turned out, made her do things she never thought she was capable of. And feel things she hadn't even known were inside of her.

With a groan, she pulled her knees to her chest and wrapped her arms around her legs. If Blue hadn't called . . . Lord, if Blue hadn't called . . . They'd have slept together, she was sure of it. And what would that have meant? She was supposed to have Blue's back, not the back . . . and the front, and the sides, and the face of the man who was trying to take them all down.

This time when she groaned, she buried her face against her knees.

As much as you're trying to melt into this bed and disappear from the realities of this situation, you can't.

Tomorrow she was going to have to face this—face him. Tell him she was drunk and not thinking clearly. Tell him that what had happened between them was a mistake. Never to be repeated again.

Scooting off the bed, she went to the door and closed it. Locked it. Then peeled off the dress that had started it all.

Seven

Cole had hit twenty miles today and his thighs were burning like a sonofabitch. He growled as he left the country road and headed into town. Just the way he liked it. Pushing his body to the absolute limit was a high and all, but it was the pain that really flipped the switch inside of him. Whether it came from a killer run, a punch to the kidneys, or a knee to the temple, he'd realized long ago pain was the best and only way to deal with his emotional rage.

Before that, before the UFC ring, he'd wondered if jail might be the place for him. Locked up. Someone else controlling his emotions and his actions.

Even at seven a.m., the small town of River Black was hopping. The sun blazed overhead, already too damn hot for being awake only an hour. The market, bank, and post office had a steady stream of customers coming in and going out;

same for the RB Feed and Tack. It was strange to be back home, the pain of the past already taking hold, reaching inside his chest and pulling out his guts. And the longer he remained, the harder it was going to get.

Maybe he should just sell his share of the Triple C to Deacon and get out. Get back to his training. After all, none of this shit mattered to him. So Everett had another kid, cheated on their mom . . . Who the hell cared? Relationships were for suckers, and happily-ever-afters lasted as long as the sex remained hot.

In just four short weeks, Cole had the match of a lifetime. The biggest one of his career. That's what mattered. The match. The win.

Realizing too late what street he'd just turned down, Cole jogged toward Marabelle's Diner. That gut inside him, the gut that had been turned inside out and upside down over the past twenty-four hours, now shrank to the size of a fucking nail head. Marabelle's had been the last place his family had eaten together. Breakfast, maybe an hour later than it was now, Cole thought. And a few hours before his mother had asked him and his brothers to take Cass to the movies.

His eyes cut to the packed diner, noticing the new sign, the new paint, the new patio. Cole was about to kick up speed and leave the place and its memories in the dust when he spotted James sitting outside on that new patio. He was at a table for two, no food in front of him, but a couple of coffee cups. And there was a dark-haired woman across from him.

Cole wasn't sure, but he thought he recognized her. For a second, he contemplated jogging over and saying hello, but just at that moment, James glanced up and spotted him. There was no look of embarrassment or shame on the man's face, but there was also no sign of an invitation to join them or even acknowledge them. In fact, after a second or two, James turned back to face the woman.

Cole kept on running. Damn, James had always been so fucking secretive about his life and where he was in his head. But in the past year, things had gotten worse. He and Cole had talked maybe once a month or so since they walked out of River Black ten years ago, but it had dropped to every four or so lately. Same with Deac. They'd all just become strangers.

Something about being back here, back home, Everett gone, the ranch's future unclear—and a possible brother they'd known nothing about—it made Cole crave more from Deacon and James. Maybe that was a pussy thing to want, but there it was.

Eyes trained on the road ahead, sweat pouring off him, he took off, sprinting back toward the Triple C.

*   *   *

"I'll be staying here longer than expected, Sheridan." Phone to his ear, Deacon headed out of the house, across the porch, and down the steps. "I may need you to come for a few days."

Which would mean opening the River Black office space and apartment he'd bought a few years back. He'd furnished and stocked it well, but he'd need to get it cleaned and have the AC checked before his assistant arrived. He couldn't have her conducting business in a hot and dusty three-room space above the Feed and Tack. River Black had a small hotel and she could stay there if she liked. He'd invite her to the Triple C, but with what was going down, he didn't think she'd be comfortable.

He heard the buzz of office life around her as she answered. "Of course, sir. Do you want me to liaise with your housekeeper? I can bring anything you may need."

"That's not necessary," Deacon said, heading for the large red barn. What he needed was a good, hard ride. It had been way too long since he'd been in the saddle. "I'll be back on Friday for the dinner with Breyer. I'll pick up a few things then."

"Oh," Sheridan said, her tone slightly confused. "Are you sure you don't want me to reschedule the dinner? If you need to stay—"

"This meeting will happen, Sheridan." His tone sharpened. "I'm not letting Breyer slip through my fingers again. I'll take the *Long Horn* in and back."

"Very good, sir. I'll make sure everything is confirmed. And shall I contact Ms. Monroe?"

He paused just outside the barn doors, which were spread wide, giving him a panoramic view of the immaculate stalls, horses that were well fed and cared for, and one of the farm dogs stretched out and snoring. "Yes," he said tightly. "And make sure Pamela knows who we're having dinner with and where."

"I'll take care of it, sir."

His eyes cut to the right, and instantly his chest tightened with awareness. The ranch's foreman was saddling her horse in the crossties. Christ, he'd thought Mac would be gone by now. Up and out and on the land. Deacon's gaze roamed over her, trying to memorize every inch. He felt like a lecherous bastard, but he couldn't seem to help himself. Dressed in a pale green tank top and tight jeans that were tucked into roughed-up cowboy boots, she was all tan skin, lean muscle, and dangerously sexy curves.

"Sir?"

"I'm still here, Sheridan," he said.

Mac's head came around, and her gorgeous blue eyes locked with his. She gave him a quick, tight smile, then returned to her horse.

"I just received the call you've been waiting for," Sheridan said. "An employee from Genetics Free should be there by two o'clock. Ty is flying him over."

"Perfect."

Mackenzie was tightening the girth beneath her black gelding, the muscles in her toned arms bunching with the effort. Christ, just staring at her made Deacon's hands twitch and his blood heat. He hadn't slept for shit last night thinking about her, how her mouth had felt on his, how her hands had dug into his skull, how her hips had ground against his cock. And the sounds she'd made . . .

His nostrils flared. He'd have to address it. Make sure she knew—and hell, he knew—that it wasn't happening again. Allowing her any kind of power over him would be a huge mistake and could end up costing him the Triple C.

"Anything else, sir?" Sheridan asked, once again cutting into his thoughts.

"No. Thank you, Sheridan."

He ended the call, then placed his phone in his pocket and strode into the barn. He thought about moving right on past the beautiful foreman who was truly a perfect combination of hard and soft, and checking out the Triple C's horseflesh. But when he reached her gelding, she turned to acknowledge him.

"Mornin', Deacon."

"Mackenzie."

"You're up early," she said with a trace of guarded humor in her tone.

"Always," he returned. In fact, he'd been up since dawn, working, handling business overseas.

"So where's the suit and tie?" Her eyes worked up and down his body, took in his jeans, boots, and white T-shirt. "You look like a cowboy in that getup."

"I am a cowboy, Mac. Nothin'll take that out of me."

Her eyes softened a touch. "I'm glad to hear it."

Deacon stared at her, knowing he should be moving along. Doing what he'd come out here to do. Ride a horse until they were both exhausted and covered in sweat. But those eyes of hers, they held him hostage. And they weren't the only things. It was something about the way the warm sunlight pushed through the cracks in the barn walls, hitting her with a thousand spotlights. She just glowed, her face, her skin, even her thick, dark hair that was braided and hanging over one tanned shoulder.

His fingers twitched as he imagined wrapping them around that braid and easing her toward him.

Damn, he groaned silently. He needed to end this. These thoughts were crazy. Beneath him. Unlike him in every way.

Her horse lifted its head then and nudged Deacon's shoulder. He reached out and gave the black gelding a few strokes on the neck. "Gorgeous animal."

"Yes, he is," she agreed, smiling as she turned back to the overo. "His name's Gypsy, and he's all mine." Her voice softened. "Thanks to Everett."

Though the acknowledgment triggered quick irritation inside Deacon, he pushed it away. She thought the world of Everett, and nothing was going to change that. Except for maybe knowing the truth about what had happened all those years ago. And he wasn't doing any sharing.

"So you going on a pleasure ride?" he asked as she reached for a bridle from a hook nearby. "Or is this work?"

"I told Blue to take the day off. The cowboys are moving cattle, so me and my hangover are going solo to fix some fences."

As she slipped the bridle over the gelding's head, she paused for a moment. "I could use some help." She glanced up, her eyes shuttered now. "What do you think? You up for it?"

There was something in the way she'd asked that made warning bells go off inside of him. "You want me to help fix something I'm just going to break later?"

Her jaw went rigid, and for a moment, Deacon thought she was going to pitch some choice curse words his way. Shoot, he wouldn't blame her if she had. But then she took a deep breath, let it out, and shrugged.

"It's an invitation, Deacon. Plain and simple." She cocked her head. "You either accept or you don't."

A loud whinny echoed throughout the barn, making Gypsy dance in place a bit. Deacon glanced past the gelding's head to a stall farther down on the left. A beautiful chestnut mare with wicked eyes had her head out. She had to be close to seventeen hands and she was glaring something fierce at him. He liked her instantly.

"What's that girl's name?" he asked Mackenzie.

"Trouble."

His eyes cut to her. "You're kiddin'."

She shook her head, her eyes suddenly bright with amusement. "Funny you spotted her, but I suppose trouble attracts trouble."

He shot her a wicked grin. "No doubt about that."

He left the overo and walked over to the mare. He waited for her to dip her head an inch, give him some clue that she had a submissive bone in her body. When she didn't—when the black-eyed beauty flared her nostrils and pulled in his scent instead, Deacon laughed.

"She do all right with your gelding?" he called.

"Far as I know," Mackenzie said. "You're coming with me?"

He ran his hand up the mare's blaze. "Fixing fences," he muttered. At the damn Triple C. "Christ."

"Is that a yes, cowboy?" she called.

Hell. "That's a yes, foreman."

"Good. Glad to have you along." She paused a moment, then said in a slightly sarcastic tone, "But maybe you want to take on something a little tamer. After all, you've been riding nothing but elevators for . . . What's it been now? Since you took to the saddle?"

Deacon glanced over his shoulder, spied her looking at him with those challenging blue eyes. His heart fairly turned over. Shit, what had he just gotten himself into?

"Ten years?" she asked, her mouth rising at the corners.

One dark eyebrow lifted. "Not that long."

"Well, she's a handful . . ."

"Not to worry, darlin'," he said easily, giving the mare a good rub on her neck. "I have a way with challenging females."

Mackenzie's eyes widened and her cheeks went pink. "You don't say," she muttered dryly, unclipping her horse.

"And riding doesn't leave you," he added, watching her. "Not when it's in your blood."

"Well, I guess we'll see about that." She started

to lead her horse out of the barn; then she stopped and glanced back at him. "Should I wait for you to tack up, city boy?"

Deacon grinned. "You go on ahead, darlin'. I'll catch up."

"You don't even know where I'm headed." She reached for her gray Stetson, which was hanging from a hook on the wall, and dropped it on her head.

Deacon's eyes ran the length of her, from boots to Stetson and everything in between. Good Lord, she made his insides melt like a tarred road in August.

"Don't worry." He grabbed the mare's halter. "I'll find you."

Her eyes danced with amusement. "Getting cocky ain't gonna help your sense of direction none. But I have to say, I'm dying to see you try."

Without waiting for him to respond, she turned and headed out of the barn, her denim-clad ass swaying like she was hearing music inside her head.

Deacon turned away from the dangerous sight with a low growl. Oh, he'd find her all right. Not just because he knew her scent now, or because he was a helluva tracker, but because he knew every inch of this land. His land. Knew where fences got busted most often, where the water gaps happened after the rain.

He opened the stall door and eyed Trouble.

"You and me, we got a job to do. You like huntin' for treasure?"

She tossed her head and snorted.

"That's what I thought." He chuckled.

But when he went to halter her, she slipped her head in the red nylon without even a whisper of apprehension.

Mac had fixed two fences and was just pulling up to a water gap when she heard him, heard the sound of hooves hitting earth a mile or so off. Tipping her hat back and squinting her eyes against the sun, she spotted him. Riding hell-bent for leather across the meadow, horse and rider looking like they'd been together for years. She shook her head and pushed out a breath. She'd known he'd find her. Just like he'd said, he was still a part of this land. No matter what had happened to make him hate it so. It was why she'd asked him along. She needed to find out why, needed to see if she could change his mind before it was too late.

She reached up and wiped the sweat from her cheek and jaw. Was she actually overheated at eight a.m.? After fixing a couple of goddamned fences? She jumped down and led Gypsy to a patch of grass, then grabbed her tools. Nope. It wasn't the sun overhead that was causing her to sweat. It was the man barreling toward her on one of the most mercurial horses at the Triple C. Standing calf-deep in water next to a downed post and a couple wires, Mackenzie just stared at him as he came toward her. Brown Stetson covering his dark hair and the top half his face, white T-shirt showing off all that muscle. Shit, she'd thought he sat behind a desk and barked orders all day long. Clearly, he was doing way more than that.

He was about a half mile away now, coming in fast, the ground rumbling like an earthquake beneath her feet. Damn, she hated how sexy he was. Hated how her body reacted to his fierce confidence and fiercer passion. Last night, alcohol fueling her, she'd taken what she wanted. Without thinking, without asking. A long time ago, a silly young girl with a bad attitude and a fondness for getting herself and her best friend into trouble had followed a certain Cavanaugh brother around, pretending to hate him, always giving him a hard time of it. When what she'd really wanted was to be noticed by him. Not as a pest or a pain, but as a girl. Maybe even be kissed by him.

Her heart stumbled in her chest. That girl's silly wish hadn't exactly been realized. Sure, there'd been a kiss. But it had been Mac who'd taken it. Lord, she'd never known that soft, full lips could be so possessive, so hungry, so feral. If she had, maybe she'd have tried something with him earlier, before he'd left the Triple C, way back when they were teenagers.

With a sharp "Ho" he pulled up a few yards away and let Trouble walk a bit. His green eyes on Mac, Deacon circled the mare a few times, nice and easy, then brought her to a stop at the rim of the water.

"Well?" he said.

"Well what?" she answered.

"What's my prize, foreman?"

His voice, so husky, so perfect in the open air, made Mac's hands unsteady with the wire cutters. "What are you talking about?"

One side of his mouth kicked up. "I found you."

She laughed. "And?"

"And I won."

Standing in the water, she stared up at him. Seeing him sitting on that horse, his green eyes and gorgeous face peeking out from under his dusty Stetson, Mac felt as though no time had passed. He wasn't the billionaire tycoon from Dallas, ready to bulldoze this land he'd just raced across. Not today. Today, he was a cowboy.

"There's no winning, Deacon Cavanaugh," she returned.

He eased his hat back and gave her a look of mock reproach. "You practically dared me to find you back in that barn, Mackenzie Byrd."

The sun shone fully on his face now, making his eyes shine like twin and very wicked emeralds. She shrugged. "Maybe I did. But there's no winning on a dare. You either accept or you don't."

He led Trouble in a small circle again. "That's not how I remember dares."

She pointed the fence stretcher at him. "That's because you're old."

His eyes widened.

She broke out laughing. "Yup. And sorry to inform you, but memory's the first thing to go."

"Shit, darlin'," he muttered, jumping down from Trouble and tying her to a tree a few feet away from Gypsy. "You know I'm only four years older than you, right?"

She walked through the water, over to the fence. "That all?"

Coming up beside her, he shot her a good-natured grin, then joined her in cleaning the dead grass and such off the broken wire. The top three wires were still in good shape. They just needed to fix the one on the bottom.

"Hand me those fence stretchers, foreman," he said. "And as far as memory goes, mine's crystal clear." She straightened out the wires and he spliced them together. "In fact," he continued. "I remember you having one of the biggest goddamn crushes on me this ranch has ever seen."

Mackenzie froze, and within seconds her heart started slamming violently against her ribs. She hadn't heard him right. Oh, please, God, let her not have heard him right.

Deacon chuckled. "Not to worry. Didn't mind it then; don't mind it now."

"What?" she practically spat out, embarrassment surging through her. Had she really been that obvious back then? She'd truly thought he hadn't even noticed her outside of all the annoying shit she pulled. "Oh, let me assure you, cowboy, there's no now."

He turned and gave her a knowing grin. "Come on, Mac."

Oh jeez. Her skin prickling with awareness and her cheeks flaming from humiliation, Mackenzie turned away and started down the fence line.

"You did have a crush on me," he called after her.

"I think you just rode right past Arrogant Town and parked in Egomaniacville," she called back.

He laughed. "Tell me it's not true, Mackenzie."

"I'm not telling you nothin'." She turned to glare at him, but her false ire turned soft when she saw him pounding a T-post into the ground. His face was hard, sweaty, and the muscles in his arms flexed under his skin with every drive.

Damn.

"So, you have a diary or somethin'? Was I in it?" He finished driving the T-post and clipped the wire to it, then turned to face her. "Did you write Deacon plus Mackenzie equals love?"

He was so close to the truth she nearly admitted it. But that would be stupid. And after last night, she'd used up all her stupid. She eyed him. "What's it gonna take to make you stop?"

His grin widened. "I want my prize."

She felt that grin all the way down her body. "Well, I don't have a ribbon on me."

"Don't like ribbons."

"Got no gold in these pockets neither."

"I don't need any more gold, darlin'."

No, she was pretty sure that was true. "Fine." She gave her best foreman's stare down. "You hungry?"

His eyes turned from humor to heat in a split second. "Always."

Good God and all that was holy. This man was making her shiver in ninety damn degrees. "Easy, cowboy. I'm talking about lunch. I got it packed. Soon as we finish all the water gaps, I'll share it with you."

"Oh, hell, that's no prize," he grumbled good-naturedly.

"What it is, Deacon Cavanaugh, is a big goddamn sacrifice. I'm starving."

"Fine," he tossed back. His eyes filled with amusement. "Then there'd better be enough. I'm starving, too."

"Trouble." Shaking her head, she turned back to the fence and stretched out the wire.

"What's that?" he called out to her.

"Your horse, cowboy," she returned with a small smile. "After we finish up here, you'll get on Trouble and follow me to the next fence."

Walking toward her with another T-post in his gloved hand, he gave her nod. "To the fence or into the fire, Mackenzie Byrd. For today I suppose I'll follow you anywhere."

Eight

Two hours later, hot and sweaty, his stomach barely appeased by the two sandwiches he'd already eaten, Deacon sat beside Mackenzie under the shade of a birch tree and watched her eat her first sandwich. Her hat was resting on the grass, and the breeze off the lake a few feet away was sending dark strands of her hair flying about her beautiful, dirt-smudged face.

Hell, a body could get used to this. Working hard alongside such a woman, his muscles being fed by hours in the saddle and under the sun instead of in the sterile private gyms in his office building and penthouse.

The thoughts moved uninvited through his mind, and he turned to the picnic, which was set up on a blue-and-white-striped cloth on the grass, and grabbed a third sandwich, along with a handful of chips and a bunch of grapes.

"You sure worked up an appetite, cowboy," Mac said, eyeing his plate.

"Thank God you had the good sense to pack enough for—"

"An army?" she finished good-naturedly. She grinned and crunched a slice of pickle.

Deacon laughed. "I was going to say a country boy."

She cocked her head, pretended to study him. "Not sure you can call yourself that anymore."

"I told you—"

"I know what you told me, but I think you've been out of the game too long." She shrugged, then popped the rest of the pickle in her mouth.

"There's a statute of limitations on calling yourself country?"

She nodded. "Yes. It's ten years."

The flash of amusement in her blue eyes made his heart flip over like a damn fish on the bank. Out of its element and unable to breathe. "That written down somewhere, or did you just make it up on the spot?"

"Oh, it's common knowledge," she said, taking her half of a brownie she'd cut in two earlier.

He watched her eat it, watched the moist chocolate slip between her teeth. "So, if I go back to the house and ask Sam about it, you think he'll back you up?"

"Oh, Sam will always back me up."

"There's gotta be someone I can ask." He dropped his chin and gave her a serious look. "Someone impartial. Someone who either isn't in love with you, doesn't think you're the prettiest girl they've ever seen, or go to bed dreaming of getting a kiss like the one we had last night."

Her cheeks flushed instantly, and she dropped her gaze. "Hey, Deacon, about that. I'm sorry—"

"No, I didn't mean anything, Mac," he started, feeling like an asshole for shooting off his mouth.

"I don't know. Maybe we should talk about it."

"No. It was a mistake. Right?" He tried to catch her eye, but she wasn't having it. "You were drinking, I was . . . there."

She turned to face the lake, her jaw tight. "Right."

Shit. The last thing he wanted was for her to feel uncomfortable. He didn't like it. And he really didn't like that she'd agreed with him about the make-out session meaning nothing.

"Hey," she said. "You gonna eat the other half of that brownie?"

"You avoiding talking about our kiss, Mackenzie?"

"Maybe."

He pushed a hand through his hair. Maybe he should avoid it, too. But his mouth opened anyway and he started babbling on. "Truth? It was amazing. Hell. It was the hottest motherfucking kiss I've ever had. It deserves to be talked about. Might even deserve to be commemorated on a plate or something."

She groaned. "The brownie, Deacon," she said again, her eyes still trained on the dessert. "You gonna eat it or what?"

"Depends."

"On what?"

"If you'll let me feed it to you."

Her head came up, and her eyes narrowed. "You have issues."

"That a yes?" He picked up the brownie, smiled at her. "How bad do you want it, Mackenzie?"

She shook her head at him. "Not bad enough to humiliate myself."

"Come on, now. Don't get all bent out of shape." He leaned toward her and waved the brownie under her nose, then swiped a bit of the frosting on her upper lip. "Every man knows that women can't resist chocolate."

She licked it off instantly. "Where did you hear that?"

"You." He shrugged. "And somewhere else, too. I'll tell you if you open up and take a bite." Deacon broke off a piece of brownie and waited. When she let him slide it between her lips, he felt his entire body tense.

"Lucky brownie," he whispered.

Her eyes cut to his. They were worried and

confused and glazed with attraction like they'd been last night.

Deacon knew he should stop this. It was so damn dangerous, playing around with her feelings, and shit, his own. But they were so close, and her eyes were on his, and her sweet, salty scent was pushing into his nostrils.

He bent down and whispered, "I know I've never tasted anything better than your mouth. No hotter, sweeter place in the world."

For several electric seconds, she stared back at him. Then she swallowed hard and looked away. "Now, who else told you women can't resist chocolate?"

Deacon grimaced, his insides tense and bleeding with the need to kiss her, taste her again. But he shoved it away.

"I learned that valuable piece of information," he said, handing her the rest of the brownie, then stretching out on the blanket, "in the sixth grade."

"Sixth grade? That's mighty young."

"Forget math and science. I wanted to kiss girls."

"So, not much has changed."

He laughed. She had no idea. "Right before a guy enters junior high, he's taught what girls really want."

She turned to look at him, her eyes no longer wary, but curious. "Is that right?"

"Oh yeah."

"From who?"

"Whom," he corrected with a teasing grin.

"Get outta here," she drawled.

He shrugged. "Hey, we're talking about school. Just triggered something in me."

"Like your schoolteacher gene?" she shot back.

He pointed at her. "Exactly."

"Come on." She laughed as the wind kicked up across the lake and blew her hair about her face.

"I'm serious."

She rolled her eyes. "Fine. From *whom* did you learn what girls really want?"

"The older guys. Juniors and seniors mostly."

She snorted. "And they told you it was chocolate that a girl really wants?"

He grinned wickedly. "Among other things."

"I'm not even going to ask," she said.

"Good, because I'm pretty sure I'd have to demonstrate a few of them. You know, to make sure you were clear on things."

Her face split into a grin. "I think I'm clear. I've got a great imagination."

His blood started to heat up. Damn woman. "Maybe you need to stop talking like that, or I might be forced to bring up last night again."

"And maybe you shouldn't be threatening to spill all those sacred male secrets," she said, her grin growing wider. "What if the big boys heard about it? You might get in trouble."

He sighed, watched as far above him, a young hawk flew back and forth, from branch to branch, practicing—preparing for a longer journey. "Clearly, I like getting into trouble."

She laughed and started cleaning up. Baggies and foil, cans of soda. Deacon moved to help her.

"Hey, remember that lemonade stand you had?" he asked.

She glanced up. "With Cass?"

He nodded. "You wanted to buy me a bolo tie for my birthday, so you charged all the hands a dollar a glass."

She looked stunned. "You remember that?"

"I'm not as old as you think."

"Cass forgot to put sugar in it."

He laughed and stuffed a few napkins in the picnic basket. "The cowboys had to smile through their puckers so they wouldn't hurt your feelings."

"You still got that tie, Deac?"

His gaze cut to hers and held. 'Course he didn't have the tie. It had been a million years ago. But in that moment, her eyes to his, under the dome of blue, he wished he could say yes.

"You know, it wasn't just from me," she continued with a soft smile. "Cass helped me pick it out."

His gut twisted at the mention of his sister. Especially here, on this spot near the water. She'd loved to play around here. "Cass hated shopping and clothes . . ."

"She really did," Mackenzie confirmed. "But she loved you." Her eyes warmed. "And she knew you. Makes buying a gift a lot more fun."

"I don't know where that tie is, Mac," he admitted a little sheepishly.

She smiled, shook her head. "It's okay. I'm sure it wouldn't stand up to the silk ones you got hanging in your closet now."

"I don't know about that."

God, he wanted to kiss her. Wanted to feel her lips against his, hear her soft moans. He wanted to lift her up and sit her on his lap, then slide his hands underneath her. Maybe she'd wrap her legs around his waist like she had last night, and her arms around his neck, and they'd taste each other, breathe each other's air, and forget about the past . . .

. . . and the future.

But then clouds moved in and the air felt cold.

"You know, losing Cass took a toll on everybody, Deacon," Mac said.

And Deacon no longer felt like the playful, carefree cowboy he'd been a second ago. He nodded. "'Course it did, Mac."

"But you're the only one who wants to end this place over it."

He stared at her for a full ten seconds before

responding. "Understand me, darlin'." His tone nearly stripped the sunshine from the sky it was so dark. "The destruction of the Triple C happened long ago. Not because of Cass's murder, but because of what happened afterward."

She froze. "What?"

He shook his head. Damn his mouth.

"What are you talking about? What happened afterward?" she said, her eyes pinned to his. She sat on her feet and faced him. "Are you talking about how the police couldn't find that 'Sweet' guy Cass had told me about? How they closed the case?"

He remained tight-lipped. What was he doing? Why was he even here with her? Fixing fences, having picnics, dredging up the past?

"Deacon, please," she nearly begged. "I know you're holding back something. I know there's more to this—all of this—everything you've done in the past six years—than just you wanting to destroy memories of Cass."

"You don't know anything about me, Mac," he ground out. "And one night of hot necking in your room isn't going to change that."

She flinched at the harshness of his words. "Wow. Okay. Well, you're right about that." She took a deep breath and let it out. "But don't I at least have the right to know why you're taking this place away from me, and everyone else who calls it home and a living?"

Deacon stared at her, feeling like the worst of bastards. This was so fucked up. This whole thing. Coming here, staying here, going to her room last night and letting things get out of hand. He could not afford to care about her feelings, her wants or her needs. At least not more than his own.

"Hey there!" came a not so friendly call from behind them.

On a soft gasp, Mackenzie turned. Deacon followed, and promptly frowned. Blue stood on the rise, hat tipped back, his horse grazing a few yards back.

How long had he been standing there? Deacon wondered. And had he heard any part of their conversation?

The cowboy headed down the incline, then straight toward them, stopping just a few feet away. His eyes went to Mackenzie first, then cut sharply to Deacon.

"Your employee's here," he said. "He's up at the house ready to swab the inside of my cheek." He arched a brow. "I figured you'd want to witness this less-than-blessed event."

Deacon stared at him. "I do."

Once again, Blue's eyes went to Mackenzie. "Then let's go."

Mac paced the rough wood floor of the kitchen. She'd refused to sit on the hard living room couch with

James, Cole, and Elena and watch as Blue got tested for Cavanaugh DNA. But she couldn't hang out in her room or go back to work either. Nerves ran up her spine and made her neck feel stiff. After what had happened the night before, and then today at the lake, she felt unbelievably confused. Deacon Cavanaugh wanted to destroy everything she loved, and yet she couldn't stop herself from wanting him. Maybe it was because she saw the good inside him, the desire to connect with her, with his brothers, and with the ranch again—the desire he tried to mask or tamp down or pretend wasn't there. Whatever it was, she was convinced he was hiding something important, and she wanted desperately to know what it was.

"Baking me some cookies, foreman?"

She glanced up, spotted Blue in the kitchen doorway and gave him a nod. "Absolutely. You'll find their small, round, and very burned carcasses in the trash. Help yourself."

He laughed. "We're just waiting on the results now." He walked in, dropped into a chair at the kitchen table. "Well, *they're* waiting," he clarified.

"Damn, Blue," she began, shaking her head. "What if you are . . . ?"

"If I am, I am."

"That answer sucks."

"I know." He shrugged. "But right now, it's the only one I got."

"Have you talked to your mom yet?"

His eyes grew stormy and he shook his head.

Mac released a breath and leaned back against the counter. "You need to, Blue."

"We all have things we need to do, Mac." He cocked his head to one side, seemingly to see her from a different angle. "Like driving cattle, seeing the ocean, learning where we come from, trying *foie gras*"—his eyes shuttered—"and coming clean about our interest in people we shouldn't be interested in."

Her brows drew together. "What are you talking about?"

"Don't act like you don't know where I'm going and why." He fixed her with a harsh stare. "What the hell were you doing with Deacon Cavanaugh today?"

Anxiety rushed up from her toes and kept going until it settled real heavy and annoying-like inside her skull. She shrugged as casually as she could manage. "Fixing fences, having lunch."

He lifted an eyebrow. "That it?"

"'Course."

"Come on, Mac," he said on a forced laugh. "I mean, it's been a while since I met a girl who made my insides explode." He grinned. "Who made me look at her like I wanted to lick every inch of her skin lollipop-style—"

"Jesus, Blue!"

He laughed again. "But I know what it looks like. And Mr. Billionaire Cavanaugh had that look all over his face, in his eyes, and in that growl he fixed on me when I interrupted things down at the lake."

"You didn't interrupt things."

He pushed his chair back and stood up. "Why are you denying this?"

She didn't know. Maybe because she wanted to pretend it wasn't there. Maybe because whatever it was that Deacon felt where she was concerned was going to be short-lived and painful. If she kept pursuing it, that is.

"He wants you," Blue said flatly.

"No." She said the word like it actually meant something, like it could combat the truth, maybe even the desire raging in her heart. "That's just him. He's a player."

"Well, I've no doubt about that. I'm just telling you to be careful. He wants you and he wants the Triple C. Now, depending on what this test says, his destruction of the one may turn out to be none of my business." His eyes darkened. "But the other . . . I'll bury him if he tries."

Before Mac could say another word, she heard a commotion out in the hallway. She expected several people to walk through the door, but the only person who did was the very one she unfortunately ached to see. The one Blue had just basically threatened to knock out if he hurt her.

Gone was his Stetson, leaving his thick black hair molded slightly to his head. His tan skin was dirty, his boots, jeans, and T-shirt, too. His black eyes were as cold as a snake's, but even so he fairly radiated heat.

Mac had never seen anything so sexy in her life. And yet as he came to stand in front of Blue, his jaw set and his imperious attitude turned up to high, she wished he'd never come back home at all.

He avoided her gaze and trained it solely on Blue. "How much?"

"How much for what?" Blue asked.

"For your share in the Cavanaugh Cattle Company."

Mac's heart dropped into her belly, and she felt simultaneously furious at both Deacon and Everett. One for making this into a grand and ugly display, and the other for cheating on his family and lying to all of them about it.

"So it's true," Blue said, his tone as even as Deacon's.

"DNA doesn't lie," Deacon replied.

Blue glanced over at Mac, then shook his head. "This is unbelievable."

She went to him at once, grabbed his hand and stood by his side.

Deacon's jaw tightened, but his gaze remained on Blue. "I'll give you five million right now."

Mac gasped, instant anger firing her blood. "He's not selling."

"Mac—" Blue began, but she cut him off quick. "Stop it, Deacon."

"Not your business, Mackenzie." Though Deacon spoke to her, his eyes never left Blue. "You can do a lot with five million dollars, Mr. Perez."

"Don't call him that," Mac warned.

"Start your own ranch," Deacon continued. "Your own life."

Mac felt as if her heart would explode inside her chest. "You're being a manipulative jackass—you know that?"

Blue's eyes cut her way again. "Actually, he's being the most honest one here."

Mac glared at him, shocked. "What?"

"He's the only one who has his cards on the table, open and honest, about what he plans to do."

She released his hand. "He wants to bulldoze this fucking ranch, Blue!" She knew she sounded out of control, but she didn't care.

"I don't know if I blame him, Mac."

She stared at him, disbelieving, then uttered, "Oh my God." She turned and caught sight of Elena coming into the kitchen.

The woman stopped dead when she saw them.

Blue saw her, too, and he sniffed. "See, lies and betrayal have a way of souring your feelings about a place, Mac."

Elena blanched, and Mac considered knocking him upside the head for purposely baiting her. He was angry at her. Had a right to be. But he wasn't going to be cruel. She wouldn't allow it.

"You wouldn't understand that, Mac," Blue continued. "But I believe my brother here does."

Deacon's eyes lit with the fire of impending triumph. "That a yes, Mr. Cavanaugh?"

"Naw. You were right before," Blue said. "It's Perez. But I'm going to have to think about it."

The answer clearly displeased Deacon, and his nostrils flared with impatience. Mac knew he probably wasn't used to hearing no from anyone.

"Offer's good for twenty-four hours," Deacon said tightly. "Then it's off the table."

"Look," Blue said in a cold yet calm voice. "I took your test because I wanted to know for certain and because I'm not a complete jackass. But I won't be pushed into making the decision of a lifetime. Twenty-four hours ain't gonna do it."

Something close to respect flickered in Deacon's sharp green eyes, and after a moment, he nodded. "All right."

Blue looked surprised. "All right?"

Deacon shrugged. "Contrary to popular belief, I'm not a complete jackass either," he said, his gaze shifting momentarily to Mac and then back again. "But I won't wait longer than a week."

Blue nodded and then stuck out his hand. "Fair enough."

As they shook hands, Mac watched, knowing that if she allowed it, if she didn't fight it, these two men had the power to dictate not only *her* future—but the future of everyone who counted on and loved the Triple C.

So fight it, she would.

Nine

"And you didn't invite him? To our Cavanaugh brothers' happy hour?"

Beer in hand, Deacon tossed his little brother a wry grin. "I would've, Cole, but when I offered, he tossed the Cavanaugh name right back in my face."

"Shit, can you blame him?" James said, his gaze moving around the bar.

Celebrating its fifth anniversary, the Bull's Eye was a pretty recent addition to downtown River Black. And obviously a welcome one, Deacon mused, if the lively Wednesday-night crowd was any indication.

After the revelation that Blue was indeed their brother, Deacon, James, and Cole had all decided to meet up, have a few beers, some food, and, if Deacon could manage it, another opportunity to discuss selling off their shares of the ranch to him.

"He found out his mother's lied to him all these

years, and Everett, too," James continued, his grip easy around the neck of his beer. "I hear they were pretty close."

Deacon's head came up. "Who told you that?"

James's gaze shuttered, and he looked away, inhaled sharply. "Think it was Sam."

Deacon snorted. "That old man talks too much."

"You think he's lying?" Cole asked, then drained the rest of his beer.

"No," Deacon said, reaching for a hot wing. "I'm sure they were as close as father and son. Hell, I wouldn't be surprised if Blue had suspected something."

"Well, he was the son none of us were—that's for sure," Cole said with a bitter edge to his voice. "Stuck around. Worked Daddy's land."

"Our land now," Deacon said.

"That's right. The four of us." James's gaze locked with his, and the stubborn coolness behind his eyes concerned Deacon.

But he only nodded. He didn't see any reason to tell his brothers about his offer to Blue. Not yet. Not until he had a firm answer.

As if reading his mind, Cole turned to him and asked, "So, did Blue give any clue as to what he wants for the ranch? What he plans to do with his share?"

"Come on, Cole," James said just as someone switched on the jukebox and an old Whitesnake song filled the bar. "He's going to want to stay. He lives here. His mama lives here. His work is here."

"And Mackenzie's here," Cole added.

Deacon felt a rumble in his chest at the mention of her name and tore into the hot wing with supreme relish.

"Well, can't believe I'm saying it," James began. "Especially about Mac. But damn, that woman could keep a man locked into this place. Forget about the money; she's turned into every cowboy's dream."

Deacon tossed the small chicken bones onto his plate, his expression as tight as his gut now. "Blue isn't interested in Mackenzie." *Not if he wants to keep that nice white smile intact.* "They're friends."

Cole snorted. "Sure they are."

"I wish I could find a friend like that," James said. "Loyal, beautiful, fearless. Women like that don't grow on trees." He grinned. *"I'll follow thee and make a heaven of hell."*

"Okay, you're cut off, Shakespeare," Deacon said, grabbing another beer and pointing the bottle's neck at the man's face. "That dark ale's going to your brain."

"I kind of like that one," Cole said, ignoring Deacon. "Sexy. And damn apropos. What's it from, J?"

"A little play called *A Midsummer Night's Dream*."

Cole turned to Deacon and grinned wide, looking

like a young randy boy, despite the near military haircut and all the tats. "What'd I say? It's summer. Night's coming on. Dream girl. Apropos." He dropped his chin and clarified. "I'm not talking about Mac, y'all. We clear? She's great and pretty and everything, but she's family."

"She's not family," Deacon said tightly and emphatically.

A dark-haired woman dressed in black jeans and a white tank top bumped into their table, sending an empty beer bottle flying onto the floor. She was short, curvy, had a real pretty face and a smile that could melt the polar ice caps. And she had all three men up and out of their seats to help her.

But Cole got to her first. Turning on the smooth Texas charm he was so famous for—and that brought nearly more women than men to his fights—he gripped her forearm, steadying her. "You all right, darlin'?"

"Oh, shoot," she said, laughing softly. "I'm so sorry."

"It's no problem, sweetheart," he drawled. "Let me help you out there."

"Thank you." She laughed again. "I'm fine. It's just these shoes." She gestured to the three-inch black leather heels she was wearing. "It's my first night trying them out."

"Well, careful as you go," Cole said. "We don't

want any accidents tonight, nothing bad happening to a pretty thing like you."

Her pale green eyes brushed past both Deacon and James before she gave them all one final smile before turning and walking away.

"I could go after her," Cole nearly growled as they all sat back down. He grinned wickedly. "Make sure she doesn't stumble into someone else's table. Let her know my hands and I are available at all hours to assist her."

Then suddenly his grin died, and he glanced back over his shoulder, following the woman's movement. "Hey," he said, the easy Texas charm draining out of his voice. "Wasn't that the woman I saw you with this morning, James?" Cole turned around and looked at his brother. "At the diner?" he pressed.

"No," James answered simply. "I wasn't at the diner this morning."

"What are you talking about, man?" Cole returned, the full beer he'd just grabbed completely forgotten. "I saw you."

James shook his head. "Wasn't me."

Cole turned and glanced over at Deacon with an expression that screamed, *He's fucking lying right now*.

Deacon turned back to James and studied his expression. Unreadable, cool, impassive. Typical James. Deacon didn't know what was going on with his brother, if he knew that woman or not, but James had always kept his thoughts and his actions to himself, unless he felt like sharing. Pushing or threatening hadn't worked back when they were kids, and it wasn't going to work now.

He gave Cole a little shrug. "The man says he wasn't at the diner."

Cole looked from brother to brother, his black eyes flashing with irritation. "Fine," he spat out. "I must've been in an endorphin haze or something."

"Or something," James added, his mouth curving into a smile as the cloud that had covered his eyes a second ago lifted.

Cole flipped him the bird, then switched back into bar-night mode. "All right, cow patties, I say we forget about why we're in this town, the new addition to the family, and what lies ahead, and invite a few of these hometown fillies to our table and see what happens."

"I'm up for seeing what happens," James said cautiously. "But that one with the heels is off-limits."

Deacon tossed him a curious grin. "I thought you said you didn't know her."

"That's right," James returned dryly, his ocean-colored eyes once again impassive.

Cole snorted, clearly done with the subject. "Whatever, Shakespeare." He turned and winked at Deacon, grinned like a cat over a canary. "Deac, that redhead with the blue dress and fine ass over at the far table has been fucking you with her eyes since we got here."

Not even remotely compelled to look, Deacon pulled back his chair and stood up. "Have fun, boys. But not too much fun."

"What? Where you going?" Cole demanded. "This is a Cavanaugh brothers moment."

"You don't need me."

"Well, shit, boy, of course we don't, but we'd like you." Cole reclined back in his chair and stared innocently up at Deacon. "I'll give you my portion of the Triple C if you stay."

"He's lying," James said dryly.

" 'Course I am," Cole said with a laugh. "What's up, Deac? You need to get yer beauty rest or somethin'?"

"Or somethin'," Deacon answered.

Cole laughed while James studied him. "I think he's going home to Mackenzie," he said.

That brought Cole out of his Cheshire cat mood and nearly out of his chair. "What?" he said, looking between the pair.

Deacon's eyes narrowed on James. How the hell could he know that? Or even suspect that? The man wasn't even staying in the house.

"Damn, brother," Cole said, his expression serious, maybe even a little pissed off. "You got a thing for Mac?"

"It's not a thing," Deacon muttered dryly. It was more like a potential obsession. A driving hunger he couldn't seem to satiate. But he needed to keep trying. Goddamn, he needed to keep trying.

"I know you two were talking about her earlier," Cole said, his tone threaded with warning. "James saying she was beautiful and tough. But that's just talk. She's got to be off-limits." He eyed Deacon. "You feel me, Deac? She was Cass's best friend. She's family—"

"She's not family," Deacon said again, this time with a decidedly sharp edge to his tone. He leaned over the table, so only the two men could hear him. "If she were family, she'd not only be carrying scars; she'd be wearing them." He turned to Cole. "You feel *me*, Cole?"

Both men just stared at him.

Deacon inhaled deeply, then let it out. "Have a lovely evening, gentlemen." He didn't wait for them to respond. Just turned and walked away, out into the night, to his truck.

On the way back to the Triple C, he tried to push his brothers out of his mind and concentrate on both the plans he had when he gained control over the Triple C and all the work he had coming down the pike at Cavanaugh Group. Including his upcoming dinner with Angus Breyer. But none of it took root. As the warm night air rushed in from the open windows of his truck, all his mind wanted to think about was Mackenzie. What was she doing tonight? Was she hanging out with Blue? Comforting him? Talking things over with him?

His lips pressed together. Were they discussing Deacon? His offer, and his terrible, unexplainable need to ruin the Triple C? Was Blue warning her to steer clear of him, that he was nothing but trouble? And could Deacon blame the man if he had?

The house was quiet when he walked through the door twenty minutes later. The kitchen light was off, and Deacon wondered if Blue was even around or if he was still avoiding his mother. Sleeping out under the stars for the second night in a row.

Bypassing the door to his own room, Deacon headed for Mac's. He knew this was just another check mark in a laundry list of asinine moves lately, but he couldn't help himself. He needed to see her. After what had gone down in the kitchen earlier, after they'd gotten the results of Blue's DNA test and Deacon had offered him the five million to walk away, he needed to know that she didn't hate his guts. Pissed off at him was fine, but hate . . .

He knocked softly on her door. He wondered if she was already asleep. He hadn't glanced at the clock in the truck, but it couldn't be later than nine thirty. When she didn't answer, he tried one more time. Last night had been a late, drunken, stressful one, so maybe she'd dropped off early?

"She's not there," came a female voice to his right.

Deacon turned to see Elena Perez down at the end of the hallway. She was in a nice set of deep purple pajamas. Her feet were bare, her hair was piled on top of her head, and she hugged a white stone mug to her chest.

"Is she out?" he asked, his tone as calm as he could make it. "Working late?" He refused to say the words "On a date?" Shit, he didn't even want to contemplate that idea.

"She left," Elena said softly.

Deacon felt the breath leave his body and icy-cold fingers dig into his spine. "She left town?" he asked.

"No," Elena said, her gaze watchful, curious. "She left the house. She didn't want to stay here anymore." She sighed heavily. "Seems that's how everyone's feeling these days."

"Do you know where she is?"

Elena nodded. "But she doesn't want you to know."

His chest tightened like someone had a vise to it. "Blue staying with her?"

She shook her head, her eyes dropping to the steaming cup in her hands. "No. Blue's staying in town. Farthest he can get from me without actually movin' to another city."

The last thing in this goddamn world Deacon wanted to feel was sorry for his father's mistress. But in truth, they'd all been screwed by Everett. Who the hell knew what had really gone down between them.

He started down the hall toward her. He knew Mackenzie was on Triple C land. She was foreman. She wasn't going to live off-site. Just wasn't done. And if she was on Cavanaugh land, Deacon would find her. Find her and apologize. He stopped in front of the housekeeper. "You make those brownies Mackenzie brought in her lunch today?"

The blatant grief in Elena's eyes lifted a touch, and she nodded. "You liked them?"

"Best I ever had," he said in all honesty. He raised a brow at her. "There any more? I'm fixin' to have me a little late-night snack."

What did she need TV, electricity, or hot water for? She had her books, plenty of candles, and the breeze off the river.

Lying on the porch swing, listening to the water move over and through the rocks, Mac tried to get lost in the mystery novel propped on her chest, but it wasn't as easy as she'd hoped. She didn't have any guilty feelings or worries about leaving the main house. In fact, she'd promised Elena she'd be back for breakfast and to get her sack lunch. But there was a very big part of her that wanted to be as close to Deacon as possible. Even after his prickish behavior toward her and his ugly and impulsive five-million-dollar offer to Blue.

She placed the book down on her chest with a sigh and stared up at the sky. The moon was at half-mast, and the stars winked something fierce at her. The lusting for Deacon Cavanaugh she couldn't fight—not after that kiss or all he'd said at the lake while he was feeding her a chocolate brownie—but his plan to destroy the Triple C, that she could.

And would.

But how? Her feelings, his brothers' feelings, none of it seemed to matter to him. He still had a care for the land he'd grown up on, but it hadn't changed his goal any. The object of his anger seemed to be, not the land itself, but Everett. She had to get him to tell her why.

Her stomach twisted painfully. There was a small part of her that didn't want to know. After what she'd learned about Everett's affair with Elena, she worried that whatever it was Deacon was holding on to was worse. Everett had been like a father to her after her own father had given his life over to alcohol. She didn't want to hate him.

The sound of a horse and rider barreling across the meadow broke through her thoughts, and she scrambled off the swing and to her feet. Wearing just a tank and loose-fitting pajama bottoms, she thought about running inside and grabbing the robe off the hook in the bathroom. But there wasn't time. Whoever it was, was coming up fast.

She was just getting to the other side of the porch when the very man she'd been thinking about came riding into view.

Trouble riding Trouble.

Why had he come? she wondered, her heart pounding inside her ribs. Had something happened up at the house? Was Blue okay? He'd told Mac he was staying in town for a spell while he figured things out.

Bringing the horse to a quick stop, his gaze cutting to the house, Deacon spotted her at once. Under the glow of the moonlight, his green eyes blazed with the heat of a treasure hunter who'd found gold.

"Don't blame Elena, okay?" he said, jumping off the horse's back and pulling the bridle over her head. "She told me you were gone, but she didn't tell me where you were."

"Blame Elena?" she repeated. "Is everything okay?"

He looked so good, black jeans molded to his powerful legs, black T-shirt molded to his sexy, broad chest. She prayed she wasn't outwardly drooling.

"Everything's fine, except you leaving without saying good-bye."

Wait a sec. He'd come here for her? Her pounding heart dropped several feet to her stomach. "Well, if Elena didn't tell you where I was, how'd you find me?"

His gorgeous face split into a wide grin. "Come on, now, darlin'." He walked over to a nearby tree and tied Trouble, affording Mac a perfect moonlit view of his stellar ass. "I grew up knowing this land. I could find every house, building, or barn blindfolded. This is my third stop." He came back her way and looked up at the small cottage. "When James and I were little, maybe around seven and eight, we used to hide from our mother here." Something moved across his face, something dark, and it wasn't the shadows. "She'd never get mad, though."

Mac came to stand at the top of the porch steps. "What are you doing here, Deacon? It's not just to get a good-bye from me, is it?"

His eyes came to rest on her. They were filled with a pained need she'd never seen before. Not on him, not on anyone. "I'm sorry. I was a jerk at the lake and when I was making that offer to Blue."

An apology from Deacon Cavanaugh? That was a rarity indeed. She nodded. "Okay."

He pinned her with an intense stare. "You didn't have to go, Mackenzie."

Her skin hummed with awareness. Why did he have to look at her like that? And dammit, why did his voice have to enter her bloodstream and turn it blisteringly hot?

"Couldn't stay there," she said. "Not after last night, not after today."

He shook his head. "Are we talking about the kissing or the offer to Blue?"

"Both. They both got me messed up." She looked around herself for a moment. "You're not going to be here for much longer. Not after you get what you want. You'll be at that ranch of yours or in your fancy office in Dallas." Her eyes found his and held. "I think it's better if we stop this right here and now, don't you?"

"No."

"Deacon—"

He bounded up the porch steps, had his arms around her in less than five seconds. "I don't want to stop this. Shit, I don't think I can."

Mac didn't struggle, didn't try to get away. In fact, her body instinctually drew closer to his. Her head dropped back, and she stared up into his eyes, her pulse racing, her skin prickling. "I need you to," she uttered breathlessly.

His eyes moved over her face. "That's very different from wanting me to."

She shook her head. "I'm going to save this ranch."

"I know. And I'm going to destroy it." His head dipped like he was going in for a kiss, but he caught himself right before their lips touched.

She whimpered both in anticipation of the extraordinary feeling and in desperation to keep herself together. "I'll fight you."

He nodded, his nose caressing hers. "Good."

Chills ran up and down her spine. "Dirty if I have to."

"The dirtier the better," he whispered, nipping at her bottom lip. "I work well in the mud."

"Don't say that," she whispered back, her chin tipped up, her tone reed thin and desperate.

"Why not? It's the truth. I know what I am and so do you." He ran his nose along her jawline and lapped at the shell of her right ear with his hot tongue. "Can I kiss you?" he whispered, making her breath catch in her throat.

"Have you ever asked any of the girls you've kissed for their permission?" she said with a groan.

He laughed softly, making her breath catch once again, while making the muscles in her sex clench. "No. But you're special. You're extraordinary."

Her heart squeezed. They were standing on the porch of a remote cottage, under the moonlight, a soft breeze moving over and through them, and yet there was an empty place inside of Mac that worried, that questioned, that knew this would end badly because of the circumstances they were in.

"Oh, Deacon. You kill me," she whispered.

He eased back, his eyes so black they looked like polished stones under the light of the moon. They possessed her with their intensity. "That's the last thing I want to do to you, Mac."

"How's this going to work?" she asked breathlessly, her eyes clinging to his. "Me on one side, you on the other. We can't possibly come together . . ."

Sexual heat flared in his eyes, and he pulled her even closer, up against his rock-hard chest and the now hard cock behind his zipper. "Oh, we'll come together, darlin'. I promise you that." His hands raked up her back to her shoulders, her neck, and into her hair. "But tonight," he growled, "you're the one who's going to be coming . . ." He dropped his head and kissed one cheek. "And coming . . ." Then the other. "And coming . . ."

As she arched in to him, Mac's mind warned her that if she went one step further with this, accepted what her body was screaming for, she was going to end up hurt. That it would be a long road back to happiness and contentment. But when Deacon took her mouth, captured it so hungrily she gasped with unparalleled pleasure, she gave in to the possibility of pain. For the promise of the greatest pleasure she might ever know.

He dragged his mouth from hers and his hand came around to cup her cheek. She saw that anguish swam in his incredible green eyes. "Beautiful, strong, fearless Mackenzie." And then his mouth covered hers, and she lost all thought, all concern, all care.

It was a feeling unlike anything she had ever experienced or imagined. His lips worked hers in hungry, coaxing drags, feeding off her mouth and the soft moans that escaped her throat. He tasted wicked, like night and heat and maybe a touch of the beer he must've had earlier, and she wrapped her arms around his neck and ground her hips into his groin, letting him know how deeply he affected her. How much she wanted for him to take her, control her.

She heard him curse, then drive his tongue deep into her mouth and out again. Her skin went hot and tight, and she whimpered for him to do it again. As he played her tongue with his, claimed and possessed her, Mac moaned and cocked her head to one side, then the other, trying to feel every inch of his heat. She stroked his tongue with her own, then suckled it hard, making him groan.

"Holy hell, darlin'," he hissed, dragging his hands from her hair and dropping them to her ass. He palmed both cheeks hard and yanked her forward, grinding himself against her, dry fucking her as he took her mouth with his tongue.

Mac's entire body burst into flames and her head felt dizzy, her breasts ached to be touched, and wet heat claimed her thighs. Her fingers dug into his hair as she kissed him back, primal and ravenous, wanting to drink him down, eat him up. Wanting to jump up, wrap her legs around his waist and thrust her core against his groin as she bit and sucked at his lips and tongue.

"Oh, Christ, I have to touch you," he rasped. "Shit, Mac." Holding tight to her ass, he lifted her a foot off the ground and headed for the screen door. "I have to get you naked, get my hands on your hot, tight skin before I lose my mind."

I'm already there, Mac thought blearily. *Gone. Dead and alive at the same time.* This was utter madness, and she was willingly participating in it. She reached behind herself like a madwoman for the door handle, but Deacon got there first. Gripping the door and pulling it back, he nearly tore the thing off its hinges.

"Shit," he said against her mouth, nipping her bottom lip as he stumbled inside. "I don't think we're going to make it to the bedroom."

"Don't care," she said breathlessly, kissing him again, her thighs drenched inside her thin cotton pajama bottoms.

One hand abandoned her ass again and smacked at the wall. "No lights?"

She licked his lips and laughed softly. "Just the

moon and my bad sense of direction. I think we're in the living room."

"Never fear, honey," he growled, holding her tight as he carried her forward. "I have a great sense of direction. I found you, didn't I?"

"Oh, yes," she moaned. Her legs were shaking, her breathing, too. Still in his arms, she released him and grabbed for the edges of her tank top. Off. She needed it off. She got the thing over her head and tossed it to the floor just as he eased her down on the long, wide leather couch.

"Besides," he said, looming over her, his fingers playing with the waistband of her pajamas as the moon's light filtered into the room in splintered lines through gaps in the blinds. "I don't need anything but my nose and my tongue to help me find the hot, wet places on your body."

She gasped as he yanked off her pajamas, tossed them onto the floor, then cursed darkly, hungrily, when he saw she wasn't wearing underwear. His eyes moved over her, then lifted to connect with hers. His mouth curved into a smile. "Oh, darlin' . . . Oh, honey . . ."

Naked and anxious for him, her breath held captive inside her lungs, her heart slamming a rhythm of unbridled need, she stared up at him.

"Tell me you want this, Mackenzie," he said, his eyes blisteringly hot as he spread her legs and settled himself between them. "Tell me you want my hands on you. My mouth on you. My tongue working you over. Please." His nostrils flared and he groaned. "Christ, tell me now, baby. Or I'm going to die from wanting you."

She stared at him, watched his gaze travel down her neck and settle on her breasts. She knew her rapid breathing was making them move. She knew that his hungry gaze was making her nipples hard and tight. His nostrils flared and he licked his lips, which made the muscles inside her sex clench painfully.

If he didn't touch her soon, put her out of her misery, she was going to start weeping. Like a little fucking girl. And she couldn't have that. She was a ranch foreman, for heaven's sake.

"I've wanted you from the first moment I saw you, Deacon." When his hot, possessive gaze returned to hers, she reached out and grabbed a handful of his black T-shirt. "Nothing's changed. Hell, if anything, I want you even more now."

It was all he needed to hear. He was over her in seconds, forehead to forehead, nose to nose, mouth against mouth. He groaned, taking her mouth so deeply she groaned along with him. Damn, the way he kissed her, it could've been illegal, it was so breath stealing. His hands raked up her arms, gripping her shoulders and massaging the muscles.

"Oh, Deacon," she rasped, wrapping her legs

around his waist and jacking her hips up. She wanted to feel him. She wanted to feel him naked, his skin against hers, rough against soft, muscle and bone, his cock against her smooth, wet sex. She wanted to feel the skin of his shaft in her hand, revel in how hard he was, delight in the heat of him, feel the precome leak from the tip as she stroked him before guiding him to her entrance.

But first she needed to get his clothes off.

Her hand tunneled between them, eager to get to his zipper, get his jeans down around his ankles. But Deacon had other plans. Dragging his mouth from hers, he buried his head in her throat, nipping at her skin before moving his big, heavily muscled body away from her touch. When she whimpered, he laughed softly, kissing his way down her collarbone.

When his mouth closed around her nipple, she jerked with the instant and shocking pleasure of it. She'd always had sensitive breasts, but the combination of Deacon's hot, purposeful strokes and his hand slowly raking down her rib cage made Mac breathless with want.

"God, I love the way your body responds to me," he said, his breath fanning over her breast. "How tight your nipple gets in my mouth, against my tongue."

As she thrust her hips up and down slowly, showing him what she wanted—where she wanted him—he dropped his hand to her lower belly. As he flicked her tight nipple, causing shards of electric heat to erupt inside her sex, he massaged the top of her mound. Kneading the wet skin and muscle beneath. It was the strangest sensation. Almost as though he were trying to fuck her from the outside. But whatever it was, it made her breath catch, made her clit swell and hum, made her almost desperate to come.

"Please, Deacon," she begged, writhing on the couch, slamming her hips upward, circling them, silently pleading with him to touch her, put her out of her misery. But he continued mercilessly, getting closer and closer to her pussy lips and the hidden bud beneath.

She felt owned, possessed. She felt wild and contained and on the verge—shit, on the edge—and she just needed release or she was going to lose it.

Deacon dragged his mouth to her other breast and suckled her nipple deep into his mouth. Mac groaned and fisted his hair. She was close, so close to flying, to breaking free. It had been so long. Too long. Or never. Because that's the way it felt to be with him.

She palmed her breast, still wet from Deacon's

mouth, and pulled and pinched her nipple as he suckled the other while kneading the flesh of her drenched sex below.

"Oh, honey," Deacon rasped, blowing his warm breath on her sensitive nipple. "Squeeze it tight. You're about to come."

Mac's breath caught. Every inch of her skin was on fire and electric. Her eyes shut tight and she tried to hold on. But it was no use. Deacon's palm covered the outside of her pussy, and as he suckled her tit deeply into his mouth, he pressed down over the sensitive wet skin that housed her clit and rubbed her fast and rhythmically.

In an instant, Mac broke apart, moaning and pumping her hips and saying his name over and over as heat surged through her blood. It was too much. No, it wasn't enough. She gulped for breath as the waves of pleasure grabbed hold and took her along for the ride. So caught up in the incredible sensation, she hardly noticed when Deacon left her breast and started trailing kisses down her ribs, her stomach, her hip bones. But when his fingers dipped into the wet crease of her pussy lips and moved down her trembling flesh, over her clit to the opening of her sex, she cried out and spread her legs wider.

"You're so pretty, Mackenzie," he said, his breath fanning over her sex.

She looked down, blinked to rid her vision of

the blur and haze of climax, and saw him between her legs, his dark, tousled head wickedly close to her pussy.

He glanced up and met her with a look so fierce, so hungry her skin tingled and hummed.

"So pink, so wet," he said as he eased two fingers inside of her.

Mac gasped at the feeling of sudden fullness.

"And so tight," he murmured.

She could barely breathe, couldn't think. Her entire being was lost to the sensations running through her at a mile a minute. And when he started slowly pumping inside of her, so gentle, yet so deliciously deep, she let her head fall back, let her eyes close, and let her thighs fall brazenly to the sides.

"God, I can't wait to eat you," he said on a growl, his thrusts gaining intensity and speed. "You're creaming all over my fingers, darlin'. Sweet . . ." His thumb found her clit, and as he fucked her with his fingers, he stroked her tight bud.

Mac couldn't believe her body, how it had already forgotten its recent orgasm and was desperately and hedonistically begging for another.

"That's right," he crooned, thrusting fiercely within her now as she gripped the back of the couch and moved against his hand. "Your walls are squeezing me, Mackenzie. Crying against my fingers. Come, darlin'."

As her breathing went rapid and heat built up within her blood, Deacon thrust a third finger inside of her. But he didn't continue to pump. Instead, he held himself there, all three fingers deep inside of her. And while he flicked her G-spot with the pads of those long, talented fingers, his thumb slowly circled her clit.

Crying out his name, Mackenzie came again, sweat breaking out on her skin, her hands trembling, her feet flexing. The waves crashed harder inside her now, shocking her system. She wanted to reach out and grab him, pull him over her, get him—his cock—inside her where it belonged. But once again, Deacon had other plans. Once again, he took her all the way to the edge, the near cooling of her body, of her orgasm, then started all over again.

His fingers eased out of her sex and she felt his hands wrap around her ankles, felt him press her knees back to her chest, exposing her completely.

Forcing her eyes open, her breath coming in stolen gasps now, she stared at him. He looked diabolical. He looked starving. He looked desperate. And he looked gorgeous—like a sex god in the shafts of moonlight coming in through the blinds.

His eyes lifted to connect with hers. Dark emerald green and dilated.

"I want you," she said, her tone as close to begging as she'd ever come in her life. "I want you inside me. I want you to let me rip off those jeans and fist you in my hand. I want to lick you, make you lose your breath, make you come."

His nostrils flared and his jaw went tight. He shook his head slowly. "Just like I told you, darlin'. The only one who's going to come is you. Again . . . and again . . . and again." His gaze dropped to her core. "Your clit is callin' out to me, sweetheart, pulsing with the need to be stroked by my tongue and suckled deep into my mouth."

His words, his gaze, made her tired flesh pulse and cry out for more. She didn't know how this was possible, how she could take any more—and, God, how he could give so much without allowing her to give to him in return. She wanted him so badly. Wanted to feel him, touch him. It wasn't fair . . . It wasn't right. Her mind spun. Did he not want her to touch him? Make him moan and sigh and lose control?

"I'm so hungry, Mackenzie," he said, opening her with his thumbs. "Just lookin' at you, how wet you are, how sweet you smell. I've got to taste you." He dropped his head and licked her.

The instant his tongue made contact with her flesh, her mind shut down and blood rushed to her lower half again. Feeling as though she might pull his hair out if she grabbed his head at this point, Mac reached down and took hold of the couch cushions. As Deacon lost himself between her thighs, ravaged her lips and sensitive clit, she mewled. Like an animal. She mewled.

"Fuck, I could eat you all night, darlin'," he said as he kissed and licked her inner thigh, his hands driving underneath her to hold her ass. "You taste so sweet."

The heat was building inside her once again, and she was afraid—actually afraid—of what would happen to her both physically and emotionally if she came again. Would she lose herself? Would she break down in tears? Would she pass out? Why wasn't he letting her touch him?

"I don't know . . ." she uttered, exhausted. "I don't know if I can do it again."

"Your body was made for this, Mackenzie," he said, his voice tense with desire. "Let me show you."

He eased her legs even farther apart, then slipped a broad finger back inside of her. Mac gasped and lifted her hips. Giving Deacon the perfect opportunity to slash his tongue over and over and over her clit.

Her fingers digging into the cushions, her head rolling from side to side, Mac felt her inner muscles clench, felt a new wave of cream wash over Deacon's finger.

"Aw, Mackenzie honey," he said between flicks of his rough, hot tongue, "There's nothing I want more than to be inside of you, fucking you like this . . ."

"Yes," she rasped, not caring anymore if she fell apart or cried or lost consciousness. She wanted him. "God, yes. Please, Deacon."

"But not tonight," he whispered. "Tonight I want you to know what it feels like to be worshipped. I want you to know that every breath, every sound, every drop of sweet cream from your hot pussy makes me the happiest fucking man in the world. I need you to know."

"I do . . . But why? Oh, God, I can't—"

"Come again, honey. Let go and come. Scream. No one can hear you but me, and fuck, baby, I need to hear it. I need to know that you need me, too."

He flattened his tongue on her clit and let her ride him, let her take herself there as he thrust another finger inside of her and fucked her in a steady rhythm.

"Oh, God! Deacon! Oh, God!" She jackknifed up, grabbed his hair and fisted it, pressed him hard against her and fiercely pumped her hips.

The tornado of unimagined, never-before-experienced pleasure slammed into her body. She was nothing but air one moment and fire the next. She stiffened, then spasmed, and tried to gulp air. And then Deacon wrapped his lips around her clit and suckled her gently.

The scream that tore from her throat echoed throughout the cottage. Mackenzie knew in that moment that her body didn't belong to her any-more. It was Deacon's. For good or for evil. And that no matter what happened between them, what damage they did to each other emotionally with their opposing goals—or what other partners they had in the future—in her heart, she was his.

Deacon sat on the bed in the cottage's very tiny bedroom and stared down at her. Worn-out, tears running down her cheeks, Mackenzie had fallen asleep thirty seconds after coming. Coming so hard Deacon had thought he might go insane from wanting her so badly.

Never in his life had he done something like that. Wanted to prove not only to her that he meant what he'd said about her being special and extraordinary, but to himself as well. That he wasn't the selfish bastard he had come to believe he was. That his reasons for being here weren't just about the Triple C anymore. They should have been. But they weren't.

She stirred, and he reached for the covers and pulled them up to her chin. Then leaned over and kissed her softly on the mouth. Tenderness pulsed through him, mingled with the desire that refused to even dim. She was so beautiful, but his attraction to her was so much more than that. She had the courage he lacked. She'd lost her best friend, the sister of her heart, and yet she'd been able to move on, move past it without wanting to take down or wipe out anything that brought back those memories.

Her eyes fluttered and she rolled to one side, gripping the blanket. "Deacon?" she said in a soft, sleepy voice.

"I'm here, darlin'."

Her eyes opened this time, and she blinked a few times before looking up at him groggily. "I fell asleep?"

"Just for a few minutes."

"You carried me in here?"

He nodded.

She smiled, looking all too luscious in that bed. "That was sweet of you."

"I do have my moments."

"More than you think, I imagine."

The way she was looking at him, like she could see straight through him, unnerved Deacon something fierce. Her effect on him was the one thing he didn't seem able to control. Which both excited and intrigued him, but also concerned him. Nothing could get in the way of his plans for the Triple C. Not even the woman before him.

He leaned in, kissed her again, and stood up.

Mackenzie's brows drew together in a frown. "What are you doing?"

"Going back to the house."

"What?" She sat up, didn't bother with the sheet that kept her breasts from his view.

His cock raged to be freed. "I'll see you tomorrow."

"Wait." She reached out and grabbed his arm. "Don't go."

He stared at her hand around his forearm. Her touch burned him, made his insides flare with lust and aggression. "If I stay, I'm going to fuck you."

"Then for God's sake, stay."

His eyes cut to her, pinned her. "Nothing I want more." Nothing, he thought, his chest tight, his cock straining behind his zipper. But he needed to get himself together. He felt like he could break down at any moment, tell her the truth of what had happened to him and to Cole and James. And goddammit, he didn't want her to know. Didn't want her to see him weak. Just kissing her made him question his plan, his need for retribution. That was just unacceptable.

He placed his free hand over hers and slowly, gently disentangled himself from her grasp. With a look of supreme confusion, she dropped back against the pillows, but in her movement, her arm knocked against the brown paper bag he'd placed beside her. He'd put it there, thinking she would probably sleep all night, hoping it would make her think of him when she woke up in the morning.

She picked up the bag. "What's this?" she asked him.

"Just a little something for you."

Her brow lifted, she opened the bag. "Brownies?" She looked up at him, her midnight-blue eyes now a gorgeous combination of curiosity, confusion, and pleasure. "What are you doing, Mr. Cavanaugh?"

He sighed. "I don't know. But I hear there's nothing a woman likes more than chocolate."

She smiled. "Funny, I think I heard that, too."

"You get some sleep, darlin'," he said. "And I'll come by around six tomorrow night."

"Six tomorrow? For what?"

"We have a date."

Her eyes widened. "Really?"

"I think we'd better."

"And where are we going?"

"Here. I like the new digs. And I like being alone with you."

Grinning, she reached in the bag and took out a brownie. "I like that, too."

"In fact, I'll cook."

She dragged her gaze away from the brownie long enough to give him a look of mystification. "You know how to cook on a woodstove?"

"I'm pretty sure I can remember how it's done."

He headed for the door. "Night, darlin'. Enjoy your brownies."

"You sure you don't want a bite before you go?" she called after him, her voice smoothly sexual.

He turned and glanced over his shoulder. "Nothing could be sweeter or taste better than you." His eyes ran over her and he shook his head. "Forget chocolate, I want you on my tongue for the rest of the night."

Her cheeks flushed. "Damn you, Deacon Cavanaugh."

He chuckled, then turned and left the bedroom.

Ten

James felt his phone buzz against his ass as he moved down the aisle at Bacon's Hardware. Pulling it from the back pocket of his jeans, he checked the number, then turned it off. Los Angeles, California, had somehow gotten ahold of his cell number, and even at seven a.m. West Coast time, refused to take no for an answer. Well, more specifically, a woman from Walking Nights Production Company refused to take no for an answer. They wanted to do a reality show all about James and his work. According to the producer, June Dupree, "the Dog Whisperer is totally out, and the Horse Whisperer is totally in."

"Damn," he muttered, dropping his phone back in his pocket. He knew he shouldn't have done that spread for *People* magazine. But they were giving two million to his charity, and though he didn't need the money himself, when it came to his horses, he rarely said no.

He'd said no to the producer, however, told her he wasn't into the spotlight, made him damn uncomfortable.

A friend of his had told him, "They're turned on by you being turned off. They love how in the shadows you are. Hard to get."

Now, Cole was someone who loved the spotlight. The brighter the better. Between the screaming fans and the punches, body checks and knees to the lower back, he was able to shut out the past. James made it a point to push back, push away his memories, too. But he liked to keep them hidden in the darkness, along with the rest of his secrets.

At the end of the aisle, he turned to head toward the back of the store. He got about three feet when a little boy nearly crashed into him. He was running hard, looking behind himself. Instead of letting him fall backward, James caught him.

"Walker!" a woman called. She sounded like she was one aisle over. "Walker Days! Where are you?" She came rushing around the corner, a baby in her arms. When she saw James holding on to her boy, some of her panic receded. She ran over to him. "Don't do that again." Then she looked up at James. "Sorry about that," she said. "He just takes off these days."

Fingers of tension curled up James's back, and he fought for control. "S'okay." He came down to one knee and turned the boy to look at him. "You stay with your mama, y'hear?"

The little boy, who probably was no more than five, gave James a big nod, his brown eyes wide with dread.

"She loves you," James continued, "and she doesn't want to lose you. It would make her very sad. Understand me, little man?"

Again the boy nodded.

James stood up, gave the mother a smile and a nod.

Looking at him a little strangely, as if she thought she recognized him, the boy's mother offered him a quick thank-you, then took her boy's hand and led him away.

As James continued down the aisle, every inch of him from muscle to skin to blood was on edge. He felt like a rubber band that had been pulled back too far and never released. When he reached the wall where ropes of different sizes hung, he stopped and fingered the nonbraided nylon.

"Why'd you want to meet here?"

He turned to face the woman. She was dressed simply, in a sweatshirt and jeans, her glossy black hair back in a ponytail. "My brother saw us together yesterday at the diner. I'm not ready to discuss this with him yet." *And he's not ready to hear it.*

"You could've come by my veterinary clinic," she said quietly, glancing around the store.

"I think this is better, and easier to explain. A chance meeting." He raised a brow at her and lowered his voice. "Do you have something for me, Dr. Hunter?"

The woman's pale green eyes filled with sadness. "I called my dad last night, after I ran into you and your brothers at the bar. I wanted to see if he'd talk to me."

"And did he?"

She nodded.

James's chest tightened. "What did the exsheriff here in River Black have to say?"

Once again, she looked around them for anyone lurking near. When she turned back, she whispered, "You've got to understand. He's very ill. I don't know if what he's saying is true or . . . not."

"What did he say, Dr. Hunter?" James repeated, his voice so low and dark it sounded almost otherworldly.

"That the man they said didn't exist . . ."

"The suspect?" he interrupted. The one Cass had called "Sweet." At least, that's the name his sister had mentioned to Mackenzie a few weeks before she was taken.

The woman nodded. "He may have been real after all."

Tiny electric shocks pelted James's insides. He couldn't believe what he was hearing. It wasn't possible. The police had assured them that they'd exhausted every avenue, swore there was no Sweet and that Cass had probably made him up in that diary of hers. The diary that was never found.

He stared at the woman who'd contacted him a few days after Everett's death. The woman who'd told him that her father was none other than Sheriff Hunter, the man who'd headed up the investigation in River Black twelve years ago. The man who had knocked on their door twice: once with the news that their sister's body had been found and a second time to tell them that the case had gone cold, that unless any new leads came in, there was nothing they could do.

"Did your father say where this man is, Dr. Hunter?" he asked through nearly gritted teeth. "Did he say why this man got away? How he got away?"

Her eyes filled with grief and confusion. "No. He wouldn't tell me anything more." She shook her head. "When I pressed him on it, he got really upset. His health is bad, as I told you, and I'm not entirely sure if what he's saying is true or just the ramblings of . . ."

"I understand," James said calmly, though inside him a bomb was going off. "But I need you to find out." He leaned in. "Because if you don't, I'll have to go see your father myself."

Her eyes went wide, fearful. "No. That wouldn't be good. I'll talk to him."

A customer was being led over to where they were. They needed to call this, and James needed some air in his compressed lungs.

He gave the woman a tight nod. "I'll be in touch, Dr. Hunter."

Then he headed past the customer and out the door of the hardware store.

"We're all here, Mac. What's this about?"

Standing on about a half dozen bales of hay, Mac took in the sight she'd managed to put together in barely three hours. Gathered inside Ben Shiver's barn just outside of town, the crowd of fifty or so townsfolk stared up at her expectantly while they ate the sandwiches and cake she'd brought in.

"As some of you are aware," she began, "well, those who were at the funeral anyway, Deacon Cavanaugh wants to destroy the Triple C."

There was a quick and loud response, everybody talking at once, discussing what they knew and what they'd heard. She hated to do it this way, go behind Deacon's back, but she told him she'd be fighting. And when he'd gone up to that pulpit and declared his intentions, well, he was asking for a grand push back.

Stepping to the front of the crowd, Ben Shiver

put up his hands and called for quiet, then turned back to Mac. "We do know. What we don't know is why."

"It's about Cass, I reckon," Mrs. Remus piped up from over by the food table before picking up another sandwich.

"Who's Cass?" someone near the barn doors asked.

"His sister," Mrs. Remus said through a bite of sandwich.

"Poor girl," Jody Pickens said with wide eyes and a grave expression. "Stolen from the movie theater when she was just thirteen years old. Those boys were supposed to be minding her."

"I heard they were too caught up in some action movie and didn't want to go with her when she asked to go to the bathroom," Mrs. Remus said.

"Stop!" Mac interrupted sharply, wanting to yell at them that Deac and James and Cole had been just kids themselves. But she needed to keep herself calm, and she needed their help. "Please. This isn't about what was; it's about what is." With a deep breath, she forced the conversation back to its true path. "Listen, y'all, the reasons why Deacon wants to destroy the Triple C don't matter. The fact is, he's hell-bent on doing it, and we need to stop him."

"But how can he?" Ben asked. "As I hear it, there are four owners of the Triple C now."

"Four?" someone called out. "Who's the fourth?"

"Blue Perez," Ben said in a wary tone. "Supposedly, he's Everett's son."

Several people gasped at this news, and Mac wondered just who the hell had let that cat out of the bag already. Damn small town.

"Gossip all you want about this later," she said sternly. "The truth is Blue might sell to Deacon, and if he does, he'll have controlling interest."

Ben shook his head. "If he really is hell-bent on taking it down, Mac, what can someone like me do about it?"

Mac bit her lip. This was it. The call to action. After last night, all she'd wanted was for Deacon to crawl back into bed with her, eat brownies with her, spoon with her, wake up and make love to her. Maybe afterward tell her what was really motivating him, what was consuming him, what the hell had happened after Cass's death. And that he wasn't going to try to destroy the one thing in her life that gave her joy. But she knew that the very thing that gave her joy was obviously the thing that tormented him. And he wasn't giving up.

"That's why I've called this meeting," she told Ben and everyone else who was listening. "To talk about ways to stop Deacon, fight him. Not alone, mind you. Alone, none of us stands a chance, but together . . ."

"The man's worth billions, Mac," Ben said.

"This fight isn't going to be about money," she told them, seeing that for the first time each person was quiet and listening. "It's going to be about heart. Introducing him to this town all over again, reminding him of what used to be before everything went to hell. Getting Cole and James on our side. And most of all, showing him who we are and how much the Triple C means to us."

For a few seconds, no one spoke. The barn was eerily quiet, folks thinking things over, wondering if it was all worth it. Then, from the refreshment table, Mrs. Remus cleared her throat.

"All right, gal," she said, putting down her plate and eyeing Mac. "What did you have in mind?"

Mac smiled with relief, then addressed the crowd once again. "First, does anyone have a connection with the Bureau of Land Management?"

It was six o'clock on the nose when Deacon pulled up to the cottage. He'd spent most of the day on Skype working on changes to his proposal for Breyer with three of his staff and trying like hell to keep Mackenzie out of his mind. Business at the Cavanaugh Group stopped for nothing, and after years of trying and failing to get the head of Breyer Builders to sell, Deacon felt it was time to make another move. Especially now that the company's shares had dropped substantially.

The dinner Friday night would be the perfect

opportunity to see where the man's head was at. The idea that he was bringing Pamela Monroe to the dinner irritated him. Truly, the last thing in the world he wanted right now was to have that woman at his side. But he couldn't go alone. Breyer was a stickler for dinner companions.

A bag of groceries in one arm and some prepared food in case he failed miserably in his attempt to cook in the other, he headed toward the cottage. The one he wanted by his side was in there, waiting on him. *Mackenzie.* Damn, he couldn't wait to see her. Touch her. Hold her hand and feel her mouth under his. Shit, after he'd left last night, he'd been so goddamn worked up he'd slept maybe all of an hour.

"Hey, cowboy."

Her voice, that sexy, husky, tough-as-nails voice called out to him. It brought his head up and his eyes searched the porch for her whereabouts. He found her on the swing, and instantly, a wave of desire washed over him.

Mine, he mused dangerously, his gaze traveling over her. She was sitting there, swinging gently, in a pretty pale blue sundress and cowboy boots. Her smooth, tanned skin made his fingers itch to touch, and her thick, dark hair, which was pulled back in a ponytail, gave him all sorts of wicked ideas.

She looked like the cover of *Western Living*

magazine, and when she stood up and walked over to the top of the stairs, grinned down at him with that heart-stealer smile of hers, he forgot all about dinner, business, Breyer, and shit, even the Triple C.

Bounding up the steps, he dropped his bags at her feet and wrapped his arms around her. "You look beautiful," he said, pulling her close, breathing her in.

"Thank you," she said, sinking in to him, her head dropping back. "So do you."

He laughed and she grinned. Damn, she made him feel . . . good. Happy? He leaned in and kissed her. Nothing too hungry, though he felt that inside him. Nothing too possessive either—though he felt that, too. Just soft and sensual, maybe letting her know where his heart was at.

"I missed you today," he whispered against her lips.

Her eyes were closed, but she smiled. "Did you, now?"

Too damn much, he wanted to say, but instead he kissed her again and wrapped his hands around her ponytail. When he came up for air, he grinned. "Honey, I think you should wear your hair like this more often." He gave her hair a gentle tug, then took the opportunity to ravage her neck. "Oh yeah, this is good."

When he released her, she brought her head up

and laughed. "You are such a bad boy, Deacon Cavanaugh."

You have no idea, Mackenzie Byrd. He lifted one dark brow and eyed her intensely. "Let me put this stuff inside, and then I'll show you just how bad I can be."

Her eyes instantly lost their heat and playfulness, and she disentangled herself from his grasp and reached down to pick up a bag. "I'll help you," she said, tucking it into her arm and heading toward the door. "But then we need to go."

"Go?" He grabbed the other bag and got to the door just in time to open it for her. "I'm cooking you dinner, remember?" he said as she headed into the house. He followed her. "If this is about my cooking, don't be afraid, darlin'. I brought a few things already made in case I screw up."

Once inside the small kitchen, she placed the bag on the counter, then turned to face him. "See, the thing is," she began, her gaze flickering around the room, "I sort of forgot I already had plans tonight."

Deacon set his bag down next to hers, then placed his hands on either side of her body, his palms against the countertop. "Is that right?"

Locked in, her back against the counter, she was forced to look at him. Her eyes dragged upward until she caught his gaze. She swallowed tightly. "I have plans. But you know, you're welcome to come along."

She was really working herself into a state, Deacon mused, watching her. Damn, she was so adorable.

"And where would I be coming along to?" he asked.

Her eyes swept the floor. "Hmmm?"

He chuckled. He couldn't help it. "Come on, honey, look at me." When she did, he leaned in and planted a quick kiss on her mouth. "Now. Where are we going tonight?"

She sighed. "The Appletons' place."

His brows lifted. "Eli Appleton?"

She nodded, then tried to get away, but he held her tightly. He wasn't even remotely done with this conversation.

"What are you doing, Mackenzie Byrd?"

She shrugged, her teeth tugging at her lower lip. "Playing dirty."

This time, when her eyes lifted to meet his, he saw flashes of wicked, wicked female in her fantastic blue gaze. He growled, wrapped his arms around her, and pulled her closer. When her arms instantly encircled his neck, he covered her mouth with his own and kissed her hard and hungry. And when she moaned, he took the opportunity to slip his tongue inside and taste her. Goddamn, he thought, she tasted like heaven.

Her fingers delved into his hair and she gripped his scalp as she changed the angle of their kiss and sucked his tongue into her mouth. Tasted like heaven . . . Shit, she *was* heaven—*his* heaven.

"Can we be late, honey?" he uttered, easing his thigh between her legs, making quick contact with her warm core.

She gasped and pressed herself against him, then started moving her hips in slow but deliberate circles. Deacon groaned and shifted his thigh so she could ride him better.

"Oh, dammit," she uttered, cursing again and disentangling herself from his grasp. Breathing heavy, her eyes dilated, she licked her lips and glared at him. "Now, what are you doin', darlin'?" she drawled.

Though his body was screaming and his cock strained against his zipper, he grinned at her. "Playing dirtier."

For several seconds she stared at him; then she grinned back at him and reached for his hand. "You coming with me or not, Mr. Cavanaugh?"

His eyes raked her. Damn woman. Of course he was coming. She had to know how she affected him. She had to know that there was no way he was allowing her to go to the Appletons' or anywhere else without him tonight. They had a date, and damn, he needed to be around her, next to her, breathing in her scent and holding her hand.

Shit, he'd turned into quite the bleeding heart.

He took her hand and led her out the door and

down the steps. "We're taking my truck," he said through slightly gritted teeth.

"If you insist."

When he glanced back at her, her eyes sparkled with mischief and happiness. His fingers twitched. Might have to put her over his knee later. Just the thought made his body jerk with tension.

He held the passenger door open for her.

But before she climbed in, she rose up on her tiptoes and kissed him. "Don't look so glum, Deacon. I'll let you get to second base on the ride home; how 'bout that?"

His jaw tightened. "Darlin'," he said, grabbing the bouquet of sunflowers he'd brought for her from the seat and thrusting them into her hands. "If I go to this shindig with you tonight, not only will I be thoroughly enjoying each one of your bases, I'll be roundin' home a few times as well."

Diary of Cassandra Cavanaugh

April 25, 2002

Dear Diary,
Today Mac and me were talking about the future. She likes to do this a lot. I don't know why. We're only thirteen years old for goodness' sake. Well, a month shy for me. Anyways, I'm always saying I don't know, I don't know, and maybe we should paint each other's toes now instead.

She thinks that's silly.

But I think pretending you know what you want as a kid is silly. Superman or Cinderella. A veterinarian 'cause you like animals, or a baseball player 'cause your dad throws you a few balls in the yard. A wife and a mom when there's not one at home and you got a crush on a boy. A boy who's too darn old for you and barely knows you exist.

But Mac has it in her head that we should have a plan. She says the stars have one for us if we don't. That makes my belly nervous when she says it. What does it even mean?

Should I make that boy know I exist? Is he my future?

Cole's calling me down to supper. Better go.

Love and kisses,
Cass

Eleven

Two hours into the barbecue and Mac wanted to pull the plug on the whole thing. Her *brilliant* idea. She'd thought that if Deacon could interact with some of the people in town, he might gain a fresh perspective—a different perspective—on his plans to destroy the ranch. But instead of people talking to him about what a hardship it would be to lose the Triple C, how their families relied on all the jobs that filtered down from the place, they were listening.

To Deacon.

Talk about *his* ideas and *his* plans to make sure everyone in River Black was not only taken care of financially but had a new job with him if they wanted it.

On *his* ranch!

Why hadn't she thought of this? She knew he was maybe ten months or so away from that place being finished. She knew how smart he was and that he always had a plan in place.

Standing next to Eli Appleton's ancient red pickup truck, a plate of uneaten food in her hands, Mac watched as Deacon flowed through the crowd, slapping men on the back and smiling handsomely at all the women as he answered questions about the property and how far along he was in construction.

"So, how much land you got over there?" Cory Craft asked him, handing him a beer.

"Nearly double what we got at the Triple C," Deacon answered. "Double the water, too."

Manning the grill, Shep Lansing handed him a loaded plate. "Here you go, Deac," he said with a grin. "This beef is your cattle, you know?"

"That right?" he asked.

Deac? Mac shook her head, feeling completely out of sorts, confused, and betrayed. Not at Deacon, but at the town. They were calling him Deac, like he was family. Or at the very least like he was River Black family. She couldn't believe it. After all she'd said to them. How eager they'd been to help. How could they just turn their backs on what Everett had created? What had put food on their tables for decades? Did they really not care about the Triple C's survival at all? Was it only about the paycheck?

"You thinking of driving that cattle right on over to your place?" Cory asked, taking a sip of his beer as someone flipped on a radio and country music spilled out over the front yard.

"That's a thought; that's a thought," Deacon answered good-naturedly. "Although I do have my heart set on Black Angus. Always wanted 'em. You think this town can handle twice the business?"

The man grinned, and several people around them chuckled. Disgusted and disappointed, Mac dropped her plate in the trash, her stomach turning over. Was it going to be this easy to lose?

A fresh Coke in his hand, Sam walked over and sidled up next to her. The Triple C's aging horse and barn caretaker, and Everett's closest friend, looked far too cheerful. "Enjoying the show, Mac?" he asked.

"You talking about them?" She nodded toward the crowd. "The Deacon Cavanaugh Fan Club?"

He chuckled. "Yup."

"Hell no, I'm not enjoying it, Sam. I'm pissed." She grimaced as her stomach did another roll and clench dance. "I don't understand how everyone could just forget what we talked about at Ben's. What about the Triple C? What about Everett?"

"Honey, everyone loved Everett, but they got families to take care of."

"So they'll just go wherever the wind blows?"

"Pretty much."

Mac turned to look at the older man. "But today—"

"They also love you." His eyes warmed. "They didn't want to hurt you."

"So, they were just blowing smoke up my ass?" she hissed.

"No, honey. I think they all wanted to believe it was possible to take down the grizzly bear, but then, you know, reality sets in." His eyes grew solemn. "Fear sets in."

"Fear?" She turned to him, the hot night wind whipping her hair about her face. "Dammit, we could've done this, Sam. Convinced him not to go through with his plans. Deacon doesn't want to take down the Triple C. Not really."

His lips thinned. "You sure about that? Because I'm not, and I've known that boy since birth."

She glanced back at where Deacon stood talking and eating. The gorgeous, charming, stubborn, hard-ass who towered above them all and had more money than God, and too much hate and too many secrets in his heart, was finishing up a burger as he told the crowd about his desire to bring in wind turbines on part of his land and the job opportunities that would create. Her heart seized and she felt tears behind her eyes. On one hand, she hated how the town had caved to fear. But on the other, she understood and couldn't blame them. On one hand, she hated that Deacon had land bought and ready and that it was so easy for him to talk about destroying something she loved. But on the other, he looked different when he talked about his place. He looked young and excited and like maybe that ranch he was building was actually a true goal realized and not just another way to hurt the C.

She took a deep breath and blew it out nice and slow. This had to be her heart talking. She hated to admit it, even to herself, but she was falling for Deacon Cavanaugh. Hard and fast. Wrong and right. And it felt real, not like the crush she'd had on him when she was a girl.

Her stomach rolled again, and this time, nausea accompanied with it. She pushed away from the truck. "Excuse me, Sam."

She didn't want to stay here, watch this whole mess she'd created fall apart any longer. She had other irons in the fire, and if those panned out as she hoped, maybe losing the town's help wouldn't be as huge of a deal in the end.

She moved through the crowd, throwing out tight-lipped smiles as people called to her, trying to make silent amends with their eyes. When she finally came up beside Deacon, he grinned brightly at the sight of her and wrapped his arm around her waist.

"Hey there, darlin'," he said.

As his warm, hard body pressed against hers, she looked up at him. "I'm not feeling very well. I think I want to head home."

His eyes instantly lost every ounce of their playfulness. He set down his beer and took her hand. "Night, all," he said without even a trace of the charm he'd been displaying only moments ago.

"What is it?" he asked, wrapping his arm around her again as he guided her toward his truck. "Headache? You look a little pale." He glanced around and growled. "It's too goddamn hot tonight."

She shook her head. "It's just my stomach."

"What did you eat?" he demanded. "Did you have a hamburger? Shit, it better not be the meat."

"Calm down, Deacon. I didn't eat anything."

He stopped beside the truck. "What? Christ, Mackenzie. That's not good either." His jaw tight, he helped her inside, rolled down the passenger window, then came around to the driver's side. Once he was behind the wheel and they were on their way, he glanced over at her. "How long were you feeling this way?"

"Not that long." The air hitting her face was warm but fresh, and she breathed it in deeply.

"I should've been by your side," he grumbled.

"You were doing exactly what you should've been doing, Deacon."

"What does that mean?"

"You know what that means."

He sighed. "Honey . . ."

"No," she said, shaking her head. She didn't look at him. She was kind of afraid to. Those breath-stealing, leg-shaking green eyes were pretty damn powerful. And trained on her, they tended to make her heart and resolve weaken. "We both agreed to fight."

"Dirty," he said.

"Exactly."

Another fresh wave of pain rolled through her gut and she couldn't help herself. She looked at him. Stared at him, this man who lingered between worlds: land and luxury, Porsches and Chevys. He was too damn gorgeous for his own good, too smart, and too angry. Angry at something that could never change or be fixed—or erased—no matter how big and mean and deep that bulldozer went.

The fear in her heart mixed with the pain in her belly. No longer was she just worried about keeping the Triple C safe; now her concern extended to Deacon's ability to release his past pain altogether. If he held tight to it, there'd be absolutely no chance for them.

"Deacon?"

"Yes, darlin'?" He pulled off the road and onto the Triple C drive. "You feeling worse? God, I hate it that you don't feel good. And I despise the fact that I can't do anything to fix it. I think I'd pay heavy to see you smiling twenty-four-seven."

"You can do something," she said quietly.

"Name it."

"Stop this whole thing."

His jaw went tight.

"I don't want to play dirty with you," she continued. "Not that kind of dirty anyway."

"Mackenzie—"

"I mean it, Deacon. Let this go. Please. It's not going to give you want you want in the end."

He didn't say anything, not until they pulled up alongside the cottage. Then he killed the engine and turned to look at her. "And what do you think I want, Mac?"

His eyes captured her, holding her hostage. She wanted to say, *Me. It's not going to get you me.* But she couldn't. She knew how she felt about him, but she had no idea how he felt about her.

Her heart pounding, her stomach clenching, she yanked open the car door and jumped out. As she headed for the steps, she felt her throat tighten. *Not here. Not in front of him.* If tears were working their way up her tight throat, she needed to get inside before the bawling went down.

"Mackenzie, wait." Deacon was behind her.

She picked up the pace. She couldn't look him in the eye. Mackenzie Byrd, ranch foreman and ass-kicker of every cowboy on the ranch, and she couldn't look Deacon Cavanaugh in the eye because he'd see her being vulnerable and weak. He'd see how much she cared about him and how every moment they spent together was just sending her farther and deeper down a rabbit hole.

He touched her just as her hand closed around the door. He turned her around to face him and said gently, "Talk to me."

"I don't want to talk anymore."

"What's going on? We were good a few hours ago. We'd agreed to fight. What's changed? You were ready to take my ass down."

She shook her head, still keeping her eyes on his chest. "I don't know." *Yes, you do. You know. You're falling for this man—this man who plans on destroying your life, your work, your home.*

"Mackenzie . . ."

Feeling the tears at the back of her eyes, she turned and grabbed the door, pushed it opened. Goddammit, she wasn't going to let him see her like this. "I just want to be alone tonight, Deacon," she said, lurching inside.

"No, you don't. You're upset." He tried to follow her, but she blocked his way.

This time, she met his gaze. "Don't do that," she warned, her voice unsteady. "Don't tell me what I'm feeling or what I want."

"I don't have to tell you a thing, darlin'. Tears are welling up in your eyes right now."

Her lips started to tremble and she shook her head. "Damn you." Then she turned around, closed the door, and headed for her bedroom.

*   *   *

What was he doing?

What the fuck was he doing?

The woman he wanted, the woman he needed and craved, was behind that door and he'd just pushed her away. He could hear her crying softly, and it ate his guts up. He didn't know how to fix this, how to stop wanting what he wanted—what he had to see done so he could continue breathing. But what he did know was that Mackenzie had captured his heart and made him feel happy for the first time in a long time.

He dropped his forehead to the door and knocked. "Mac?"

She didn't answer him.

"Please open the door," he called. "I won't say anything more about tonight or the ranch . . ." He rubbed his forehead back and forth. "I just need to see you. I need to know you're all right."

He heard nothing at all for about a minute and a half, and he started to think she wasn't coming, that maybe he was going to have to camp out on the porch like he and James used to do. Then he heard footsteps.

"You should go back to the house, Deacon." From behind the wood, she sounded quiet, strangely calm. It sent a wave of fear through him.

"Can't go. Don't want to." He shook his head, even though she couldn't see him.

"Deacon, I don't know what I'm doing, what *we're* doing."

"We're spending time together, enjoying each other."

"But why?"

"Because it feels good." Fuck, he wanted to rip down the door, take out this barrier between them. "There's nothing wrong with that."

"It's going to get me hurt."

Deacon's eyes closed and he drew in a deep breath. He hated to think it, didn't want to even tempt fate by thinking it, but she was right. There was a whole lot of hurt to be had here. For the both of them. If only that made him want to stop seeing her—made him stop wanting her, needing her. But he was pretty certain nothing was going to do that.

"Open the door, honey," he said. "Let me just say one thing to you."

For several seconds, the only sounds Deacon could hear were the wind in the trees and the water slapping rock down at the river. Then there was the scuffle of Mackenzie working the door, the lock snapping back, and the wood creaking open.

His eyes lifted, and when he caught sight of her, his breath nearly left his body. She'd changed out of her pretty sundress and into a black tank and matching pajama bottoms. Her dark hair was loose, falling about her shoulders, and her eyes . . . those stunning midnight blue eyes were red-rimmed and vulnerable. She looked like a dark, beautiful, sexy angel, and the blood racing around in his heart dropped several feet.

Against the door, his hands fisted. He ached to reach for her, pull her into his arms and kiss that damn troubled look off her face, but he wasn't going to risk having her shut him out again.

"Can I come in, darlin'?" he asked, leaning against the doorframe, looking at her through his dark lashes. "I won't say anything more. I just want to hold you."

Her eyes softened and he could see it clearly, see her clearly. She felt it just as much as he did, this connection, this powerful, outrageous, desperate, and potentially painful connection that was destined to ruin both of them for good—and for anyone else who might happen by and try to forge a relationship with them. Deacon's bitter heart squeezed. Shit. He needed her. He needed her like he'd never believed he could need anyone.

"Let me hold you, Mac," he said again. "That's it. That's all. I swear."

She bit her lip, stepped back and allowed him entrance. He reached for her hand as he walked in, and she gave it to him willingly. Without a word, he headed straight for her bedroom, his nostrils pulling in the scent of her with each step as his body heated and tightened. God, he wanted her. More than he'd ever wanted any woman ever. But tonight he was going to be as good as his word. He would wrap his arms around her and hold her until she fell asleep.

All he took off were his shoes before getting into her bed. He stretched out with a pillow at his back and opened his arms to her. Her expression as she stood over him killed him. Wanting him, hating him, needing him. Damn, balancing on the edge of vulnerability was a crazy thing. And he was right there with her. He wanted to tell her that— that he was just as messed up as she was. Just as confused. But she seemed to cast off her fears and anxiety, and she crawled in beside him and snuggled up against him.

For several long seconds, Deacon just drew her scent into his lungs and listened to the sound of her breathing, reveled in the feel of her head against his chest, her arm slung across his middle, and her thigh draped over his groin. He tried not to think about how addictive this could be. How the longer he kept this up, kept it going, the harder it was going to be to walk away.

Or shit, see her walk away from him.

"Mackenzie?" he uttered, his voice a soft growl.

"You promised, Deacon," she said, though her

arm gripped him tighter and her hand burrowed under his back.

Sensing she might be cold, he grabbed the edge of the sheet and pulled it up to cover her. "It's not about any of that. It's about us."

"Us," she repeated a little sadly.

"Tomorrow night I have a business dinner in Dallas."

She stilled. "You're leaving." It wasn't a question.

He hated how quick her brain went to the negative, but hell, what did he expect? "I want you to come with me."

Her head came up and her eyes locked on his. "To Dallas?"

His gut tightened and every inch below his belt, too. If she'd just move up a bit, better yet, crawl up his body like a tree, he could taste her. Kiss those pink lips until they parted and a hungry moan escaped.

"We'll fly in and out on the *Long Horn*."

Her eyes widened. "Your helicopter?"

"It's an easy trip. You'll love it."

Without another word, without an answer, she put her head back down on his chest and curled into him again. He could feel the cogs of her brilliant mind turning. He didn't know what he'd do if she refused him. Coming to River Black, he hadn't given his date for the dinner with Angus

Breyer much thought outside the fact that he required one. Over the past year, Pamela had done the job well. But now Deacon couldn't even imagine taking anyone but Mackenzie. Couldn't imagine touching, talking with, or tasting anyone but her. Hell, just the thought of leaving River Black without her made his insides churn.

His nostrils flared. To give in to that need was dangerous as hell, given the circumstances, but he wanted her, needed her beside him. No. It was more than that. He wanted her to see his life, what he did, who he was outside of this world, this ugly world of River Black and the Triple C—this world that couldn't sustain them.

He rubbed her back through the sheet in slow, easy circles, and when she groaned softly, his entire body went hard. Painfully hard.

"Let's get out of here, Mackenzie," he said. "Away from the ranch, away from everything. Just for a bit. Just be us."

"God, that sounds good," she whispered, her voice heavy with emotion.

"Say yes."

Ten seconds of solid silence followed, and Deacon felt his guts contract to the point of pain.

"Say yes, Mackenzie." *Say yes before I die right here and now. Before I lose what's left of my mind.*

And when she did, when she finally did, the palpable relief that spread through him was shocking.

"One more time," he uttered. "Say it one more time."

Deacon knew that no one should ever have that kind of power over another person. It made you react before you thought things through. He'd never operated that way. But as Mackenzie wrapped her sexy body tighter around him and sighed the word "Yes" against his chest, he pushed his concern away.

"Sleep now, darlin'," he said, kissing the top of her head.

She didn't say anything more, and neither did he. And when he heard her breathing run slow and steady, he closed his eyes and followed her.

Inside the cramped but clean hotel room out on Route 12, Blue stared at his laptop screen for a moment, then clicked on the picture of the small ranch just outside of Austin. It seemed to have everything he was looking for. Land enough for a few thousand head of cattle, a grain silo, several outbuildings, a three-bedroom house, and it was far enough away from River Black and the Cavanaughs yet still in Texas.

He clicked on a picture showing the interior of the main house. It had a good amount of light, nice floors, but it needed some work, some updating. And someone who knew something about furniture and decorating and all that shit he'd never remotely cared about.

Tipping his chair back, he stared at the photographs as they ticked by. Nice home, good land. Was he really going to do this? Walk away from his friends, Mac, his mother? Take money from Deacon and sign away his rights to a ranch that he'd never even thought of staking a claim to yet never thought of leaving either?

Spotting another ranch about fifty miles outside of Dallas, he was about to click on it when a message popped up on the screen.

Everything all right, Cowboy? Haven't heard from you in a while.

Blue's gut tightened and his skin hummed. Just like it did every time he IM'd with Cowgirl. The chance encounter on a discussion board for saddles about six months ago had led to an off-site discussion on ranching. She had a dream of owning one, but lived and worked in a big city. It was about all the specifics she'd offered in their six months of knowing each other. What big city, he didn't know. She'd told him right away that she couldn't reveal herself. Told him she wasn't married or anything like that, but that her work was the kind where she needed to stay anonymous.

Normally, Blue would've walked away from something like that. He hated secrets and lies, but her openness about everything else and her desire to listen, hear what was on his heart, had just drawn him in.

Cowboy? You there? I'm worried about you. I know your boss passed away. If you don't want to talk, that's cool. Just let me know you're okay.

Blue stared at the message. Did he tell her? He always told her everything personal—without using real names and places. But emotions, events . . . This just felt different somehow. What had gone down with Everett, and worse, his mom. He couldn't be specific, and to give Cowgirl a clear picture, he kind of needed to be.

Just complications at work, Cowgirl. Family issues. All of it keeping me busy.

He waited for her response. It came quick.

Is "busy" code for turning your insides out? Making you crazy? Making you wish you were anywhere but there?

Blue smiled. *You know me too well, Cowgirl.*

<Smiles> How was the funeral?

Sucked.

I wish I could've been there for you.

Shit, he wished it, too. He wished it all the damn time. He wanted to see her, meet her desperately. They had such a connection, such heat. But he'd agreed to keep their relationship like it was. For now.

I've missed you, Cowgirl.

I've missed you, too. You want to tell me what happened? How you're feeling?

I want to tell you everything. Face-to-face. Whisper it against your mouth.

<sigh> <grin>

He grinned back and typed.

I mean it, you know. I want you here with me. Shit, I just want you.

I know. I feel the same. But I can't. Not yet.

He'd asked her a hundred times why not. Why she felt she couldn't reveal herself to him, but he never got a straight answer.

Talk to me, Cowboy. Just imagine me there with you.

Shit, he'd done that a million times, too.

Have you ever been lied to before, Cowgirl? Something so big, so life altering that you don't know who you are anymore . . . ?

He continued to type, his fingers flying over the keyboard, like they always did when he spoke with her.

Twelve

Headset on, blades rotating, confirmed for take-off, Deacon hovered for a moment, then pulled up on the collective. His eyes cut momentarily to his copilot. Wearing jeans, boots, a black tank, silver shades, and her headphones, she made him wish his chopper had autopilot.

"You look good in my bird," he said with a grin.

She heard him in her headset and turned to look at him, smiled back in that I'm-slightly-freaked-out way. "I don't know about good. Terrified's more like it."

He chuckled. "Darlin', I wouldn't let anything happen to you."

"We could've driven," she said, her hands fisting around her seat. "That fancy truck of yours was available."

"You'll love it. In fact, knowing you, I'm bettin' that after this trip you'll be wanting to learn to fly him yourself."

"I'm bettin' on the possibility of vomiting."

"Airsick bags are in the compartment to your right."

She glanced over as they rose into the air. "What? There is no compartment to my right."

He chuckled. "Sit back and relax, darlin'. Enjoy the view."

It was two o'clock in the afternoon, and the sky was nothing but blue and yellow and forever.

"Is this all your land?" she asked him, craning her neck to see every which way, sounding slightly less panicky than before.

"Yup."

"It's vast."

He didn't want to bring the conversation to his ranch and how close it was getting to completion. Not today or tonight or tomorrow. Not until he had to. "You feeling better? Nerves gone?"

She turned, and this time when she smiled it was broad and relieved. "I think so. It's amazing up here. It feels like we're a part of the air or something." She laughed. "I'm sure that sounds stupid."

"No," he insisted, something pinging inside his chest. He'd wanted her to love it. Love what he loved. It made him feel strangely whole and happy. Now who sounded stupid? he thought grimly.

"So, this dinner?" she said, releasing a deep breath and sitting back in her seat. "Who's it with?"

"The owner of a company I'm trying to buy. His name is Angus Breyer."

"What kind of company?"

"Property holdings mostly."

She turned to look at him again. "Why do you want to buy it?"

The *Long Horn* caught some wind and Deacon quickly steadied her out. "The properties are very valuable. I want to make . . . improvements on them, then resell them."

She was studying him—he could feel it—trying to understand what he was saying. Exactly what he was saying.

"This Mr. Breyer," she said. "He already say no to you?"

Damn, she was perceptive. Deacon turned and eyed her. "How could you possibly know that?"

She shrugged. "You've obviously put a lot of work into this. Meeting him outside the office. Leaving the Triple C in the middle of a major is-sue. It's just your way, Deacon Cavanaugh."

Deacon tensed, wondering if she was taking things there. Bringing up the ranch and his need to have control of it at all costs. "What's that, Ms. Byrd?"

"When you want something, you go after it un-til it surrenders."

He could feel the heat in her words and he grinned. Pushed back, played back. "And then I take it out to dinner."

"Hey, buddy," she returned with moderate heat. "I didn't surrender." She put her hands behind her head and sighed. "I'm just coming along for a mini vacation."

"Taking a break from work is a good thing. I don't do it nearly enough."

"I'll bet. You're a workaholic, aren't you, Deac?"

"Probably." His gaze cut to hers. "You?"

She laughed. "Probably."

He laughed along with her. "Blue taking over as foreman while you're gone?"

She sobered slightly. "Yep."

"He seems like a decent guy," Deacon allowed.

"He's the best."

Deacon turned and growled at her. "I said decent."

She dropped her chin so he could see her eyes behind her shades. They were dancing with amusement. "How many times do I have to tell you that you don't have to be jealous of Blue?"

Seriously. Autopilot would really be good here. "Can't help it, darlin'. He's had so much more time with you."

"Well, that's being rectified right now, isn't it?"

Deacon glanced back at her again. Looked her over as his chest went tight and the hands holding the *Long Horn*'s controls wanted to be holding her. "Shit, Mac," he said. "I really want to kiss you."

She pointed at him in mock seriousness. "No kissing in helicopters."

"Says who?"

"I read the safety rules online this morning."

"You did not."

"Hell yes, I did. I wanted to be able to fly this thing if you fainted or something."

"Honey, I don't faint." He turned to her and grinned. "And even if I did, one morning's reading ain't gonna do it."

"Yeah, I suppose I'd need lessons or something."

"I'll give you lessons."

She raised an eyebrow. "Teach me to fly."

His body reacted to her words and he groaned. Just then, he heard a male voice in his cans.

"Dallas/Fort Worth to *Long Horn*. Come in, please."

"This is *Long Horn*," Deacon returned. "Over."

"Flight plan to Cavanaugh Towers accepted. Please proceed."

"Roger, Dallas/Fort Worth. Over."

That drew Mac's attention. "What was all that?"

"We're coming in for a landing."

"That exchange wasn't in any of my reading material this morning," she said lightly, almost wickedly. "I have so much to learn, Mr. Cavanaugh."

He groaned again. Maybe they should've driven.

Or hell, taken his jet. Then he'd have his hands free. "Damn you, woman," he grumbled.

She laughed. "So where do we park this pretty bird? The airport?"

He smiled to himself. "No. Somewhere a little more convenient."

As he flew them over the city, between buildings, Mac grew quiet, interested in her surroundings. She pointed things out and squealed when she thought they were getting too close to a skyscraper. And in few minutes, they were headed for the tallest building of them all and the helipad on top.

"Oh my God. What's this?" she exclaimed, pointing at the *CE* down below. "Where are we?"

Deacon hovered over the pad, grinning at her awe and maybe preening a bit, too. He'd never taken anyone on the *Long Horn*, he thought, bringing her down. Never brought anyone to the office. Not like this. Never wanted to. Until Mackenzie.

He set the bird down nice and easy and switched off the engine. Then he turned to look at his beautiful, enthusiastic guest. "Welcome to Cavanaugh Towers, Ms. Byrd."

To say that she had entered a whole new world was an understatement.

As soon as the chopper blades stopped whirling, the rooftop doors slid back and two men came out. His door already open, Deacon called to them. Ty and Bell, Mac believed it was. The one named Ty came around to her side and helped her down. He was young, maybe late twenties, and had a superinfectious smile that went well with his California-surfer-boy looks.

Thick, wet heat suffusing her, Mac walked around the chopper and met Deacon on the other side. She'd seen him in his suit and tie when he'd come to get her and, of course, on the helicopter. But there was just something about him wearing those clothes in this environment that sent curls of awareness running through her. The reaction surprised her, as she always thought of herself as a cowboy-only kinda girl.

The fact that Deacon not only owned the building, but was the man in charge, became apparent the second they walked through the rooftop doors. Ty and Bell had stayed behind with the *Long Horn*, but two more people, assistants maybe, met them just inside. One was a young man in a suit carrying two bottles of cold water, and the other was an older woman who asked Deacon if she could take his briefcase and anything else he didn't wish to carry.

Good Lord, it felt like they were celebrities or royalty or something. She wondered if Deacon had this kind of treatment every day. If he liked it, or if it made him a little crazy having people fawning.

"Mackenzie." Deacon gestured for her to take his hand, and when she did, they headed straight into a tiny metal elevator.

"You're quiet," he said to her, flashing her with those incredible green eyes and a heavy-duty grin.

"I'm taking it all in, Mr. Cavanaugh. It's pretty amazing. You in this massive office building that has your name on the front. Helipads and people catering to your every need . . ."

"And to your every need, Ms. Byrd," he said, his voice dropping to a husky whisper. "Anything you need, just let me know."

Her cheeks went hot. Hells bells, what in the world would she need? Her eyes ran up the length of him. Tall drink of water in a tailored suit. Well, except maybe him. She grinned.

"You're smiling at me, Mackenzie."

"The suit . . . I just never thought it would do anything for me . . ."

He had her in his arms in an instant, turned her so her back was against the metal wall. Then he leaned in, and his lips found her ear. "That's all I want, Mackenzie. To make you feel. Make you happy. Make you want me like I want you."

That last bit was wrapped up in a devilish smile. A smile she could feel all the way down to her toes.

Heart racing, her stomach doing some serious flip-flops, she wanted to scream at him. *Kiss me, damn you! You wanted to in the helicopter; now's your chance.*

But then the elevator stopped and the door opened. She saw several people walk past, determined expressions on their faces. "I think we're here," she said.

His eyes fierce, Deacon backed up and took her hand again. "Come."

Her entire body was humming with heat from his words, his nearness, just *him*, as she followed him out of the elevator and down the hall. No one spoke to him, but a few people nodded. It was only when they entered a separate wing of offices that people took notice.

"Welcome back, Mr. Cavanaugh."

"Good to see you, sir."

Deacon acknowledged all of them, but didn't stop to introduce her to anyone. Finally, he led her through a set of double doors. Inside was an office the size of three of her river cottages and a desk the size of a small car. Rugs blanketed the floor, and two black leather sofas faced each other with tables and lamps on either end. Windows made up one entire wall, and as Mac drew near, she saw that there was a covered balcony and a lap pool. Holy cats, this really was his building.

"Your office is incredible," she said, checking out the view, the tiny world below.

She felt him come up behind her, felt his warmth, his rock-solid chest. "No, you're incredible."

Smiling, she turned around. "So, what now? A dip in the pool? A flying lesson? We could get a Popsicle. You know one of those ones you can break in half and share. And I'll even take the broken one. That's how nice I am."

"I couldn't have you do that," he said, running his hand through her hair, making her shiver. "You're my guest. I'll take the broken one."

"All right, but you get to pick the flavor."

He sniffed with mock arrogance. "Grape. Don't even have to think about that."

"Really? Grape." She looked him over. "I just don't get grape from you."

"Honey, it turns your tongue purple."

Mac was laughing hard when the door opened and a woman strode in. For a split second she looked surprised to find Mac there, and even more surprised that there was laughter present, but she covered it well and quickly.

"Good to see you, sir," she said in the most professional tone Mac had ever heard in her life. "I've confirmed your dinner reservation, confirmed with Mr. Breyer, and I'm packed and ready to go."

"Very good, Sheridan," Deacon said as Mac moved away from him slightly, so they didn't look like they were in the middle of making out in his office. She wasn't sure why she cared about this, but she did.

His eyes alight with amusement, Deacon watched her. "Mackenzie Byrd, this is my assistant, Sheridan O'Neil."

Mac stepped forward and offered her hand. "Hi."

The woman was incredibly beautiful, her auburn hair pulled off her face, making her gray eyes pop. She dressed impeccably, and when she clasped Mac's hand, her smile was both lovely and genuine.

"It's really nice to meet you, Ms. Byrd," she said.

"You too. And please, it's just Mackenzie. Mac actually."

The woman nodded her understanding, then said, "We have a car waiting downstairs. If you'll come with me."

Where the hell was she going? Suddenly nervous, Mac glanced at Deacon, who was now standing behind his desk, looking way too powerful and sexy to be around people who might find him as hot as she did.

She nearly rolled her eyes at the moronic thought.

"Sheridan is going to take you to the house," he said. "I have a few things to do here. But I'll be right behind you."

Oh. She hadn't realized she'd be on her own for a while. Was it silly and girly of her to want to stay in his office, stretch out on one of his black leather couches and watch him work? Yeah, probably.

His eyes bored into her, making her shiver. "I won't be long. I promise."

She nodded, gave him a small smile, then turned to Sheridan. "Downstairs, you said?"

The woman nodded. "This way."

Mac followed the woman out of his office, through what was no doubt her office, and into the same private elevator she and Deacon had used to come down from the roof. After the door slid closed, the woman turned to Mac with another of those way too beautiful smiles, and Mac couldn't help but wonder just how closely this Ms. O'Neil worked with Deacon.

"The ride to Mr. Cavanaugh's home isn't long," she said. "We'll be there in less than ten minutes."

We? Oh. "You don't have to take me to Deacon's place," Mac told her as they rushed down toward the lobby. "I'm sure I can handle it on my own. And you probably have a ton of work to do."

"It's no problem, and it's Mr. Cavanaugh's wish that I accompany you."

Oh my. "And everyone does what Deacon wants, right?" Mac had meant it as a joke, but the woman looked slightly confused.

"Of course," she said.

Good Lord, this was a far cry from the small-town life of River Black.

The elevator dinged softly when they reached the lobby, opening to reveal a bustling atrium. As they walked side by side toward the glass doors leading outside, Mac took in all that was Deacon's. Cavanaugh Towers was like a hotel with its banks of elevators, newspaper and coffee kiosks, and hundreds of people heading in and out. It was damn impressive.

"Besides, I'm done for the day," Sheridan said as she opened one of the glass doors and motioned for Mac to go through. "After I get you settled, I'm actually heading to your River Black."

"Really?" Mac replied, her surprise unmasked.

The hot, damp Dallas air assaulted her for the second time that day, and she wished she had taken that cold bottle of water the assistant guy had offered her on the roof.

"Gary's over here," Sheridan said, leading them toward a black stretch limousine.

Mac's mouth dropped open. The driver was dressed in a black suit and gray tie and was waiting by an open back door. He nodded to both Sheridan and Mac.

"Ms. O'Neil, Ms. Byrd," he said as Mac slipped inside, followed by Sheridan.

Mac had never been in a limousine before. It was roomy, that was sure, with a lot of black leather and tinted windows. She sat on one side near a small bar setup, while Sheridan sat on the other, facing her.

"So, why are you going to River Black?" Mac asked as the driver pulled away from the building and onto the street.

"Mr. Cavanaugh wants me to open the office he has there. It's above an RB Feed and Tack, I believe."

An office? He had an office in town above the Feed and Tack? Since when? "To do what?"

She gave Mac an apologetic smile. "I'm sorry. That's confidential."

Of course it was. Mac tried not to show her frustration at not knowing something about the man she was here with, the man she was staying with, and hopefully sleeping with. She shook her head. "No problem."

"Have you ever been to Dallas, Ms. Byrd?" Sheridan asked, expertly shifting subjects.

"A handful of times when I was younger."

"Do you have any family or friends here?"

"Just Deacon."

She nodded, her stunning gray eyes unreadable. "If you need anything, Mr. Cavanaugh has three members on staff at his residence. And, of course, Gary is at your disposal."

"I'm sure I'll be fine," Mac insisted.

"I'm sure you will, too," she said with a genuine smile. "You seem very capable, strong. You're the foreman at the Triple C, I believe?"

Mac nodded. This woman spoke of the ranch like she knew a good amount about it. And being Deacon's assistant she probably did. Mac wondered what she would say if she asked Sheridan about Deacon's plans for the ranch's destruction. Would the woman show any sign of knowing, or would she simply say again, *Sorry—that's confidential*?

She guessed the latter.

Crossing her legs at the ankles, Sheridan sat up very straight and focused her attention on Mac. "That must be a big job. And exciting."

"Both and very," Mac confirmed. "Bossing cows and cowboys around all day long." When Sheridan smiled, she did too. "Truly, I love it. I hope to never ever be without it."

A shadow crossed Sheridan's eyes, but she just nodded. She did know, Mac realized with a squeeze to her gut as the car moved up an incline and then came to an easy stop.

"Here we are," Sheridan announced.

Gary was quick with the door, and when Mac stepped outside and saw the building they were parked in front of, she nearly gasped. Her head tipped back as she took in all the stories of glass and metal. This was blatant and breathtaking opulence, and the furthest thing from home cooking and open prairie there was. Boy, Deacon had not only run fast, but he'd run far.

A male voice called out, "Ms. O'Neil."

Sheridan smiled at the short, stocky doorman as they passed through another set of glass doors and into another shockingly beautiful lobby. Clearly, Sheridan knew the auburn-headed doorman pretty well, which sent threads of irritation—aka jealousy—through her. Seriously, was there something more between her and Deacon?

"Red, this is Ms. Byrd," Sheridan said, heading for the elevator.

"Afternoon, Ms. Byrd," the man said, his brown eyes flashing with good nature. "Pleasure having you here."

Mac smiled in return. "Nice to meet you, Red."

The elevator was once again private, and when Sheridan used a key to start it, Mac knew they were probably headed for the penthouse. She was starting to notice a pattern here. The billionaire bachelor pattern. And though she was curious and in awe of the whole thing, she wasn't at all sure if she fit into it.

When they reached the top, the doors opened and they were inside the most incredible apartment Mac had ever seen in her life. Thick-planked dark hardwood covered the floors of the wide foyer and continued into a massive great room. Floor-to-ceiling windows made up nearly ninety percent of the walls, and anyone who enjoyed a view would understand why. Downtown Dallas spread out before her at an almost perfect height. Mac imagined that at night, it was probably the most breathtaking thing ever, not to mention sexy.

Deacon's furnishings looked comfortable, yet modern, with lots of leather. And to Mac's surprise and delight, much of it, from the couches to the rugs and tables, had a very decided Western feel. Inside that expensive suit, a cowboy still dwelled.

"Afternoon, y'all."

A woman dressed in a fitted black T-shirt and black pants walked down the hall toward them. She had short, spiky black hair with gray steaks running through it and pale blue eyes that seemed to smile before she did.

"This is Carol Highcourt," Sheridan said. "Carol, this is Mr. Cavanaugh's guest, Mackenzie Byrd."

Bright white teeth flashed. "Hello, Ms. Byrd. Welcome. Can I take your bags?"

"That's okay," Mac told her. "It's just the one. Thank you, though."

She nodded. "How about something to drink, then? It's darn hot out there today."

"It is," Mac agreed, feeling strange about being catered to. She didn't want to insult anyone or have them go out of their way, but she knew this was the job the woman before her had been hired to do. "Maybe after I put my things away?" she suggested.

"Perfect." She looked at Sheridan. "Something for you, Ms. O'Neil?"

"I'm good, Carol. Thank you."

Carol turned back to Mac. "I'll show you to your room, then."

Sheridan turned to Mac and touched her arm lightly. She had long, elegant fingers to go with her long, elegant self, and once again Mac wondered moronically if she and Deacon had ever gone out, or maybe had a hot office romance. It would really chap her ass if they had. Especially with how Deacon had sent the woman to escort her home.

"I'm going," Sheridan said. "Again, anything you need, Carol's your woman. Enjoy your time in Dallas, Ms. . . . ." She paused and smiled shyly. "Have fun, Mac."

Damn, she really kind of liked this woman. Sheridan O'Neil was not only gorgeous and obviously brilliant and accomplished, but she seemed damned nice, too.

She gave her a genuine smile. "Thanks, Sheridan. I appreciate it. And maybe I'll see you when I get back to River Black." *With Deacon. The sexy boss you may or may not have dated and/or slept with.*

Mac mentally rolled her eyes. Okay, this needed to stop now.

"Hope so," Sheridan called as she headed toward the elevator.

"Oh and hey," Mac called after. "Don't forget to pack some country clothes. You'll need 'em."

Sheridan turned around once she was inside the elevator. "Country clothes?" she said, pushing the button. "What would those be?"

But before Mac could answer, the steel doors closed on Sheridan's suddenly confused expression. Odds were, the woman would bring along a pair of jeans. She'd figure it out from there.

"Ready, Ms. Byrd?" Carol asked, snagging Mac's attention.

She led Mac down a long hallway. On one side of her were windows leading to an outside deck with gardens, a pool, lounge area, fire pit, and a brick-and-stainless-steel grill. It all looked brand-new and impeccably maintained. On the other side of her were rooms. Most of the doors were either closed or nearly so, so Mac didn't get a chance to see inside. But she was going to guess they were probably bedrooms.

"Here we are." Carol stopped in front of double wood doors, opened one, then moved aside so Mac could enter first.

Mumbling a quick thank-you, Mac stepped inside the loveliest—no, the sexiest—room she'd ever seen in her life. She would've never chosen it but found herself drawn to it. It was shockingly beautiful. Everything was white—bedding, couches, chairs, lamps—except for the floors, which were the same dark wood, and the short, fat vases of red roses on nearly every surface.

Mac's first thought was Deacon. Had he decided on this room? Had he asked for those flowers? Or was it all Carol's doing? She desperately wanted to ask, but she refused to look like a sixteen-year-old girl who wanted to know how much her boyfriend talked about her. No matter how much she felt like one inside.

"Your private bath is through here," Carol said, gesturing to a door on the far side of the room. "And your closet is here. Can I hang your things for you?"

The closet looked as long and as large as the bathroom. Mac glanced down at her bag. "Thanks, but I can do it. I just have one thing that hangs anyway. My dress for tonight." She'd brought a nice black cocktail dress she'd bought a few years ago and had worn only once. There weren't tons of fancy parties or dances to go to in River Black, nor were there shops that sold that kind of finery.

"I'm sure it's lovely," Carol said with a gentle smile. "But if you're so inclined . . ." She gestured to Mac, then slipped inside the closet.

Mac followed her, then gasped when she stepped inside. Lord, she'd been right. The closet was nearly the size of her bedroom in the foreman's house.

Which in and of itself was pretty nuts. But there was more to make her eyes bulge, her breath catch, and her curious, conspiracy-theorist brain ping. On the right side of the closet, hanging in a neat row, were a rainbow assortment of couture dresses.

Mac turned to Carol and just raised an eyebrow. It was like something off one of those runway-modeling reality shows she sometimes watched late at night if there was a decent amount of ice cream in the freezer.

"Feel free to wear anything you like," Carol said, her easy grin broadening.

"I'm confused," Mac began, trying to keep the strain of jealous chick out of her voice. "Deacon has dresses here for his guests?"

Poor Carol's eyes bugged out of her head. "No, Ms. Byrd," she said, aghast. "Of course not. This is for you."

Okay. Jealous Girl kicked to the curb. "Come on."

The woman nodded. "The store delivered them just a few hours ago."

"But why?"

Her eyes returned to their normal size. Maybe even softened a little. "Mr. Cavanaugh wanted to make sure you had access to the newest styles, if you needed them. Or wanted them." She went over to the other side of the closet and removed a strip of cloth that was draped over a long, heavy cabinet. "There are shoes as well."

"Holy shitballs!" Mac exclaimed as she took in twenty or so of the most spectacularly beautiful pairs of heels she'd ever seen.

Carol laughed.

Mac turned around and faced the woman, her face flushing with every second that ticked by. "Sorry."

"Don't apologize, Ms. Byrd," she insisted. "I appreciate a ballsy woman. As well as a woman who knows a nice set of footwear."

Mac turned back. While the whole thing was a bit intimidating, crazy, and truly unnecessary, she really did have a few girly bones in her body. And right now, they were urging her forward to see the pretty.

With a soft sigh, she reached down and picked up a little piece of open-toed silver heaven. She wore heels pretty much never, but she sure liked the idea of it.

Her head came around again and she asked Carol, "How the hell did he know my size?"

"Mr. Cavanaugh is nothing if not thorough, my dear."

Her heart pinged again. She kind of didn't want to know what that meant. Didn't want to know if this was standard practice or not. Instead, she went back to the right side of the closet and fingered the sleeve of a green halter dress. "This is lovely."

"It is," Carol said behind her. "But I think you'd stop traffic in that strapless blue next to it."

Mac's eyes cut to the blue. "Oh, my. This is . . . Wow . . . It's beautiful."

"Try it on," Carol encouraged. "And while you're doing that, I'm going to whip up some refreshments. Maybe a cocktail. It's gotta be five o'clock somewhere in the world. Come on out if you're inclined."

"Carol?" Mac said, turning.

"Yes, Ms. Byrd?"

"I really appreciate this," she said with sincerity. "All of this. But I just want you to know that you don't have to do anything special for me."

"Sure I do." Her eyes glittered. "Mr. Cavanaugh's orders, honey."

Mac sighed. "Orders, huh?" She gave the older woman a conspiratorial smile. "And what were those orders, if you don't mind me asking?"

The woman smiled. "Make you feel completely at home."

The ping. It was back. But this time, it didn't go away. It spread warm, like honey, through her. "Well, it's nice that he treats his guests like that."

"I wouldn't know, Ms. Byrd."

Mac's brows drew together. "What do you mean?"

The woman's smile broadened. "You're the first guest Mr. Cavanaugh has ever had."

When Deacon arrived home an hour and a half later, he was greeted with something he'd never heard before.

Laughter.

And it was coming from his kitchen.

For just a moment, he leaned against the wall in the foyer and listened. Mackenzie. She had this very specific laugh, like her whole body felt the happiness or joy or humor that had been offered to her. His gut tightened. Was it right to bring her into this world? Bring her smile and good nature, quick wit and sharp mind into ruthlessness and shadows? She laughed again, and this time his entire body felt it. Yes, she belonged here. Because she belonged with him.

As he came around the corner, Carol spotted him from her perch behind the stone island. She stood abruptly. "Mr. Cavanaugh."

Seated on one of the barstools, Mackenzie glanced over her shoulder, and when she saw him, her eyes lit up.

Shit, he could get used to this, he thought.

"Welcome home," she said as he walked toward them.

He came up behind her, his gaze raking over her. She was dressed simply, but sexy, in jeans, a white tank top, and bare feet. He ached to lean down and kiss her. But he didn't think she'd feel comfortable with a display in front of Carol.

She lifted her bottle of beer to his lips. "Want a sip?" she asked.

His body tightened, and his eyes locked with hers as he allowed her to serve him. He growled softly as the cold, sharp liquid hit his tongue.

From behind the island, Carol cleared her throat softly. "Can I fix you something, sir?"

Deacon's eyes clung to Mackenzie's. "Thank you, Carol. But I believe Ms. Byrd is going to share with me."

"A sip. That was all that was promised. All you get from me, Deacon Cavanaugh." Mackenzie grinned so wickedly, his cock swelled.

"Just one more?" he asked, his tone husky, his meaning clear.

Her cheeks flushing pink, she lifted the bottle to his lips once more. When he clamped his hand around hers and drained the thing, she gasped. "Hey! Greedy—"

Deacon had the empty bottle on the island and Mackenzie off her chair and in his arms in less than five seconds. He wanted to make her feel comfortable around Carol, but frankly, he wanted her more. His gaze ate her up, and he lowered his mouth to hers. Gently, he shared the last of the beer with her. Moaning, she wrapped her arms around his neck and swallowed.

His entire body racked with heat-laced need. Deacon pulled her closer, his arms wrapping her so tightly, they crossed at the wrists. She tasted so good, warm and wet and crisp from the beer, and when she drew back and looked up at him with dilated eyes under lids at half-mast, he was ready to take her right there.

"Deacon," Mackenzie uttered, then turned to look at Carol.

The woman's eyes were as big as salad plates, but even so, she refused to look at him. "I'm just going to . . ." she rambled, pointing to somewhere out of the room they were in. "Laundry and . . . there's some things to snack on here . . . but then you're going out to dinner . . ."

"Thank you, Carol," Deacon said, his attention back on Mackenzie.

"Yes, thank you, Carol," Mackenzie added, then, when the woman hurried out, burst into a fit of giggles as Deacon dropped his head to her neck and nibbled his way up one cord of muscle.

"Poor Carol," she said between breaths.

She tasted so sweet. He lapped at her earlobe. "You scared her away."

"Me?" she cried, her fingers digging into his shoulders. "Please. If it was anybody, it was you and your beer bottle shenanigans!"

His mouth moved to her ear. "Did you just say the word shenanigans in my house?"

"Damn right, suit." She moaned as he licked the shell of her ear, then suckled on the lobe. "This house needs shenanigans and a helluva lot more country going on."

"Then you're going to have to stay a lot longer than a night."

She drew back and looked at him. Her eyes seemed to be studying him, questioning him. Then she shrugged. "I can do plenty of damage in a night." She grinned, ran her fingers over his tie, then flipped it out of the top of his suit. "I have to say, Mr. Cavanaugh, you look damn fine in this getup."

"Thank you."

"Can't decide which way I like you best. Jeans, tee, and boots or starched collar, suit—and a tie I can use to pull you closer."

He dropped his head and kissed her again, deep and hungry. He just couldn't seem to stop. Wanting her. Tasting her. Was this how an addiction began?

"Or maybe I like you the third way best," she whispered against his mouth.

"What way is that?" he growled, his cock so hard he didn't know how long he could contain it.

She smiled. "Wearing nothing at all."

"Oh." He drew his head back. "Come on, Mackenzie," he groaned. "Don't make me take you right here on the island."

"I'd be tempted to make you," she whispered sensually, "if poor Carol and her weak heart weren't going to be strolling past at any moment."

"Carol has a weak heart?"

"I don't know." When he laughed, she grinned. "But I don't want to risk it."

"I like having you here." He nibbled her lower lip. "I mean it. I think you should stay. And not just to bring in the country."

She looked momentarily flustered. Then she cocked her head to the side and said, "Well, I do have a month's worth of dresses and shoes to wear."

Ah, yes, the clothes he'd ordered. "Did you find something you like?"

She gave him a quizzical, almost reproachful look. "What's that all about?"

"Did you?" he pressed.

" 'Course I did. I'm a girl, Deacon Cavanaugh." She eased back, rested her elbows on the island and gave him a mock terse look. "There are two things in this life us females can't resist. Chocolate, shoes, and chocolate."

"That's three things," he pointed out.

"Chocolate deserves to be repeated."

He laughed, his brain conjuring images of her in nothing but a sexy pair of heels—and him licking melted chocolate off her body. Goddamn, he was a goner.

"But I have a dress," she said. "I brought a dress with me."

"So wear it." He reached out and ran his fingers through her hair. So soft.

"What do you mean?" she asked.

"Listen, darlin'. I didn't order all that shit to piss you off or to offend you. I just thought you might like it."

Her mouth quirked and she just stared at him. He was tempted to start kissing her again, and if it led to stretching her out on the island and making her forget about dresses and shoes and ranches and any kind of life before now, then he would be one happy man.

"What?" he asked when she just kept looking at him.

"Two diaries."

He lifted one eyebrow.

A small smile played about her perfectly pink mouth. "Two diaries filled up with nothing except you." She pushed away from the island and wrapped her arms around his neck again. "I never thought we'd get here."

His eyes burned into hers, and he said with utter conviction, "Neither did I, Mac. But damn, I'm glad we did."

Rising up on her toes, she kissed him. A deep kiss that matched his previous one, but this time, she dipped her tongue into his mouth and played with his teeth.

His body primed and ready, Deacon gathered her up tight and met her kiss for kiss, stroke for stroke. They were both groaning with need when Carol took that exact moment to walk through with a basket of folded laundry.

"Oh," she exclaimed. "I'm sorry . . . I—"

Deacon drew back an inch. "Carol?" he said, his eyes pinned to Mackenzie's. She looked as fraught as he felt.

"Yes, sir?"

"Do you have a weak heart?"

"No, sir. Fit as a fiddle."

He watched Mackenzie's wet, worked-over mouth curve into a smile.

"Wonderful," he uttered, closing in on her once again. "Now, please take the night off."

Thirteen

Sheridan O'Neil didn't fly in helicopters unless forced. And then she made sure she was medicated. The whole thing just didn't make sense aerodynamically. Or was that logically? She wasn't sure. But whatever it was, she wanted no part of it.

What she did trust to get her from place to place, however, was her Subaru Impreza. Granted, it took her a few hours longer, but it never failed. Or, she mused, as rain pelted her windshield, let her fall out of the sky to her death.

The afternoon was coming to a close, and she wondered while listening to the third chapter of *Zombie Fallout* if she would see the town of River Black come upon her soon. She'd never been in this part of Texas, but she'd heard it was incredibly beautiful. It was. Even under the shade of gray clouds and a crying sky she could see the hills of green dotted with wildflowers.

She wondered if it was raining in Dallas, too, and if it would cause problems for Mr. Cavanaugh's dinner. She knew that finally closing this deal was important to him. Maybe more than just important, though she'd never asked. She liked Deacon Cavanaugh, thought he was a brilliant businessperson, and appreciated how he supported her ambitions. But in all the years she'd known him, she'd never seen him as he was today.

As the rain downgraded to a sprinkle on her windshield, she lowered the speed of her wipers. It was no secret that Deacon Cavanaugh was good-looking. Or that every woman in the office stared and maybe even drooled when he walked by, but he never gave anyone more than a polite nod and a quick, uninterested smile.

Until today.

When he'd called and asked her to cancel things with Pamela, said he was bringing someone else to dinner instead, Sheridan had wondered about the new woman. Wondered if she was like Pamela. The same type. Ten feet tall, bone thin, artificial smile, performed well, and completely at the boss's disposal—which frankly, as a woman, kind of pissed Sheridan off. But it wasn't her business or her place to make those feelings known.

White fencing emerged on her right, a dark cloud burst overhead, and the rain started pounding anew. She turned up chapter four and settled herself in to listen. But a few minutes in, she was completely jarred from the story when she ran over something in the road.

"Shit," she uttered, glancing back. "What the hell was that?"

From what she could see with the lack of light and all the rain, it appeared to be a pothole. She turned back around, gripping the steering wheel, and just prayed she hadn't blown a tire. But as all cruel jokes went, she felt the lurch almost immediately, then heard the *thump, thump, thump.*

"Dammit." She pulled to the side of the road and got out of the car. Rain fell in pinpricks all over her skin and through her clothes as she headed to the rear. The rain had slowed again, but it was still enough to soak her in a matter of minutes. Spotting the dead tire, she hurried back to the driver's side, and climbed in.

Her teeth chattering, she grabbed her cell phone and quickly dialed AAA. Then she waited. And waited. No ringing.

No ringing?

She tried again. Dialed nice and slow, then held it to her ear. But there was nothing. No ring. No reception.

"Dammit," she said again.

She glanced around. Ranch land for miles. She was just going to have to wait out the storm, then walk to town. Or maybe to the ranch's house. Whichever was closer.

Turning her car off and locking the door, she tipped her seat back and just let the sound of the rain soothe her frustrated spirit.

"Damn, Carol," Mac uttered to herself, turning around in the full-length mirror in her ultralush bathroom so she could see the back of the navy blue strapless. "You know what you're talking about, lady."

She turned around again and stared at herself, wondering how she'd managed to become the sexy, curvaceous glamour girl staring back at her. With its sweetheart neckline and twist-front detail, the A-line skirted dress just kissed the floor. It made her look like she was going to the Academy Awards or a very fancy dinner with an incredibly hot man.

It was just that beautiful, and boy, did it fit her perfectly.

Her eyes cut to the discarded black dress hanging on the hook on the bathroom door. Poor thing, she mused with a grimace. It hadn't stood a chance. After her shower, she'd slipped it on. She'd done her hair—soft curls, gathered over one shoulder—and smoky, sexy makeup while wearing it. Even picked out shoes from the Deacon Cavanaugh collection to wear with it. But when she'd stood in front of the mirror, she'd just looked . . . blah.

And there was no way she was looking blah tonight.

Unable to resist the temptation of couture, she pitched the black dress and slipped on the blue.

As she was gathering up a few essentials and dropping them in her small purse, someone knocked on her bedroom door. Her heart lurched into her throat. That couldn't be anyone but *him*. Carol was gone for the night, and Deacon had let his chef and groundsman go, too.

The knock came again, and it sounded rather manly and impatient.

She grinned, then called, "Come in!" With one last look in the mirror, she took a deep breath and left the bathroom.

Deacon was walking in just as she was coming out, and *good God in heaven*, the man looked so beyond gorgeous Mac nearly fainted on the spot. Her gaze traveled up and down his body. Sure, she was a country girl. Admired a man in denim and chaps over most anything else, but right now, looking at black-haired, green-eyed Deacon Cavanaugh in his sharp, no doubt custom-made suit, which fit his long, lean, muscled body to perfection, and the crisp white shirt and cream silk tie that brought out the deep, sexy tan in his skin, she was seriously considering rethinking that.

The childhood crush that once dwelled inside her had died. What hummed through her now was a very grown-up, very serious, very dangerous sexual attraction. She wanted this man, wanted him thoroughly and completely. She wanted him naked and poised above her, those large, tanned hands spreading her legs wide before the other large part of his anatomy slid deeply inside of her.

Green eyes surrounded by black lashes moved lazily over her. Uncomfortable with her own lusty thoughts, and unsure of what he was thinking, if he liked what he saw, she blurted out, "You'd better be fixin' to start telling me I look pretty."

Amusement flashed hot in his eyes, and a slow smile spread on his lips. "No. That wouldn't be even close to how you look tonight, Mackenzie. You are drop-dead-from-a-heart-attack stunning, honey, and it will take the most supreme effort on my part to keep my hands and mouth off you tonight."

Her heart leaped into her throat, and she blushed happily. "Thank you, sir."

"Shit, darlin', don't thank me. If I had my way, we wouldn't be going anywhere tonight. I'd be spending the next three hours taking that beautiful dress off you with my teeth." His nostrils flared. "Damn, I don't mind showing you off, but I'm not sure I won't growl at anything that keeps their eyes on you for longer than five seconds."

Her skin went hot instantly, and her breasts felt

heavy. She wanted that, too. In fact, there was truly nothing she wanted more than him. "But duty calls. Or is it business?"

She watched his strong, handsome jaw tighten. "Business," he ground out.

She wanted to lick that rigid jaw, feel just the hint of stubble against her tongue. Taking a deep breath, she forced a calm, easy tone to her words. "So, where are we going? Somewhere fancy?"

"Yes."

She started toward him. "And how should I act? Quiet? Demure? Sophisticated?"

He watched her every step of the way with wolf-ish eyes. "Just be yourself, Mackenzie."

"All right," she said, coming up alongside him with a grin. "But don't forget you said that."

He took her hand and led her out into the hallway. "I don't forget anything."

His words made her shiver as they walked toward the elevator.

"Like the crush you had on me," he said.

"Good. That thing was epic."

Inside the elevator, he pressed the button for the lobby, then turned to face her, held her hands in his. "I like that you had a crush on me."

Standing so close to him, her heart stuttered inside her chest. "Do you, now?"

He nodded, his eyes hooded and sexy. He just killed her with the way he stared at her.

"I was too old for you then, of course," he said. "But I always admired the way you handled yourself. How strong and brave and fearless you were."

She didn't buy it for a minute. "If I remember correctly, you thought I was a pain in the ass and a bad influence on your sister."

His eyes danced with heat and amusement. "But a strong, fearless pain in the ass."

She laughed.

"Thank you," he said, his fingers lacing through hers.

"For what?"

"Coming with me tonight. Coming to Dallas."

Her heart squeezed in the wonderfully painful way that screamed, *God, I'm so desperately into this man.* "Thank you for asking. By the way, did I tell you how good you look tonight?"

He shook his head.

"Well, you do. Finer than frog hair. And you smell . . . really good, too."

His eyes filled with amusement. "I have to kiss you," he said. "But I don't want to muss. So . . ." He leaned in and brushed his mouth against her neck.

Her pulse jumped.

"Oh, darlin'," he uttered against her skin. "If I make it through tonight without finding a dark corner and your zipper, it'll be a goddamn miracle."

Her skin and blood on fire, she laughed. When

the elevator door opened, he led her out—not into the lobby as she'd thought—but into the garage.

Sheridan woke with a start, realizing that, one—and most obviously—she'd dozed off; two, the rain had stopped; and three, she was somewhere near River Black with a flat tire and no cell service.

She sat up.

The clouds were trying to push away and make room for the impending sunset. She checked her cell again. Tried to get a signal and a dial tone. Frustration and disappointment rattled through her. She was a planner, a list maker, and look at her. In a car with a flat and no spare tire. She was thoroughly disappointed in herself.

Thunder sounded from far off, and she looked up, frowning. Another storm was really going to screw up this already screwed-up situation? She needed to get to the office, make sure everything was in order, that she had everything Deacon wanted prepared. But it wasn't the weather making that sound. Making the ground rumble and shake. She leaned forward so she could see out her windshield better.

Wow.

Horses. About a dozen of them. They were thundering across the land, coming toward her, or the fence line. Their eyes were huge, and their drenched manes slashed against their necks.

Sheridan quickly got out of the car and strode over to the side of the road where the grass met the concrete. She shaded her eyes, trying to get another look at the amazingly beautiful sight.

As they neared, she saw that there was a lone rider with them. A cowboy. Must be. He wore the jeans and the boots and the hat. And the way he rode . . . it was like he was part of the paint horse under him, an extension.

Knowing this might be her chance to get to a phone or town, she lifted her arms and waved them around until she was sure he saw her. Breaking from the pack, the man galloped over to the fence line. As his horse snorted, he stared quizzically down at her, making Sheridan's breath catch in her throat.

He tipped that hat back an inch. Eyes the color of the Mediterranean blazed down at her.

"You need some help, darlin'?" he asked.

And the voice. Heaven help her, the voice. It was husky and ultramasculine, and she'd never heard its equal. As she stared up at him, her skin tightened around her bones and she had to remind herself to speak.

"I'm looking for the Triple C Ranch," she said, her tone reed thin.

"Well, you found it."

Relief spilled through her. So, she was on the actual property. Thank God. "I'm here for Deacon Cavanaugh."

Something moved over the man's face, but she couldn't guess at what it was because he'd turned his horse in a circle before she was able to study it properly.

"That so?" he said tightly. "You one of his ladies?"

Her breath came out in a rush. "No. Oh, God. No."

His brows lifted in question. As in, *Who the hell are you, then?*

"I'm his assistant."

"Ah." Understanding dawned. And if she wasn't mistaken, curiosity.

"Sheridan O'Neil," she continued.

"Good."

Good? "Excuse me?"

The flash of understanding was now replaced by amusement. "Nothin', darlin'. I can show you the way if you'd like."

"Right. See, the thing is, I don't have a spare tire. Which is incredibly irresponsible of me, I know. But there it is." She was completely aware that she was babbling, but the guy unnerved her. "I've been trying to call AAA, but cell service out here seems to be impossible—"

"Easy, darlin'. We don't need wheels. We got Cherry here." He patted the horse. "You'll sit up front."

All the color drained from Sheridan's face, and she took a step back. "No, thank you. I appreciate the offer, but I'll wait. Or, you know what? Actually, I could walk. How far would you say it is?"

Brown eyebrows lifted over sea blue eyes. "You never been on a horse before, Sheridan?"

The way he said her name, all warm and soft like he knew her intimately, made her stomach turn over. "I prefer to keep my feet on the ground."

Chuckling to himself, the man slipped off his horse and came over to the fence. He placed his arms on top of it, showing off tanned, muscular forearms.

Sheridan inwardly sighed.

"Come on now, darlin'. Come over here."

Sheridan glanced back at her car. At the sad tire. Then turned and walked over to him, stopping when she got to the fence. She could see him up close and personal now, and if it were possible, he was even better-looking than he'd been on that horse. And those eyes . . . liquid-blue fire. For the first time in her life, Sheridan thought she might actually enjoy being burned.

"Let me give you a ride up to the house," he said. "You got my word nothin'll happen to you."

"Your word," she repeated. "I don't even know you."

He stuck his hand through a gap in the fence. It was big and tan and callused, and Sheridan just knew that if she touched it, certain parts of her body were going to tingle uncontrollably.

"My name's James Cavanaugh."

Sheridan froze, her mind running that big reveal over and over again. Until it came up with, "Deacon's . . ."

"Brother," he finished.

His hand was still extended, and she didn't want to be rude to her boss's kin, so she placed her hand in his and pumped it a couple of times. Yep. There it was, she thought madly. Something far past tingling. It was actually a lot like what she imagined a bolt of lightning through the gut felt like.

Her eyes lifted to meet his. Deacon Cavanaugh's brother. She didn't know much about Deacon's family, as he rarely, if ever, shared anything personal. But she knew he had two brothers. This one, James, and another, Cole. But they were pretty different. Where Deacon was dark and imposing, this man was like something you saw on a movie screen. Thick, tousled light brown hair, high cheekbones, heavy mouth, straight white teeth, body like a god, and eyes so startling blue-green, she wondered if they were real.

"Come on," he urged, still holding her hand. "Come through the fence and let's go for a ride."

She gestured to the car. "My bags."

"We'll get them later."

Once again, Sheridan looked back at her car. What else could she do but walk or wait? With a trepidatious heart, she slipped through the fence, and followed the man to his beautiful paint horse.

But before she got on, she turned to face him, pointed at him. "No trotting."

"Promise," he said, then placed his hands on her waist and lifted her up in one ridiculously easy move.

It made her feel feminine and not at all worried about that bag of mini peanut butter cups she'd inhaled on the drive from Dallas.

"Or galloping," she said, looking down at him. Jeez, she was high off the ground. "Or cantering."

He jumped up and slung one leg over the horse's bare back, then settled in behind her. "How 'bout a nice, easy walk?" he said close to her ear.

Good Lord, was that more tingling?

She managed to nod. "A walk sounds good."

He made a soft clucking sound, then grabbed the reins in one hand and wrapped his free arm around her waist.

For the first time in Sheridan's life, she stopped breathing.

Fourteen

If he thought she'd looked hot in his chopper this afternoon, it was nothing compared to the way she looked in his car with the city lights flickering around her.

Deacon had given his driver the night off and taken the Aston Martin instead. It was his favorite. The car that had never seen a driver other than himself, or a passenger for that matter. He'd been anxious to see Mackenzie in it, her long legs extending to the floor, her curves against the leather seat. But instead of the excitement he'd read on her face during the ride in the *Long Horn*, she now seemed pensive.

"You all right, darlin'?" he asked as they raced down the street toward the restaurant.

"Of course," she said unconvincingly.

"You're not nervous, are you?"

"No. No nerves."

Okay. This wasn't good. He came to a stoplight

and brought the car to an easy halt. "Look at me, Mackenzie."

She blew out a deep breath and turned to find his gaze. If it was possible, she was even more beautiful than she was a moment ago, despite the worry he saw flicker in and out of her blue eyes.

"What is it?" he asked. "Are you feeling okay? Because we can turn around and go back to the house. I'll deal with Breyer another night." Deacon couldn't believe how easily those words had just rolled off his tongue. A deal he'd been wanting done for far too long.

"No. I'm fine. Really." She released a breath, shook her head. "I'm just having some crazy anxiety." Her eyes cut away from him. "So far away from where I'm in control, you know?"

He nodded. "Sure."

"I know tonight's important to you, and I just don't want to make a mistake or get all country with these fancy—"

"Hey." Deacon reached over and touched her cheek. "I meant it when I said be yourself. And I really meant it when I said I'm glad you're with me."

Her eyes lifted. "What about when you said I looked amazing? Did you mean that?"

His lips twitched, relief moving through him as her anxiety seemed to dissipate and her teasing humor took its place. "Oh, yeah." He took her hand, lifted a brow. "Help me drive?"

Her eyebrow drew up questioningly. "You'd trust me with this ultrafine piece of machinery?"

"Honey, I think I'd trust you with a lot more than that." Even though he wanted to keep his eyes on her, he had to turn back to the road as the light turned green.

"Like what?"

He gunned the engine. "You really going to make me say it?"

Her voice softened. "Only because I think I need to hear it tonight."

Damn, the woman was killing him. Bit by bit, piece by piece. Tearing down what used to be and rebuilding him different, happy, maybe even vulnerable. He wasn't sure how he felt about that last bit. But he was plenty sure how he felt about her. He put her hand on the gearshift, then covered it with his own. "My heart, Mackenzie. I think I'd trust you with that."

Under his palm, he felt her take control of the shift and slip his car into first.

He groaned and squeezed her hand. "Damn, darlin'. You really are the perfect woman."

Then he hit the gas and took off down the street.

After the momentary blip of apprehension back in Deacon's ridiculously beautiful Aston Martin, Mac had returned to her usual confident self. Deacon's words, his vulnerability on the drive over, had touched her like nothing else could, and as they sat side by side at the restaurant's best table, she found herself either gazing at him stupidly or rubbing her leg against his.

Deacon, however, was the very essence of cool, unruffled business mogul. Over drinks and appetizers, he'd already gifted his prey with a new and improved offer. An offer Mr. Breyer had taken a glance at, then put aside to focus not on Deacon but on Mac.

"No Ms. Cutter tonight?" Deacon asked him, turning his attention away from Mac.

"Not tonight," Mr. Breyer said, taking a drink of his scotch and water.

"Well, no date required," Deacon said.

"Oh, I have a date." Breyer grinned at Mac. "She's running a little late."

Mac liked Angus Breyer. Somewhere in his early sixties, the tall, good looking man with salt and-pepper hair was funny and charming, and though he clearly enjoyed the company of women, it wasn't in a creepy way.

"Seeing someone new, Angus?" Deacon asked, one hand on his drink, the other finding Mac's thigh under the table.

"I think so," the man answered. His gaze returned to Mac. "How's the wine, Mackenzie?"

Mac smiled at him. "Best I ever had, Mr. Breyer. You have excellent taste."

He laughed, his eyes flashing. "I like this gal, Cavanaugh."

"Join the club," Deacon said, squeezing her thigh, making Mac pull in a quick breath.

As the waiter placed salads before them, Angus picked up his fork and asked her, "Do you prefer Mackenzie or Ms. Byrd?"

Taking a bite of tomato, she told him, "Mac actually."

"Oh, I like that. No frills." After a few more mouthfuls of salad, he continued with his questions. "And is it true that you're the foreman of a ranch, Mac?"

"I am."

"And you enjoy it?"

Deacon's hand stilled on her thigh as she answered. "Very much. Nothing else I'd rather do."

"That's good," Angus said, his eyes flickering toward Deacon. "I'm a firm believer in doing what you love. No matter what the costs, what the risks, or even what you're paid."

Deacon pulled his hand from her leg altogether and reached for his drink. "Mackenzie will always do what she loves," he said. "She's not one to be swayed by money."

Angus raised one graying eyebrow. "Unlike the two of us, eh, Cavanaugh?"

His salad completely untouched, Deacon regarded the man across from himself with cool eyes. "Money has never interested me. It's just a by-product. Power on the other hand . . ."

"And destruction?" Angus cut in. "That can certainly be a draw."

The man's tone held zero malice. In fact, Mac detected a thread of sympathy there and wondered about it. Wondered what he knew. She looked over at Deacon. He seemed completely at ease, though his eyes were pinned to Mr. Breyer.

"We all have a need to fill," Deacon stated. "Or a score to settle. Or a deal to make. And when the offer becomes too great to resist, the motivation behind it is usually forgotten." Deacon's brows lifted. "Same goes for the risk of losing possible future dealings to something as insignificant and foolish as sentimentality."

Her breath suddenly caught in her lungs, Mac turned and stared at Deacon. She'd never seen him like this. So detached, so pointed. It made her shiver. Not with awareness anymore, but with concern. This was the business Deacon, the mogul, the shark. And she thought that if this man was the one who was brought out to take down the Triple C, she didn't stand a chance against him.

Mr. Breyer turned to regard her. "What do you think, Ms. Byrd? Are future dealings—and perhaps great ones at that—enough to sway your heart away from all that it knows, all that it's created?"

Mac wasn't sure what to say, or what was truly being insinuated or threatened by either one of them. Breyer could've been talking about her and Deacon and the Triple C. And for the first time since the reading of Everett's will, she didn't have a quick answer. She was falling in love with Deacon. And she'd fallen in love with the Triple C forever ago. What would win out—power, destruction, or sentimentality? She had no idea. Frankly, in that moment, she wasn't sure about anything.

"I think this conversation is moving in an uncomfortable direction," Deacon said, his cool tone lifting, easing into practical gentleness.

Still looking at Mac, Mr. Breyer's eyes warmed. "I apologize if I've made you uncomfortable, Ms. Byrd."

Picking up her salad fork, she stabbed a tomato and smiled. "No need, Mr. Breyer. I think we all understand the reason for this dinner and that you and Deacon are at an impasse. I'm just along for the ride." Her grin widened. "And, of course, the food."

Angus chuckled and turned to Deacon. "I really like her."

"Yes, I see that."

Once again, his voice changed. Heat and possessiveness threaded it now, confusing her, yet drawing her back to him again. And when Mac glanced over at him and caught that hungry stare, her skin went predictably hot. *Oh, this man*, she mused. Who was he really? The stone-cold deal-maker from a moment ago? The man who'd been so worried when he'd thought she was sick during the barbecue, the man who'd brought her flowers, flew her to Dallas? Or the man who thought bull-dozing his childhood ranch was truly going to change anything?

The first two she could accept. But the third . . .

"Ah, there she is," Mr. Breyer exclaimed, glancing past them. "Far later than I'd hoped, but I think I'll forgive her this once."

Deacon eased Mac to him and whispered close to her ear, "Prepare yourself for something barely out of her teens."

Mac laughed softly.

"Good evening, everyone. So sorry I've kept you waiting."

Deacon's head came around so fast Mac was sure he must have pulled a muscle. When he cursed softly, she wondered what was going on.

"Pamela?" he said in an icy tone.

The woman who stood to Deacon's left was—in a word—fabulous. Tall, reed thin, straight blond hair cut smartly to her chin, and eyes the rich and sensual color of honey. She wore her black dress like a second skin, and the way she carried herself hinted at a fashion model background.

Mac didn't feel any pangs of jealousy for the

way the woman looked. After all, she was also wearing couture. She did, however, feel a few jolts of irritation for the way the woman was staring at Deacon. Pretty much like she wanted to simultaneously throttle him and tear his clothes off.

"Hello, Deacon," she said, her voice as smooth and sugary as caramel.

Mac touched her molar with her tongue to see if she had just developed a cavity.

The woman turned her attention to Mac then. And after taking in her dress, face, and hair, she gave Mac a perfectly lovely smile. Super demure. Super-supermodel fabulous.

"And who is this?" she asked.

"Mackenzie Byrd," Mac said, extending her hand.

"Mac, this is Pamela Monroe," Deacon said in a strangely sour tone.

Mac turned to Deacon with a silent question mark in her eyes. He clearly knew the woman. How well, she had no idea, but he either didn't like her or he had gone out with her before or had a fling and was pissed that she was here.

Mac hoped it was the first one.

The woman slipped her tiny mannequin hand into Mac's slightly callused one. "It's nice to meet you."

Mac nodded. "Likewise."

"Pamela is one of Dallas's premier fashion designers," Angus said, his eyes moving between his supposed date and Deacon as the small group of musicians near the dance floor began to play.

So, it was true, Mac thought with a groan. Ms. Monroe was in the fashion industry. Lord, she prayed the dress she was wearing wasn't one of that woman's creations. Once again, she wondered just how well Deacon knew her. He looked annoyed as hell that she was there, and frankly, she didn't seem like she gave a rat's ass about hanging out with Angus.

"Would you care to dance, Mac?" Mr. Breyer asked, pushing out his chair and coming to his feet.

Mac turned to the man and gave him a grim smile. Something told her he'd arraigned this. That asking Ms. Pamela Monroe to join him for dinner was a way to mess with Deacon. And damn if she didn't want to find out why.

She turned that grim smile into megawatt charm. "You know the two step, Angus?"

He looked positively insulted as he came around and held her chair. "I'm a Texan, young lady."

Mac laughed and stood up. Even with the desire to know what was going down with Deacon and Pamela Monroe, there was something inside of her that didn't want to go, didn't want to leave Deacon alone with the woman. But she pushed that silly girl bullshit away and took Mr. Breyer's arm.

"All right, Angus," she said as he led her toward the floor. "Let's see what you got."

People dealt with rage in different ways. Cold, calculated words, silence, or physical confrontation. Deacon subscribed to the former. When Angus and Mackenzie were safely out of earshot, the older man's arms around her, guiding her across the floor, Deacon's gaze came to rest on Pamela Monroe, who was sitting in the vacant seat to his left.

"What do you think you're doing, Pamela?" His voice called to mind Antarctica in the dead of winter.

His tone clearly unnerved her, but she tried to hide it. She raised her ultrathin shoulders a centimeter. "Angus called and asked me to join him."

"Try again."

"Fine." She released a breath and seemed to relax into her standard sophisticated demeanor. "I wanted to see her. The woman you replaced me with."

"There was no replacing anyone. You and I have been each other's plus one for several years. It was a mutually agreeable arrangement with no shelf life."

Her eyes flashed with heat. "And what is this? You and the gussied-up cowgirl? True love?"

Deacon stared coldly at her. He wasn't going to discuss his relationship with Mackenzie with anyone. Least of all Pamela. "Because this is the last time you and I will be speaking, I'm going to apologize for canceling without explanation or proper notice. And I'm going to wish you the best of luck in all your future endeavors."

She looked stunned. "You can't be serious."

"Oh, I'm very serious," he said, his gaze cutting to Mackenzie on the dance floor. She was dancing with Breyer, smiling. He ached to be with her, touch her.

"You're dumping me for the hometown houseguest?" she seethed. And when he turned to look at her, she nodded. "Oh yes, I know all about it. The fashion world is a small one, darling, especially here in town. When a call comes in for an entire couture collection to be delivered to you, I'm notified."

"Tell me, Pamela," he said, sitting back in his chair and observing her. "Was the person who notified you the same one who tells the press every time you and I are out together?"

The answer was in the flare of her nostrils and the flash of black rage in her eyes. "I'm giving you one last chance to reconsider. She's a hick, Deacon. What could you possibly have in common with someone like her?"

Blood ran cold in his veins. "Never insult her in front of me again. Do you understand?"

His tone was deadly calm, and after a moment, she nodded.

"Now, if you'll excuse me." Deacon stood and tossed his napkin on his chair. "This hick cowboy is gonna dance with his beautiful date. I'll send Angus right back to you."

Angus Breyer could really dance. His movement was gentle, yet firm. And he could lead like nobody's business. Problem was, Mac kept glancing over at the table, at Deacon and Pamela, and losing track of her footwork.

"You all right?" Angus asked. "I didn't step on your toes, did I?"

Feeling silly, she returned her gaze to his. "No, no. It's just . . ." She paused, rolled her eyes. "I was checking out your lovely date."

"Pamela Monroe."

She nodded. "She's seems . . . nice."

Amusement sparkled in his eyes. "Does she, now?"

"Sure. You two know each other a long time?" Fishing was not her best sport, but she was really giving it her all.

"A few months," he said, then guided her under his arm in an easy turn.

He caught her back up just as Mac said, "And how did you meet? Did Deacon introduce you?"

"Why don't we just keep dancing, Mac?" he said.

"Angus?"

"Yes?"

She grinned. She couldn't help it. He was a pistol. "You and me, we don't have a business to fight over. We're just dancing partners. Dancing partners who can share information."

He chuckled, his eyes warm. "All right. I met her through Deacon."

Her heart soared up into her throat. "When?"

"A few months ago." He swayed easily to the music. "She accompanies him to these kinds of things."

Oh, perfect. She stared at the older man. Funny, good dancer, intelligent, and clearly one sly bastard.

"You brought her to mess with Deacon, didn't you?" she said.

Not one ounce of guilt crossed his features. "My regular companion wasn't feeling well. It seemed an interesting choice."

"And a very beautiful one."

"She is beautiful." He smiled broadly. "But she doesn't hold a candle to you."

Mac shook her head at him. "You're nearly as smooth as your enemy over there."

Not once in the hour or so that they'd been at

the restaurant had Mac seen this man appear un-ruffled. *Until now.* Even his hold on her loosened.

"Deacon Cavanaugh and I aren't enemies, Mac," he said, his eyes sober now. "It'd be easier if we were. But no, we've known each other a long time. In fact, first job he had out of college was with me."

"What?" Good Lord, it was like another stone to the temple.

"He didn't stay long. Too ambitious, too brilliant, too damn talented not to start his own company. In truth, I'd like to sell my business to him. He knows it like no one else, and I'd like to sit on a beach somewhere, drinking mai tais and watching future Mrs. Breyers walk by."

"So . . ." she prodded. "What's stopping you?"

"He doesn't want the buildings for himself, or even to sell them to a third party. He wants the land they're on."

Mac's mouth fell open.

Angus must've seen it because he nodded. "Sound familiar?"

Her heart squeezed, too, and she lowered her voice. "You know?"

"Not everything. I knew about his father when he came to work for me. That he had some issues with the man. He was more open then. And I know Everett Cavanaugh just recently passed. I know Deacon bought land out there several years ago. Wasn't hard to put all those puzzle pieces together."

"Then why not just say no?" she asked him. They were barely moving now, so deep in conversation. "Why do you keep engaging with him?"

"Remember when we were talking about sentimentality in business?" When she nodded, he said, "Seems I have an Achilles' heel."

"Mind if I cut in?"

Mac's heart jumped, and her skin hummed with the sound of Deacon's rough, sexy voice.

Eyeing Mr. Breyer with a lethal dose of irritation, he added, "Your date's getting lonely." Then he took Mac's hand and led her away.

Fifteen

The moment he had her in his arms, Deacon forgot everything that had come before her. The music meant nothing. People eating and drinking and laughing, Angus and Pamela: It all felt inconsequential next to her.

"I missed you," he said, his hand flexing where he rested it on her back.

Her eyes lifted to meet his, deep blue and swimming with heat. "I've been gone five minutes."

"Exactly," he growled.

She smiled, and the warmth that small movement exuded reached out and grabbed him by the collar, yanked him in. He was becoming utterly and completely addicted to her. Her scent, her skin, her laugh, her eyes, but most of all, her company. He felt right within it, at peace. Like he wasn't always fighting to keep himself unreachable. Did he think it? Shit, did he admit it? That he felt safe with her?

"But you couldn't have gotten lonely in five short minutes," she said in a playful voice. "You had the lovely Pamela to keep you company."

"True."

Her eyes narrowed, but they were heavy with amusement. "I'm going to step on your feet."

A happy, lust-filled grin tugged at his mouth. This. This back-and-forth, this endless flirtation, knowing you were it for each other. It made him insane with desire. And yet he would always play back.

"I'm just trying to stoke your jealousy, darlin'." As he moved to the soft jazz, he dropped his head and drank in her scent. "It makes your skin flush, your eyes glow, your hands itch to knock me out, and your pussy soaking wet."

She gasped but didn't pull back. "That's not jealousy, Deacon."

"No?"

She shook her head, her hair caressing his jaw. "That's me staking my claim. That's me letting you know how badly I want you, even though I'm pissed beyond words that your ex-girlfriend is here—"

"She's not my—"

Mac drew back and put her finger to his lips.

Deacon swiped at it with his tongue.

Her nostrils flared, and her eyes darkened. "It's me being desperate for you even while I contemplate leaving this restaurant and grabbing a cab or a bus and heading back to River Black."

Deacon stopped dead. As other couples danced around them, he held her in his arms and ground out a fierce query. "What did Angus say to you?"

"Don't blame this on him."

"What did he say, Mackenzie?"

She didn't speak at first, just stared into his eyes, trying to read him. "He told me he was your boss a long time ago."

"And?"

"He thinks of you fondly."

Deacon snorted, then began to move once again.

"It's why he continued to have these meetings, Deacon," she continued. "He thinks maybe you'll change your mind about what you want to do with his properties."

So, the man had gone as far as to tell her that, had he? Hardball was Angus Breyer's middle name, but Deacon truly hadn't given the man enough credit.

"So it's not just the Triple C?" Mackenzie was saying, pulling him back.

"What?"

"Your need to destroy," she said softly. "It's not strictly a Triple C fixation."

Deacon's jaw worked. "Don't be taken in by Angus Breyer and his fatherly chat. The man's as much of a shark as I am."

"What do you plan to do with his properties if he finally sells them to you?"

He wasn't about to lie to her. Never was going to lie to her. "Level them. Bulldoze. Sell the land."

She shook her head. "What is it, Deacon? And I'm being totally serious here. This need to tear down other people's life's work?"

His gut tightened at her words. "His buildings are crumbling, Mackenzie. The land will be worth double, maybe even triple when it's clean. Listen to me. What I'm doing with Breyer has nothing to do with the Triple C."

Her eyes searched his. "Are you sure?"

"Dammit, Mackenzie, we agreed not to bring this here."

"I know. But it followed you, Deacon. It followed us. I have this terrible feeling that it's always going to follow us." She shook her head. "How could it not?"

He released her only to take her hand. "Let's go."

"What? Where? You haven't finished here."

He was more than finished. He led her off the floor. "I've given Breyer my final offer. There's nothing more to say."

"Final? What—"

"This will be our last dinner, him and me."

"But you've been trying to buy this company for so long. I don't understand."

"No, you don't." His blood running hot and fast in his veins, Deacon strode out the door and into the bustling Dallas night, his hand wrapped around hers as if it had a mind of its own.

His hands propped on either side of the door, James watched the woman as she gathered materials from Deacon's room, placing them in several different files. She'd been at it for hours. He'd left her, then come back to check on her. He wasn't sure why, but he blamed it on being polite to Deacon's employee. After all, he normally steered clear of anything that was buttoned up to the neck and said things like "color-coded" and "triplicate."

"Are you bunking in here?" he asked her, wondering if she ever undid those buttons.

She didn't glance up. Her eyes were trained on the papers in front of her. "No. In town," she said, sounding preoccupied. "Mr. Cavanaugh's office is there, along with a small apartment. I may stay there or the hotel. We'll see."

Deac had an office in town? Shit. He wanted to be pissed, even annoyed that his brother had kept something like that from him, but calling out Deac for keeping secrets would pretty much be the pot calling the kettle black.

"How you planning to get over there?" he asked.

"I've been trying to reach AAA for several hours, but no luck. I'll probably call a cab."

He laughed.

Which made her look up. She had an angel's face and, if one noticed those things—one who shouldn't be noticing those things—a highly suckable bottom lip.

"What?" she said. "No cabs?"

"You might get one out here . . . tomorrow."

That bottom lip pushed out. "Seriously?"

"Darlin', you're in the sticks."

"Right." She seemed to think about this, then put her head down again and got back to work.

"I'd be happy to take you into town." What was he doing exactly? Good Samaritaning it for what purpose? He didn't get involved with women. Well, not for anything outside of mutually enjoyable sex.

"That's really nice of you," she said. "But I'm sure it's a long way, and my butt is kind of hurting me from the first ride."

She looked up, and for the first time James saw a flash of wickedness in those closely guarded gray eyes.

"I've got a truck, Sheridan," he said "It's no trouble."

She chewed her lip. "Well, if you really don't mind."

"Don't mind at all." He pushed away from the door. "Just come on downstairs when you're ready."

"Thank you." Her gaze remained on his face

for a moment or two before she nodded, then once again, went back to her work.

It occurred to him as he strode down the hall that unlike many of the people he encountered these days, she didn't have a clue who he was. All she knew was that he was Deac's brother. And damn if that didn't make her even more intriguing.

The lights of the city flashed by as Deacon drove like a bat out of hell. Mackenzie watched him, his hand on the gearshift, ever ready. She wanted to touch him, put her hand over his, but she was afraid of getting stung.

She'd gotten too involved at the restaurant in a situation that should've warranted some self-control on her part. It was his business, for goodness' sake. The choices he made were his own. She should've stayed out of it. But when it came to him, to them, it was like trying to stop a meteor from hitting the earth. The only way to do it was to shoot the thing down.

"I'm sorry, Deacon."

"What for, Mackenzie?" His voice was tight, his eyes trained on the road.

"Getting into it with you back there. Acting jealous." She shook her head, remembering. "In front of a business associate." Ugh, not to mention every patron in the restaurant and the pissed-off fashion designer.

"You really think you know me."

His cold tone worried her. This was exactly why she'd been anxious on the way to dinner. Screwing something up for him. Acting like a naive country gal who wanted everyone to know Deacon Cavanaugh belonged to her. She shouldn't have said a word to Angus Breyer. That was Deacon's private business. Had she truly screwed something up? Had he not meant it when he'd said it was his final offer to Breyer?

"I feel like I do know you," she said, then sighed. "Hell, Deacon. I wasn't trying to ruin your night or start a fight with you." She groaned. "Or maybe I was. But if anything, it was a fight for you."

Deacon yanked the wheel to the right and skidded off the road onto a patch of gravel near a deserted playground. He had his seat belt off and his eyes on her in less than five seconds. "I'm not pissed off because of Breyer or Pamela or anyone in that goddamn restaurant, Mackenzie. I couldn't give a shit about any of them."

Her insides reeling from the jolt of the car and the fire in Deacon's eyes, Mackenzie gripped her seat. "Then what is it? Why are you so angry?"

"This." He reached out and touched her face, ran his fingers up her jawline into her hair. "You. I want you. Fuck, I wanted you so badly back there that I didn't give a shit about that deal. I didn't give a shit about anything."

Her mouth dropped open. "Oh."

"Yes, oh," he said on a growl, his fingers tightening in her hair. "What does that say to you, Mackenzie?"

She shook her head. "I don't know."

"Yes, you do," he retorted hotly. "Tell me. What does it say that I'm more enraptured with you than I am with a deal I've wanted for more than three years?"

Her heart was pounding so hard in her chest, she could barely think straight. "That you're as into me as I'm into you."

"Yes." He released her and sat back in his seat with a groan. "And that I'm losing control over myself."

Shaking her head, she huffed out a breath. "You're not alone in that, Deacon. God, we're both running hot for each other. You're all I can think about. That's why everything I hear, everything I'm told scares the shit out of me." Her throat went tight and her hands started to shake. "I want to run from you. Get out of your eyeline. Forget I saw you again, pretend my heart isn't screaming for yours to capture it right this very second. It would be so much easier. But I can't." When he turned to look at her, she shook her head at him a little manically. "I can't."

His jaw working, making his cheekbones flex, he popped her seat belt. "Come here," he uttered hoarsely, then reached for her, lifted her up like she weighed absolutely nothing and placed her in his lap.

The sports car barely had room to support what he'd done, but neither of them cared. Before her ass even hit his lap, Deacon's mouth was on hers, capturing her in a deep, hungry kiss that made Mac cry out in pleasure. He tasted like wine and the night air, and she'd never felt so desperate in her life. To touch him, feed off of him, know what it was like to have him over her, pushing her knees back as he entered her.

Her hands went to his face as his tunneled under her dress. She moaned as he raked his large, warm hand up her calf, over her knee, and in between her thighs. She knew where he was headed and what he would find there: evidence of her unending desire for him.

"Oh, darlin'," he groaned against her mouth, nipping at her bottom lip as he ran his fingers over the silk barrier of her underwear. "Your panties are soaked. Which must mean . . ." He nudged aside the fabric and sent his thumb through her hot, drenched slit. "Hot, tight, swollen little clit."

Her sex clenched at his words, and she gasped, her fingers digging into his scalp. With a hungry growl of possession, he pushed his tongue inside her mouth and licked at her teeth as he circled her sensitive bud with the pad of his thumb. Heat surged through her body, turning her blood electric and ready to spark. She arched into him, wanting his fingers inside her, thrusting deep inside her pussy like his tongue was doing to her mouth.

"Oh, darlin', if I don't fuck you soon, I'm going to lose my mind," he uttered, pinching her clit gently before circling it with his thumb once again.

"I want you so badly, Deacon," she rasped. "I need you inside me, so deep I won't be able to breathe or think."

His kiss intensified, and as he rubbed her off in small, fast circles, causing a rush of cream to rain from her sex and coat his fingers, she moaned over and over again. God, she ached to touch him, hold his cock in her hand and stroke him until he felt as ravenous as she did. But he held her there, captive on his lap, fucking her mouth, sucking her tongue as he made her skin run fire hot and her body shake.

"Tell me what you need, Mackenzie," he uttered against her lips, his voice so pained it made her muscles clench and her throat tighten again.

"Make me come, Deacon," she whispered, so close to the edge she forgot where she was, who she was—only that she was with him. Her man. Deacon. "Kiss me hard and stroke me soft."

He groaned with her words and captured her mouth again in a series of shattering kisses. There was nothing like his hands on her, in her. And his kisses, they stole her mind and made her heart slam against her ribs, trying to escape and get to his.

His fingers gentled as he felt her on the precipice of orgasm, lightly flicking her bud, coaxing it to swell even further. Mac's breath came in quick gasps as she bucked against him, trying to meet his demanding kiss. When the dam inside of her broke, when lightning crashed against her mind and her heart, she pumped fiercely against his hand and cried out against his mouth. And he answered her by driving his tongue deep and rubbing her clit in long, quick, gentle strokes, over and over, lighter and lighter, until she whimpered and sighed and sagged against him.

Still kissing her with utter devotion and deep hunger, Deacon eased his fingers from her and his hand from under her skirt. Mac felt utterly boneless. Her eyes closed, all she heard were the sounds of cars rushing past outside in the dark night and Deacon's restless breathing. She wanted him. Like she'd never wanted anything. She wanted him to feel how desperate she was for him, how her heart ached for him.

She turned in his arms slightly and moved her hand down his chest, tunneling between their bodies. She got to the waist of his pants before he growled at her and ripped his mouth away.

Stunned, breathless, her eyes blinking to focus, she looked up through her lashes. "What's wrong?"

"Not here."

His command was gruff and sexy, and it was all he said before he opened the car door, lifted her up as he slipped out, then placed her back on the seat and closed her door.

Nestled into the driver's seat, Mackenzie watched openmouthed as he rounded the front of the car, then got in the passenger side.

When the door was closed and he'd belted up, she turned to him, confused. "What are you doing?"

"It's what you're going to do. Drive." He sounded close to biting someone. Her inner thighs trembled at the thought. "I'll direct you," he added.

"You're serious?" she said, still staring incredulously at him. "You want me to drive this hot piece of metal back to the house?"

He rolled his head to face her. In his vivid green eyes was an untamed, dangerous hunger. "Honey, I'm on the edge here. Take us home so I can take you to bed. My cock is screaming for you."

Air stalled inside her lungs and her sex clenched in response. But she didn't waste time. She wanted him, too, and getting to drive the Aston Martin was just a happy bonus. She quickly changed the seat's position, righted her seat belt, and with an excited grin, shifted into first and peeled away from the curb.

Sixteen

Watching her drive his car, watching her work the pedals with those heels and work the stick with her small, yet highly capable, hand had made Deacon so insane with lust that the very moment she killed the engine in his garage, he whisked her off to the private elevator. He growled as the doors closed, shoved his key in the lock and slammed his fist against the button that displayed a *P*, completely unconcerned that his headlights might very well still be on. Mackenzie was grinning wickedly at him, and his skin was burning from all the heat her body, her kiss, and that climax were giving off. All he wanted was to get them both naked.

With a groan of hunger, he pressed her up against the elevator wall, kissing his way from her collarbone to her neck, taking in the sound of her interminable passion.

Her hands went to his hair, fisting and massaging. "Can anyone see us in here?" she whispered almost frantically.

His hands raked up her back, stopping when he hit zipper. "No. No camera, no nothing."

"Good." She grinned, grabbed the back of his shoulders and whirled them both around.

Surprised at her speed and strength, Deacon raised one black eyebrow, then cursed as she pressed him back against the wall. "What do you have planned in that beautiful mind of yours, darlin'?"

"How do I stop the elevator?" she asked, her eyes dilated, her breathing rapid.

"Behind you," Deacon said, his cock so thick, so hard. His groin was throbbing. "The silver button with the *H* on it."

She turned, reached over, and hit the button. The car jerked to a stop. Her eyes returned to his, and slowly and unbearably sexy, she sank to her knees.

Deacon felt as though his insides were going to erupt. His hands fisted at his sides and his cock strained inside his zipper.

Her head tilted back and she looked up at him with liquid-blue eyes. "You sure they won't come looking for us? Thinking we're in trouble?"

"They wouldn't dare," he said. "That's why there's a phone."

Her mouth curved up into the most beautiful, sexually wicked smile he'd ever seen. And Deacon thought he could lose it just from that. But then she ran her hands up his thighs, over his groin, over his prick, and to the waistband of his pants. She made quick work of his belt and zipper, and when his cock sprang free, hard as marble and so filled with blood, it looked the darkest he'd ever seen it.

Her nostrils flared at she stared at him. She licked her lips. "You're very . . ." She glanced up and smiled.

"Honey, it's been hard for you since that night you drunk-kissed me."

She laughed softly. "Then I'd say it needs some special attention, wouldn't you?"

Deacon never answered. Mackenzie's hands were on him, and she was running her fingers up and down his shaft, so light, so soft, he groaned and pushed into her. Again, she did it, light and gentle, up and over the tip, then all the way down until she reached his sac. As she cupped him and rolled his testicles in her palm, Deacon's insides contracted and he swore brutally as droplets of precome shimmered at the head of his cock.

"Look what you do to me, Mac," he said, his voice taut. "One touch and my prick's crying."

She stared at it, the evidence of his desire for her. Then, with a quick swipe of her tongue to her bottom lip, she lowered her head and kissed him.

Deacon could've come from just that alone.

But she didn't stop with the kiss. Her tongue

ventured out to flick across the wet tip, moaning when she tasted him. Deacon's entire body went rigid. He wanted to grab her head and thrust himself in her mouth, but he held himself back, watched as she flicked her hot little tongue down his shaft, then lapped at his balls.

"Christ," he rasped, slamming his fist against the metal wall of the elevator. What torture. What perfect, cock-teasing torture.

And then her hungry mouth closed around him and she sucked him deep, taking everything he had and more, all the way to the root. Deacon stilled, feeling his body tightening, his balls drawing up, his seed desperate to find its wondrous target at the back of her throat. Shit, he wanted this to last, and yet he wanted to come more.

His fingers threaded in her hair, and as he thrust easily into her mouth, she moaned and played with his sac. She was so lively, so eager, her body moving with his. Glancing down, Deacon saw that the top of her dress was starting to inch down. He could just make out the top half of each of her nipples, and the sight caused another wash of precome to escape his hungry prick.

Mackenzie groaned and sucked him down, causing him to thrust harder and deeper, causing her to move an inch closer. Causing her breasts to pop out of their confines and grant him the sight that would be his downfall.

Full, pink tits.

"Fuck," he roared, pumping furiously inside of her. "If I come in your mouth . . . It might be too much—"

He lost his words. Shit, he lost all thought as she stroked him harder and sucked him deeper and encouraged him to work her mouth like he wanted to work her pussy.

With a deep groan, he came, flooding her eager mouth with hot jets of his come. And God help him, as she drank him down, taking everything he had to give her, her nipples went rock hard.

Even as the wash of climax moved around and through him, Deacon felt barely satiated. He wanted to ease her off of him, tell her to wrap her legs around his waist, and thrust himself deep inside her pussy. But after the car and the elevator, he wanted to get her back to his mattress and her legs spread wide.

As she drew back with a moan, Deacon knew that this was just the beginning for them. And when she looked up at him and smiled, he thought his heart would break from want. He gently lifted her to feet and pulled her so close to his side she gasped. Then he hit the button to resume the elevator's ascent and they surged upward.

As they walked through the dark house together, stumbled down the hallways, kissing each other madly, Mac felt a rush of power and lust snake through her once again. After taking him on her knees, drinking him down, all she could think of was him, having him, again and again. He was the most perfect taste she'd ever had on her tongue, and just recalling his expression when he'd come, when she'd swallowed every last drop of him, sent shards of electric heat straight to her sex.

Deacon's hands moved up her back, his fingers working to find the zipper of her dress, growling as he clasped it and drew it down all the way to her hips. Exposed, free, hungry, Mac could barely contain her excitement. Having him inside her, pushing deep into her sex as he kissed her, whispered to her, possessed her.

Deacon broke their kiss with a groan of frustration, and Mac realized breathlessly that they were in a bedroom—his bedroom, no doubt. How had they gotten there so fast? And how hadn't she noticed a doorway and a complete change of scenery? With eyes that refused to fully focus and wanted only to be trained on Deacon, she glanced around the room. Lit by the moon and the hall light, his bedroom was huge and modern and masculine and boasted an entire wall of windows that displayed the incredible lights of downtown Dallas. The furniture was mostly black and brown leather, and the hardwood floors seemed a lighter cherrywood than everywhere else in the house. Black-and-white photographs decorated the light gray walls, and when Mac's gaze caught sight of the bed, all her perusal of the residence was over and unimportant.

The king-sized platform cherrywood frame was ultramasculine, as was the white comforter and black pillows, but it looked comfortable as hell, and Mac couldn't wait to pull back the sheets and climb in.

She felt Deacon's hands on her waist and sighed as he stripped her from her dress and wet panties. She felt no embarrassment being naked in front of him. They were so past that now. So addicted to each other, naked seemed like the perfect way to exist.

Still standing there in his sexy suit and tie, Deacon moved his eyes covetously over her from top to bottom, taking in her tanned skin, curvy body, which was clad in only those three-inch silver Louboutin strappy sandals.

"You make me dizzy," he said, his eyes so dark green they seemed to be all iris.

"You make me wet," she returned boldly.

His jaw went hard and his nostrils flared. "I can scent it. You. Now I want to feel . . . feel your cream rush over my cock."

Heat surged into her, and she felt wetness leak from her sex and trail down her inner thigh.

Grinning in a hungry, savage way, Deacon started to take off his clothes.

Licking her lips, savoring the taste of him that was still on her tongue, Mac drew back and sat on the edge of the bed, preparing herself to witness a truly mouthwatering sight. His eyes locked to hers, he shrugged out of his jacket and tossed it over one of the leather club chairs. Then he gripped his tie.

As he loosened it, eased it down his chest, anticipation flickered through her like overactive lightning bugs. After all they'd done, all they'd both tasted and touched, she'd never seen him naked, never seen his waves of muscle and broad shoulders, hard, tight ass and taut hipbones.

Just thinking about it made her nipples harden into tight, sensitive buds.

Deacon continued the mouthwatering striptease by unbuttoning his shirt. As every inch of smooth muscle was revealed to her, Mac bit her lip and tried not to groan. But when he shouldered out of the thing and threw it aside with the rest, a small keening sound escaped her throat.

Her eyes wide and hungry, she considered placing her hands under her ass to keep from rushing at him. She wanted to help him undress, maybe even rip the fabric off of him, but she wanted to watch him even more. Once the shirt was gone, his pants dropped from his lean, muscular hips, easy and quick.

"You are so hot, Mr. Cavanaugh," she said in a husky voice. "I want to touch every inch of you, kiss every inch of you." She smiled to herself at her brazen words. "Lick every inch of you."

His eyes lifted and locked on her, and the heat she saw in his green gaze made her heart trip up.

"Not if I lick you first," he said.

He rushed her, his face tight and hungry, his cock so hard it looked like a column of marble, and pressed her back on the bed. She gasped as he splayed her legs and shouldered himself between them. He gave her no time to prepare or think. His head dropped and his tongue pushed up into her pussy, spearing her.

Mac cried out. She hadn't expected such a delicious invasion, yet she opened her legs even wider to give him better access. Groaning, he fucked her slow and deep with his tongue as his fingers stretched her pussy lips. Loving his madness, his need for her, loving every second of it, every thrust, she threaded her fingers in his thick hair.

He groaned as he drank from her, his breath fanning over her sensitive flesh. Mac lifted her hips and circled them, letting him know how crazy he was making her, how desperate she was for him. The cool sheets at her back mixed with the heat raking up her torso and pebbled her nipples. She was going to come again. She could feel the buildup, feel her mind starting to go.

God, she wanted him inside her when she came.

Wanted to see his face, lock eyes with him as she cried out and melted.

As if he felt it, too, Deacon gave her clit one last luscious feathering, then started moving up her body, kissing his way, lapping at the tiny well of her navel, running his teeth lightly over her ribs, nuzzling her nipple with his nose.

Mac's insides were flaring with heat, shaking with want. "Please, Deacon," she begged. "Come inside me. Fuck me. Please."

"There's nowhere in the world I'd rather be," he whispered against her wet nipple. "God, Mackenzie, I think you own me, darlin'."

His words wrapped around her heart and squeezed. Could that really be true? she wondered hazily, as he licked and suckled and coaxed her nipple into a hard, aching bud, his hand tunneling between them. *Could he feel that much for me? That deeply?*

Could he be falling for me? Like I've fallen for him?

Suddenly frantic for him, to connect with him, she moaned and squeezed her ass, pumping her hips, trying like hell to find him, get him inside her. But Deacon was in control, licking her nipple in quick, hard flicks as she rubbed the steel head of his prick against her entrance. He was so hard, so thick, her sex creamed in anticipation.

By the time his head came up and his eyes

locked with hers, she was near to madness. Every inch of her skin was on fire, tingling, loving the feel of his much bigger body over hers. And then he pushed her knees apart and whispered one perfect word.

"*Mine*."

His hands now bracketing her head, he drove into her.

A strangled gasp claimed Mac's throat, and she held still for a moment, adjusting to the size of him. His long, thick cock filled her so deeply, pressed against every nerve ending, setting her muscles contracting and rippling. Blood rushed in her ears, and when he started to move, slow and easy and languid, she wrapped her arms around his neck and her legs around his waist.

"Oh, darlin'," he rasped, his eyes locked with hers. "You're so tight. If it wasn't for all that honey your pussy is coating me with . . ." He groaned, drew back, then sank into her again.

Mac felt sweat break on her forehead and tears prick behind her eyes. They came from everything inside her, everything she'd ever wanted or dreamed about having someday. This man, his large, heavy, deliciously muscled body, was poised over her, working himself in and out of her, pistoning her into a frenzy as his hungry eyes clung to her like an emotional life raft. Was it real? And was it for only one night?

Did she care?

As his thrusts quickened, hitting the soft pillow of her womb, she moaned and tightened her legs around him. She knew the answer was *Yes*. She cared. So much. She wanted him for longer than a night. She wanted him forever. But this was here and now, and she could feel it and touch it and taste it.

Her hands and nails raked up his smooth, sweaty chest, to his neck, over his hard, sexy jaw. She couldn't get close enough, couldn't get him deeper, even though she felt so full, so close to climax. She wanted his heart beating inside her chest. Nothing else would do.

"Oh, damn, Mackenzie. You're so tight, honey," he groaned, his lip curling, his tone low and raw as he gripped her ass and drove into her over and over. "Even after the elevator, I don't know how long I can hold on."

"Don't hold on," she managed to utter through gasps for breath. "I can't. I'm going to lose my mind. Oh, Deacon, just like I've lost my heart."

He cursed and buried his head in her neck, licking the sheen of sweat and moaning. Every muscle on his body was flexing and bunching, and when he drove deep once again, then started rolling his hips over and over, Mac could no longer keep herself together. The pressure was too great. It surged up from her toes and burst inside her pussy.

"Come, darlin'," he said, raking his teeth over the cord of strained muscle in her neck. "I can feel your honeysuckle walls trembling around me, milking me, bathing me in your sweet cream."

"I'm yours, Deacon," she cried. "Yours. Always. God, always."

"Tell me again, Mac," he demanded, rolling his hips. Between gritted teeth, he said, "No, tell me as you come."

His head lifted and his eyes met hers. Then he started thrusting, so deep and so wild, his hands fisting her ass, lifting her just a little bit higher, Mac could only cling to him as her clit throbbed and release took hold.

"Now!" he growled.

"I belong to you!" she screamed as she came, her body bucking, her back arching, her fingers digging into the skin of his back.

"Oh, God," Deacon hissed. "Fuck! Too tight. So damn hot. You're creaming around me, darlin'. Your walls won't stop vibrating."

His mouth lowered and crushed hers, and as he came, as hot jets of seed rushed into her sex, he kissed her hungrily, desperately, almost violently.

Tears snaking down her temples, Mac pumped her hips, meeting him with every last stroke, taking every bit of him inside her until they slowed. Still kissing her, Deacon rolled his hips easy and gentle. Mac clung to him. Everything she could get wrapped around him, she did. She'd never felt so safe, so satisfied, and God . . . so in love. As he continued to kiss her, kiss away the blazing heat between them for something softer, gentler, and infinitely more vulnerable, Mac rubbed his back. Nothing intense, just sweet, soft strokes up and down, real lazy as she moaned her pleasure and contentment into his mouth.

This man made her happy. The happiest she had ever been in her life, and she never wanted to let go.

It was when her fingers brushed something strange that a thread of that contentment, that ease, retreated. It was something she hadn't noticed before. Maybe because the room was dim except for the moonlight. Maybe because she'd been so damn worked up. But there was something on the back of his shoulder . . . The skin was raised and scarred. Curious, she dragged her fingers over it.

"What are you doing, Mackenzie?" Deacon asked, his voice still thick with arousal.

"What is this?" she asked him. She brushed her fingers over it again. It felt familiar somehow. "Do you have a scar?"

Deacon went suddenly rigid and slipped out of her. He sat up, his eyes wide and the darkest green she'd ever seen. Like a forest on a moonless night.

Mackenzie's heart started to pound. Not out of sexual need anymore, but out of concern.

"Deacon?" She sat up, too.

"Yes, Mackenzie?"

He looked . . . caught. His nostrils were flaring. Why wasn't he looking at her anymore?

"What's going on?" She scrambled to her knees.

"Nothing," he ground out.

Her mouth went dry. She'd never seen him like this. Fear clinging to him, and something else . . . embarrassment? Shame? Her fingers twitched, the fingers that had just moved over the raised skin on his back. "Let me see it."

"No. It's nothing. Just a tattoo."

"A tattoo," she repeated.

"A hawk released from a cage. I got it right after I left home. The guy who did it was a newbie to ink and he scarred my skin."

Why didn't she believe him? "I want to see it."

His eyes flipped up to meet hers. "No."

The look he gave her chilled her to her bone. She started to move around him. "Why not?"

He blocked her way. Like an animal snarling over his dinner. What the hell was going on?

"Deacon, you're scaring me. Please tell me what's happening. Why you're reacting like this."

"You don't want to know."

"Yes, I do! Goddammit. Look what we just did. How close we were. Stop hiding from me."

He was silent for a moment; then he said in the darkest of voices, "Fine. You want to see it? You want to know the real reason I'm taking down the Triple C, Mackenzie?"

Heat, prickly and oppressive, slammed into Mac, and tears welled in her eyes. She couldn't explain why or where they'd come from. They were just there. She held her breath captive inside her lungs and nodded.

Slowly, Deacon turned around, gave her his back. Eyes slightly blurry with moisture, Mac swiped at them, then focused on what was before her. Lean, tan, and muscular, Deacon had smooth skin everywhere except his left shoulder. The tattoo was indeed a hawk, but it wasn't the ink that had her flinching, had her stomach churning. Had her eyes going so wide, they hurt.

"Oh my God," she whispered hoarsely. "Oh, dear God, Deacon. Who did this?" Bile rose in her throat as a terrible thought came into her mind. "Not Everett."

"No," Deacon said. "Not Everett. But he may as well have."

What? Oh, God . . . "What does that mean?" she rasped. Her reached out and ran her fingers over the damaged skin on his shoulder.

"He didn't stop it," Deacon said, his tone so black, so bitter, it hurt her ears. "He knew how deep my mother was falling, how angry she was becoming. He knew how she blamed us for what happened to Cass. How she punished us for it.

Day after day. With anything she could get her hands on."

Tears streamed down Mac's cheeks. Oh, God . . . "Your mother . . ." That's what she'd felt under her fingers. She'd known that mark. Had felt it on the hide of every head of cattle . . . "She branded you."

Diary of Cassandra Cavanaugh

May 1, 2002

Dear Diary,
I met someone today!

He was buying penny candy at the dime store, too. I can't tell you much about him yet because he said we should keep things a secret. I've never had secrets from my family or from Mac before, but it feels kind of good. Like for once I know something they don't know. For once I feel special and wanted.

Maybe I'll just tell Mac. She is my best friend. Let her know that she's not the only one with a crush on an older boy in River Black.

Or maybe I'll just tell her his name. What I call him anyway.

Sweet.

Off to eat some ice cream on the porch,
Cass

Seventeen

Lying on his side, his head propped up on his hand, Deacon watched Mackenzie sleep by the light of the moon spilling in through his wall of windows. She was the most beautiful sight he'd ever beheld. On her back, her dark hair spread out on the pillow behind her, the sheet pulled only to her waist, her hands clutched to her heart, she breathed deep and easy. A flash of possessiveness hit him. Directly in the heart. His once cold, dead heart.

Sleeping alone had been his norm, his way of life, and he'd never had thoughts to the contrary. But now, as he dropped to his back and eased her closer, as she sensed him there and turned, cuddled into his side and sighed, he couldn't imagine his life any other way.

But things were going to be different now. It couldn't be helped. Now that she knew the truth—the black, painful, hideous truth. He'd felt the shift inside her, seen it in her eyes.

After he'd told her about how his mother had blamed him the most because he was the oldest and knew better, how she'd started with beatings, then ended up with that burning-hot iron in her hand, Mac hadn't been able to speak. She'd just wanted him to hold her. Hold her while she cried against his chest, then dropped exhausted into sleep. He knew she was angry, sickened, and that she probably pitied him. But what he didn't know was how this new knowledge might change things between them. He had no intention of abandoning his plans for the Triple C. Would she understand his passion now? Would she support him in his cause? Or would this chasm between them widen?

Alarm spread through him, threatening to steal the virginal joy in his heart, but even in her sleep Mackenzie wouldn't allow that. She wrapped her arm around his chest and pulled herself even closer, the heat off her body slowly melting the aggressive blasts of cold apprehension and fear of what was to come in his cells.

Standing before a dirty mirror in a near-closet-sized room just outside the makeshift area, Cole taped his hands. Normally, someone else did that. Along with massage and stretching and mental prep. But tonight he was doing everything himself. There was going to be no one in his corner, no one slapping his ass if he won, no one carrying him out if he got that ass kicked.

It was like the old days, and it was perfect.

After being back at the Triple C for nearly a week, he was starting to experience some strange shit. Competing feelings inside his body. It was like the place he'd run from all those years ago both invigorated him and tore him up deeper, and as he was pushed into making a decision about its future, he found himself angrier and more volatile than ever.

Thank God he had friends in the underground. It was the one place volatile wasn't feared but encouraged.

Hands taped, he opened the door, heard the deafening sounds of the crowd and welcomed the wash of relief it brought as it simultaneously strengthened his blood and cleared his focus.

A guy he didn't know stuck his head in the door. "You ready?"

"Beyond." Cole moved past him and down a short hallway.

He needed this. To keep himself sharp and sane. And though it had become an addiction of sorts, it was the only way out of his guilt. For an hour or two, anyway.

The sea of faces and the booming sounds of their catcalls and cheers were suddenly erased from his consciousness, and all he saw was the guy in the ring. Though he'd never seen the man who took Cass, who took her life—and who was never brought to justice—every opponent he faced took on the role of his twin sister's killer.

Christ, there wasn't a day that went by that Cole didn't think of her. Not a day that went by that he didn't sweat or bleed and push himself to the point of pain to distract himself from his never-ending guilt over her abduction. Because in his mind, he would always be to blame. She'd asked him to come with her, stand outside the bathroom door. She'd hated to go places alone. But he'd wanted to stay and watch the movie. He'd told her she'd be fine. He'd been a weak-hearted shit.

He ducked and moved through the ropes.

He wasn't weak anymore.

His eyes connected with his opponent. "You ready to go?"

Like Deac, he, too, had needed to get away from the Triple C and its memories for a few hours. Not with a woman who should be off-limits to him, a woman he couldn't stop himself from lusting over, but for the sweet relief of blood sport.

As she floated in the pool, her arms crossed and resting on the stone edge, Mac went through the events of the night before in her mind. Hell, the events of the past week. It was like a bomb had exploded, and all the pieces were still up in the air, floating around, some soft and harmless, many with fiercely jagged edges.

Her poor Deacon. She couldn't even imagine what he'd been through. What they'd all been through. How those boys had been completely unprotected. And she'd been home grieving. She should've been there, no matter what Everett had said.

Her stomach clenched. Was that why Everett had wanted her to stay away? He knew what was happening and didn't want her witnessing. Or interfering.

Did he blame the boys, too?

Her heart was no longer soft for him. Yes, he'd taken her in and given her a job, and she was grateful for that. But what he'd allowed to happen on his watch, to his children, turned her stomach, and she would never champion him again.

"How long you been in here, darlin'?"

Instantly, her body hummed with awareness. Still resting on the lip of the pool, she glanced over her shoulder to see Deacon, clad only in a pair of swim trunks, stepping into the water.

Her gaze moved over his tanned skin and waves of muscle. He was so beautiful. "Not long."

"I woke up and you were gone." He swam up behind her and wrapped his arms around her waist. "I didn't like it."

"I'm sorry." She leaned in to him, every part of her growing warm at his touch. "I just needed some time to think."

With a growl, he turned her around to face him. His dark hair was bed-tousled and so sexy, and his eyes, those beautiful green eyes, were wary. "About?"

"Everything," she said, wrapping her arms around his neck. "God, I understand now, Deacon."

His brows lowered in confusion.

"Why you want to destroy the C. All that Everett created." Her throat tightened and tears pricked at her eyes. "Because he destroyed you."

His face paled and his eyes went raw with emotion. He didn't answer, just pulled her closer into his arms.

Mac clung to him, ran her hands up his muscular back, ran her fingers over his scarred skin. Anger poured through her. She should've been there. She should've been there to protect him . . . them . . .

"Did she do this to James and Cole?"

He shook his head. "We were all whipped on a regular basis, locked in our rooms or the barn at times. And the terrible things she would say . . . They pretty much destroyed Cole. But the branding iron, it was an impulsive moment with me. Her eldest son. The one who should've protected his little sister."

His words were like a blade running her through. Goddammit. She pulled back to look at him. "Why didn't you tell me?" she implored him, blinking back tears. "Why didn't any of you tell me? I could've helped. I would've wanted to help. I would've stopped her. Somehow."

His eyes softened and he took her face in his hands. "You were still a kid, with your own shit to deal with. You couldn't have done anything. And hell, we didn't want you to know, never wanted to burden you with this."

"Everett knew," she said, as much to him as to herself.

"Yes."

"You blame him more."

"My mother lost her mind the day Cass's body was brought home. And her reason. She was just a shell. I have to believe she didn't know what she was doing."

Mac shook her head, fierce, painful anger coursing through her. "Don't defend her, Deacon. I never will. Or Everett either."

His eyes moved over her face. From her cheeks to her eyes to her mouth. Then he leaned in and kissed her. A slow, sensual, emotional, almost drugging kiss. "Thank you, honey."

"For what?" she breathed against his mouth, her heart squeezing inside her ribs.

"Getting angry." He kissed her again, so softly, she sighed.

"Oh, Deacon," she breathed.

A small smile appeared on his lips, and he pressed her back against the edge of the pool and slipped his thigh between her legs. "You have no idea how much it means to me. How much you mean to me," he said, soft and hungry as his eyes flickered up to connect with hers. "But I could show you. Will you let me show you, darlin'?"

Her entire body shivered in the heated pool and under the heated gaze of this man who had captured her heart so long ago and now held it gently, firmly, capably in his hands.

"Why are you wearing all these clothes?" he whispered between one deep, dragging kiss then another.

"It's a bathing suit," she whispered back, smiling. "You bought it for me."

"Right. And you look sexy as hell in it. God, I love you in blue." His eyes dropped to her mouth. "But I need it off you right now. I need you naked. I need you."

Her pulse quickened, and she glanced up at the sliding glass door. "Here? You gave Carol the night off, not the morning, remember?"

"I'm going to give her the week off." His hands encircled her waist. "Wait. No, forget that. She needs to get used to this."

"This?" Mac repeated, her heart squeezing at his words and their possible meaning.

He tilted his head and kissed her again. Took her

mouth so soft, so sensual. "This." His right hand broke from her waist and ran down her belly, slipping beneath the thin waistband of her bikini bottom. "And this."

She gasped as his fingers brushed over her sex. "You're bad, Deacon Cavanaugh," she whispered against his mouth, lapping at his top lip with her tongue.

He groaned. "And you're hot." He cupped her. "And wet." Then slid one thick finger inside of her.

Blood rushed to her sex, and she instantly wrapped her legs around his waist. She wanted him, yes. Hell, her skin was on fire. But more than that—any of that—she wanted him to know she understood him now. That his secrets were safe with her and she would never hurt him.

His eyes came to rest on hers. And as she stroked his shoulders and the scar beneath his tattoo, he gently thrust inside her.

"Tell me you don't have to go, Mackenzie," he said, his jaw tight, his breathing kicking up. "Tell me work can wait, but this can't. We can't."

She opened her mouth to speak, to answer him, but only a moan of pleasure escaped.

"Tell me you're mine," he continued, changing the angle of his hand and going deeper inside of her. "Tell me you know you're mine."

The sound of the courtyard door opening made Mac freeze. She released a soft gasp and tried to move away from Deacon. But he held her fast. Hell, he didn't even flinch.

Out of the corner of her eye, Mac saw Carol at the doorway. She was far enough away not to see what was happening under the water but smart enough to know something was probably up. She remained where she was and called to him.

"Sir?"

Deacon's eyes pinned to Mac's, he said in a completely normal voice, "Morning, Carol."

Mac's eyes widened. Oh, Lord, he wasn't . . .

"There seems to be a situation," she said.

Deacon slipped a second finger into Mac's sex. Oh, Lord, yes, he was! Her eyes bulged and her breath caught.

"What is it?" he called back, his eyes glittering with wicked heat.

"Online gossip sites are all buzzing with the news of you and Ms. Byrd."

His mouth curved into a sexy grin. "That's pretty quick, but not completely unexpected."

Her nipples hardening beneath her swimsuit top, Mac bit her lip to stop another moan from escaping.

"The news is not very favorable toward Ms. Byrd," Carol continued. "About her background, clothing, manner, that kind of thing."

Background, Mac thought, her head dizzy as Deacon kept thrusting into her—so gently the water remained calm around them.

"I wonder who could've written something so scandalous," he said, giving Mac a wink.

At that moment, Mac didn't care. About who wrote what, or Carol or the past, future . . . Her body was screaming for release.

"Must be someone intimately acquainted with Ms. Byrd and my fashion choices," Deacon continued, his voice completely unaffected by what he was doing to her. "I knew Pamela loved the paparazzi, but damn, she works fast."

When his thumb grazed her clit, Mac inhaled sharply. Her legs tightened around his waist, and she had to concentrate on not thrusting as she felt the beginnings of climax take hold.

"We're not worried about it, Carol. We're not worried about anything right now."

"But, sir."

Nostrils flared, Deacon nearly barked, "Yes, Carol?"

Mac wouldn't take her eyes off him. She was clenching around his fingers. Could she come like this? Without a sound or a movement?

"There's something else," Carol said. "There was a call for you a moment ago."

"No calls," Deacon ground out.

"It was a Blue Cavanaugh?"

Mac froze. So did Deacon. But he still didn't release her. In fact, he pulled her in closer.

"Did he say *Cavanaugh*?" Deacon asked, his eyes darkening as he stared at Mac.

"Yes, sir."

"Thank you, Carol. You can go."

When the door closed and they were finally alone, Deacon's eyes blazed down into hers. He didn't say a word as he thrust his fingers deep and rubbed her clit with the pad of his thumb. Her mind too far gone, Mac couldn't focus on anything real. Heat surged to her sex, and she gave in to the delicious waves of climax, closing her eyes, pumping her hips, and moaning as her muscles fluttered around his thick digits.

But reality came quick. The cool morning air soon licked at her skin and all that Carol had said pricked at her mind. She opened her eyes. With a groan, Deacon eased his fingers from her tight sheath and wrapped his arms around her waist.

"I think someone has made his decision," he said, looking at her with a strange combination of eagerness and dread.

She clung to him. "Are you sure you want to know what it is?"

"Yes," he said tightly.

Her heart shrank to the size of a pea, but she pushed the feeling aside. Had she actually thought that with the release of his secret would come the demise of his goal?

Oh, foolish, foolish girl.

She didn't know what to do. Not with so much

up in the air, so much undecided. But she did know that there were no answers to be found here.

This time, when she eased herself away from him, he let her go.

"I think it's time to head home to River Black, Deac," she said softly. *Leave the fantasy here.* "Face what needs facin'." Then she turned and started swimming toward the pool steps.

Eighteen

"You didn't have to do this," Sheridan told James as he drove her Subaru a little too fast out of the town of River Black and toward the Triple C Ranch.

"It's no problem," he said, giving her a cool smile. "You needed your car."

He seemed to be the man of cool smiles, smiles that didn't exactly reach his eyes. "I know. But I could've had AAA or even the towing company in town bring it to me." Honestly, it was a nice gesture, and she appreciated it. But she wasn't exactly sure how to take it. She wasn't used to people doing anything *just to be nice*, and as she opened her window and let the warm morning breeze blow over her skin, she wondered if James Cavanaugh had an ulterior motive.

"Listen," he began as if he'd heard her thoughts. "You're Deacon's assistant, which makes you part of the family in a way. And we take care of our own out here."

She turned to him, took in his masculine profile and hard jaw with its sprinkling of stubble. "I didn't know Mr. Cavanaugh and his brothers were so close."

His eyes cut to her for a moment, and Sheridan felt her chest go tight. They were honest to God the most stunning eyes she'd ever seen.

"Maybe not so much now," he admitted. "But we were."

Sheridan itched to ask him more about it. For years, Deacon had been tight-lipped about his family and why they were estranged. Even the death of his father had been a quick, emotionless conversation. She'd never understood that part of his life, and maybe she really shouldn't as his employee. But being out here, in the sticks as James had put it, made her incredibly curious about his life pre-mogul.

Especially now that she'd met one of his brothers.

"Get a lot of work done last night?" James asked, drawing Sheridan's attention back to the present.

"I did." After James had taken her to the Feed and Tack, made sure the hotel down the street had a reservation for her—even asked her if she'd like him to bring her some dinner from the diner across the way—he'd left. Sheridan hadn't been hungry, just eager to continue her work. Which hadn't gone all that smoothly as her mind kept bringing up images of a certain horse rider.

She'd have to watch that.

"Your brother has major issues with organization," she said, trying to introduce some light humor into their conversation.

"Bet you don't," James returned.

Her chin lifted automatically. "Absolutely not."

He chuckled softly. "I'd like to be more organized in my business."

"Maybe you need to hire more help."

"Maybe."

"Well, I'd be happy to show you a few things while I'm here if you'd like," she answered.

"That's kind of you, Sheridan," he said, turning into the long Triple C driveway. "But I'm not sure I'll be staying on for very long."

Sheridan felt a trace of disappointment move through her, and she shoved it away. "Need to get back home? To your work?"

He smiled. "Yes and yes."

"To a woman?" The words were out of her mouth before she could stop them. Panic jumped in her blood. She wanted to sink into the seat. What was wrong with her?

James's slid his dreamy, ocean-blue gaze her way. "No woman."

Good Lord, that look had her chest tightening. Had her feeling like taking a breath wasn't as easy as it should be.

"I'm very sorry," she mumbled, mentally rolling

her eyes as they headed over the rise toward the main house. She hoped he wouldn't mention this to Deacon. "That was absolutely none of my business."

For the first time since they'd got in her car back at the Feed and Tack, James didn't answer right away. His eyes forward, hands fisting on the steering wheel, his focus had been completely stripped from her and was homing in on something ahead of them.

"What the hell?" he uttered, lifting his chin.

"What's wrong?" Sheridan followed his line of vision and saw several semi-looking trucks parked on the grass near the fence line.

There looked to be eight or so.

"Did someone order new furniture?" she asked.

"That's not furniture," James said, stepping on the gas, his tone more serious than she'd ever heard it.

He came to a stop behind one of the trucks, killed the engine, and tossed her the keys. He was out of the car in seconds. Sheridan followed, hurrying after him as he strode toward an older man in a Stetson, a very handsome younger man with bulging muscles, close-cut blond hair, tattoos, a black eye, and a busted lip and what appeared to be one of the truck drivers.

James headed straight into their semicircle. "What's going on?"

The driver spoke first. "We have 'bout a hundred mustangs to place with y'all. Just waiting to unload."

James turned to the blond man. "Cole? Talk to me."

The inked-up man shrugged. "Seems our foreman signed off on moving these wild horses from their temporary shelters to Triple C property."

Standing back a few feet, Sheridan could actually feel the tension rolling off James. She didn't know what had happened, but she did know that Mackenzie Byrd was the Triple C's foreman.

"This ranch might be sold," James said to all three of them. "Or shit, maybe even demolished. What's going to happen to them if that's the case?"

"Look, partner, the order's been signed," the driver said. "If there's a problem, take it up with the Bureau of Land Management."

As the man walked away to confer with the other drivers, James turned to Cole and shook his head. "Mackenzie."

Cole nodded. "Seems like. Deacon told me before he left that they were going to fight each other on this. Any way they saw fit. Mac's always been a fighter. One of the many reasons Cass looked up to her."

Cass. Sheridan had heard that name before. A long time ago. She was Deacon's sister. The one who'd been abducted back when they were kids. Sounded like she and Mackenzie were close friends.

"Speaking of fighters," James began, eyeing the man and his black eye. "Remind me later to ask you what the hell happened to your face."

"What are you talking about?" Cole said, moving his head from side to side. "I'm as pretty as ever."

"Listen, James," said the older cowboy, who'd been quiet up until that point. "They got nowhere else to go."

"Come on, Sam," James responded.

The man shrugged. "Even if we wanted to send them back, it ain't gonna be today."

James took a deep breath. "Damn woman. She's using me in this fight of hers. Knows I won't sell— thinks I won't sell—if there's horseflesh involved. Fighting dirty with Deacon," he grumbled. "*A horse! a horse! My kingdom for a horse!*"

"*Richard the Third,*" Sheridan blurted out, then wished she hadn't when James's head came around so fast it was almost a blur.

His eyes narrowed on her.

She shrugged. "Sorry." She should've just gone inside, up to Deacon's room, and finished sorting files instead of following his brother into whatever problem had just arisen, eavesdropping.

James's eyes changed from firecrackers into a look of supreme curiosity and wanton heat. "*Richard the Third,*" he confirmed. "You know it."

She shrugged gently. "A true conflict between good and evil. In the mind and heart of one man."

He just stared at her; so did all the other men.

"Who's this?" Cole asked.

"Sheridan O'Neil," James told him. "Deacon's assistant."

"Lucky Deac," Cole said with a killer grin that had to make every woman who was on the other end of it unsteady in both body and heart. "Nice to meet you, Sheridan."

"Thank you, Mr. Cavanaugh. It's good to meet you too." She smiled back, then turned to James. "If you'll excuse me, I'm going to the house." She started away. "Work to do." She waved without looking back. "Have a good day, everyone."

As she hurried forward, her heart beating far too fast in her chest, she could feel his eyes on her. It was strange. Him and her and whatever had just passed between them. But it was something better left alone. James Cavanaugh was the brother of her employer, not a man to palpitate over.

She was nearly to the front walk when she felt his searing gaze pulled from her, and his voice call out, "Let's get 'em unloaded, boys."

The flight home in the *Long Horn* had been a quiet one, as was the ride to the Triple C in his truck. Deacon knew his mind was overrun with thoughts of the night before, of Mac's anger and tears that morning, and of Blue's possible acceptance of his offer. But his heart was trying to push its way in there too, force him to look at the effects of his actions if he truly followed through on his plan to destroy the ranch.

He pushed it back.

His jaw tightened. He needed this. Needed it to move on with his life. Needed it to breathe normally again.

Beside him, listening to the radio and staring out at the sun setting brilliantly over the rolling hills and sheets of man-made lakes, Mackenzie was clearly deep in thought as well. She'd noticed the shift in his mood after Carol's news and the return phone call where Blue had requested a face-to-face meet to discuss Deacon's offer. She'd seen his soft, vulnerable side sink back beneath his skin and the calculated beast inside of him rise to the surface.

As they pulled into the Triple C, drove under the sign, he reached out and took her hand. It was warm and soft, and when she gripped him back tightly, he felt a surge of worry cross his heart.

"You all right?" he asked, heading up the easy hill.

She stared straight ahead. "No."

Fuck. "Ah, Mackenzie . . ." *Please don't.*

She turned to face him, a panicked look on her beautiful face. "Let's not go in, Deacon. Let's turn around and go to town, or the cottage. Or we could go for a ride. Me on Gypsy and you on Trouble."

"Hey, hey . . ." He pulled to a stop in front of the house and killed the engine. "Please calm down."

But she didn't. Not even a bit. "Don't do this," she said breathlessly, her face pale and drawn, her eyes wide with worry. "Don't go in there."

He hated her words and the fear in her eyes. Goddamit. He wanted to give her everything, everything she desired and needed. Anything that would make her smile again. But he couldn't give her this. "Honey, I just want to hear what the man has to say."

"No, Deacon . . ." She shook her head disbelievingly.

"It's true. I owe him that."

She turned from him, took a deep breath and let it out. "We both know it doesn't matter what he says."

"Come on, Mac—"

"No." She popped her seat belt. "You're immovable, Deacon, utterly and completely committed to this cause, and I'm sayin' don't do it. Your obsession with this place—"

Ire moved up his spine. "There's no obsession, Mac," he said tightly. "I just want it gone. I need it gone."

She shook her head. "I don't think so. I don't think that's what you really want. I've been going over and over this in my mind the whole way home. I think you actually want to save it, the Triple C—"

"That's ridiculous," he interrupted with a bitter laugh.

"It's not," she insisted, facing him again, her eyes imploring him. "Destroying this place goes against everything you've ever told yourself you wanted. Everything you've told yourself you need to do to move on with your life." Her eyes softened and she gave a small shrug. "That's where I came in. You were going to let me fight to save this place, even encouraged me to."

Deacon's jaw hardened along with his heart at her words. "I pushed you to fight because you wanted to save it as badly as I wanted to destroy it. I respected that, and I supported you because that's what you do for the person you love."

She gasped, her head drawing back and her eyes going wide. Deacon wasn't shocked at himself for saying it out loud, for admitting it. Hell, he knew what was happening to him, even before she knew the truth—what he felt every damn time he looked at her. How much he'd wanted to keep her at his place, hear her call it home. Their home. He wanted her in a way that both thrilled him and scared the shit out of him.

"You love me?" she asked, finding her voice.

"Yes. Hell, yes. You know I do."

Her eyes searched his. "And yet you still want to do this?"

He ran a worried hand through his hair. "My

love for you has nothing to do with my hatred for this ranch. One is new and beautiful and fresh and clean, and the other is in my mind and my bones and my blood—and fuck, on the back of my shoulder—making me ache, making me sick. That won't go away until this ranch goes away."

Pain moved across her eyes and she released a breath. "I know you believe that, honey," she said softly, gently. "I know you do. But it's just not true. You're only destroying the thing that represents your pain. It'll never go away unless you let it, unless you forgive."

Deacon recoiled. "Forgive?"

"That's right."

"And who should I be forgivin', Mac?" he ground out.

"Your mother . . ."

"No."

She bit her lip. "And Everett."

"Christ! Never!" He turned away, then turned back, glared at her. He'd thought she understood. With all he'd told her, all he'd revealed, he'd believed she might walk away from her own crusade and let him have his vengeance.

"They're gone, Deacon," she continued. "What is there to destroy?"

"Just stop, Mackenzie," he warned.

But she wouldn't. "I know what you've suffered, and I hate them both for putting you through it. I don't idolize Everett anymore, and shit, I don't even need this ranch to feel like I'm home. But I love you, and if you do this, it won't end your pain. It'll grow it."

"You don't know that," he said through gritted teeth. "You don't know what it will do to me. Maybe you don't know me at all," he added ruthlessly, carelessly.

"Listen to me, Deacon Cavanaugh, and listen good." She pointed a finger at him, her body tense with anger and frustration. "You need to understand that with or without this place, no matter what happens, you're whole. You're safe. No one is going to hurt you again. The past is over, done, dead." She barely stopped for breath, her gaze clinging to his. "You and your brothers are staying here, longer than you expected to. Maybe that's a good thing."

Deacon sneered. "My brothers want this place gone as much as I do."

"I don't believe that. You're all as drawn to the Triple C as you are repulsed by it."

"No."

"Now that Everett's gone, things could change; they could be different."

"Goddamit, Mackenzie! I don't want them different!" he exploded. "I don't want them at all."

Silence flared inside the truck's cab. Both of them were breathing heavy. Both had desperate, impassioned expressions. But it was Mac who finally spoke.

After staring at him for a moment, she shrugged, then smiled a little sadly. "Okay, Deac."

Okay, Deac? Okay? What the hell did that mean? Was she just too pissed at him to keep the conversation going? Or was she giving up on trying to change his mind? Or God . . . his gut rolled hard and vicious . . . was she just giving up?

He reached for her, desperate to hold her. "Mac."

But she pulled away. Without even a look in his direction, she opened her door and got out.

Deacon followed suit, scrambling out of the truck and heading down the driveway after her. "Mac, come on," he said.

She stopped and turned around. "Go on, Deac." She gestured to the house, the porch. "Blue's waitin' on you."

Deacon glanced up, his gut so tight he was having trouble taking a breath. He felt like he didn't know who or what he wanted anymore. Everything he believed, that he'd told himself for years— everything that had kept him going and no doubt fueled his success—was blowing up in his face.

Blue was standing on the porch in his white Stetson, watching them. Waiting to give Deacon an answer.

Shit, an answer Deacon already knew was coming.

He turned back to Mackenzie, his eyes as god-damn soft as his tone. "Come talk to Blue with me."

She looked at him like he was nuts, or maybe like she pitied him.

"Baby, I need you by my side."

"I don't belong there, Deacon."

His heart dive-bombed into the earth under his feet. "Mac, don't talk like that."

Her midnight blue eyes held more strength than sadness now. "It's the truth. You need to make this choice on your own, then face the outcome."

"Are you saying that outcome is losing you?" he ground out, his blood now running cold in his veins.

She took a deep breath. Let it out slowly. "I love you, Deacon Cavanaugh. So much. But I won't live in anger and hate and bitterness with you."

"Mac—"

She shook her head. "I got work to do. A ranch to see after."

She walked away, heading back toward the truck. Staying where he was, Deacon watched her go, an emotion he hadn't felt in more than twelve years—not since Cass's death—assaulting every damn part of him.

The deep ache of loss.

*   *   *

When she reached the truck, Mac turned around. She was hoping to find Deacon staring after her. Shit, or running after her. But vengeance was a ruthless, irresistible master. And it had claimed Deacon long ago.

As he strode up the steps and shook Blue's hand, a part of Mac died. How was it possible that the two people closest to her in the world were agreeing to this madness? Was Blue that deep into his rage and pain that he could turn a blind eye not only to his friend, but to everyone who needed the ranch to survive?

Including his own mother?

Mac was about to turn and walk away when both men glanced over at her. Each looked at her with a different set of soulful, questioning, resolute eyes, but neither moved.

Forcing her heart out of her throat and back down into her chest, Mac reached into the truck and grabbed her bag. Eyes forward, she slung the heavy leather over one shoulder and headed for the barn, for Gypsy, the one male in her life who would never let her down.

Nineteen

In the past two days, Deacon had managed to get a total of four hours sleep. It wasn't like he hadn't tried for more. Shoot, he'd tried. Everything. Music, booze, knocking his head against the wall. But nothing brought on the sheep. Sometime between three and four a.m., he'd pass out from sheer exhaustion, but by five he was up again and out of the house, heading for the barn. It was a damn sickness. His need for her. His need to see her.

Granted, he wouldn't go all the way to her place, just to the other side of the river. Then, he'd sit there, watch as the sun rose all butter yellow over her cottage, wishing like hell she would take his calls, agree to see him. That she'd invite him back into her arms and her bed.

He'd always leave in a huff, real pissed, his chest in knots. Coming back to the ranch, he'd run Trouble into a hard-core sweat, then hose her down while he cursed himself and the unending belief that leveling the Triple C would heal the rampant pain dwelling inside of him.

Finally, he'd stumbled back into the house and stood under the shower's painful spray. But ten minutes of ice water sluicing over his back and shoulders, making every inch of him tight, and still he couldn't shake the heaviness of anger and bitterness inside him.

If anything, since he'd made the deal with Blue, those feelings had only gotten worse.

"Do you want me to make more than one copy of the DNA test results, sir? And would you like it sent to anyone else besides the attorneys?"

Deacon turned in his chair, eyed his assistant across the room. They'd been in the office above RB Feed and Tack for a couple of hours. Now that Blue had agreed to the buyout, there was a lot to be done. Deacon was trying to force his game face on, but the mask kept sliding off.

"Two copies to us," he told her brusquely. "One to the attorneys. And, Sheridan, we need to get Blue Perez's . . . Blue Cavanaugh's," he corrected himself sharply, "bank information to complete the wire transfer."

She nodded, and Deacon noticed for the first time that her eyes weren't meeting his as soundly as they usually did.

"I haven't had the opportunity to congratulate you, sir," she said.

"For what?" he pushed out tiredly.

"Controlling interest in the Triple C? The agreement with Mr. Cavanaugh."

"Right. Thank you." His tone displayed his lack of enthusiasm perfectly. He'd have to watch that in the future. Sheridan didn't need to know any more of his personal business than she already did.

"And when is Mr. Cavanaugh signing away his rights to the property?" she asked.

"I believe that'll happen day after tomorrow," Deacon answered. "Ty will be flying the lawyers out."

"Very good."

Was it? Was it good? Was it anything? Deacon felt impatient as hell. He just wanted it all done and over. The signing, the demolition, the damn Triple C sign ripped down and hauled away. Maybe then he'd stop questioning himself at every turn. Maybe then he'd find some peace.

All that was left was convincing James and Cole to walk away, and he truly didn't think that would be a difficult task. Both of them seemed more than ready to return to their lives. Hell, Cole had taken off while he and Mac had been in Dallas, and James had all but disappeared. Deacon hadn't seen the man in a couple of days. Maybe he was already out of there, off to Hollywood or one of those whispering gigs of his.

"Sheridan," he said. "You sent the flowers to Ms. Byrd, right?"

"Yes, sir. She would've received them yesterday."

Yesterday. And he'd heard nothing. His jaw tightened. He'd sent irises. Three dozen. They reminded him of her eyes in the light. He'd even written that in the card. Goddamn pussy. She didn't want him anymore. Why couldn't he get that through his head already?

Maybe because his heart belonged to her now.

"And you had the offer drawn up and sent?" he asked.

"Yes, sir." She looked over the paper. "I have a copy here. Foreman at Redemption Ranch, salary at two hundred thousand per year, house designed and built on any part of the property she chooses." She looked up, worried. "There wasn't anything else you wanted to add?"

Marry me?

Be mine forever?

Forgive me?

"No, that's it," he grumbled, turning back to his desk, grabbing his iPhone. "I want you to start pricing demo companies in the area." He stared at an e-mail from Angus Breyer. It had come in early that morning and he'd read it about thirty times. The seas had parted and that hardheaded man was finally ready to sell. Shit, when it rained it poured.

"Specifically, what would they be taking out?"

Sheridan continued, typing away on her laptop. "All of the structures on the Triple C? Main house? Bunkhouses? Cottages? Barns?"

Deacon flinched, his eyes straying from the e-mail, his mind conjuring images of Mackenzie asleep in her bed in the cottage where he'd held her, kissed her, where he'd first started to realize just how desperately he wanted her.

The cottage he and James used to play in before the sun broke and his world got blanketed in darkness and . . . bitterness.

Gritting his teeth, he shoved those thoughts away. Those pitying, useless thoughts. Mackenzie loved him; he knew it—just as he knew he loved her, too. She'd understood his anger and his hatred of Everett's land. Shit, she'd been in a rage herself over it, yet had counseled him to forgive and move on. So it stood to reason that in time, she'd come to forgive him, too.

His gut twisted so painfully he groaned. Fuck, he missed her.

"What about the land itself?" Sheridan continued in her clipped, professional tone. "Do you want to dig? Remove pastures? Water? Fencing? How many head of cattle do they have there? And are you moving them to your other property?"

Deacon dropped his phone on the desk and turned to face Sheridan. But he never answered her question. The door to their office burst open, and an uncharacteristically pissed-off James stalked in. His eyes immediately went to Sheridan, then shifted to Deacon.

"Hey, J," Deacon said, trying to assess the heat in the man's sea blue eyes.

Crossing the room in three heavy strides, James dropped into the chair beside Deacon. "Really, brother?"

"What?"

He shook his head. "You offered her a job at your revenge ranch?"

Instantly on the defensive, Deacon leaned back in his chair, crossed his arms over his chest. "How do you know about that? Did she come to talk to you?"

"I went to her. That woman and I needed to talk."

"Why?" Deacon fairly growled.

"She signed off on a bunch of wild mustangs," he said. "They're galloping across the Triple C's land as we speak. It's where I've been for the last two days. Settlin' 'em. Makin' sure we got plenty of water."

Shock barreled through Deacon. "When did all this happen?"

"While you were in Dallas." He, too, leaned back in his chair. "So, what does she expect me to do? Stick around this place for God knows how long? I have a life. Work." His lip curled. "Damn woman knew I couldn't sell to you with those mustangs on the land. They got nowhere else to go."

For a moment, Deacon just stared at his brother,

his mind processing everything the man had just said. Wild mustangs. Wild goddamned mustangs. He shook his head. Then a grin broke out on his hard-angled face. He couldn't help it. Mackenzie Byrd was one helluva player. Smart, savvy . . . unflinching in her resolve. Hell, if she wasn't such a damn fine foreman, he might be inclined to hire her on at Cavanaugh Group.

"I get why you wanted the C taken apart, Deac," James continued. "Shit, I was almost there with you." His eyes flickered toward Sheridan, then came back to Deacon. " 'Course, you do have controlling interest now . . . Thanks for giving Cole and me the heads-up on that, by the way."

Sheridan stood up, grabbed a couple of files and headed for the door of the office. "I'm going for coffee. Anyone want anything?"

Deacon shook his head.

Turning, James gave her a rare smile "No. Thank you, Miss O'Neil." After Sheridan closed the door behind her, James turned back to Deacon with an icy glare. "You are so damn stupid—you know that?"

"Hey," Deacon began. "What the hell?"

"Destroying the Triple is one thing, but destroying the one amazing thing you got in your life . . ." He shook his head. "Fucking stupid."

Heat flooded the pit of Deacon's stomach. "What are you talking about?"

"You and Mac."

His heart pinged inside his chest. Damn blood-pumping bastard. Just her name drove his entire body off a cliff. Nostrils flaring, he looked away, then back. "I'm not destroying us," he snarled. "I'm protecting us."

The look James tossed his way was censure at its finest. "How you figure that?"

"We can't have anything if I don't get this out of me, this demon who rules every decision I make. When the Triple C is leveled, it'll go, it'll be gone for good, and Mac and I . . . we can be happy." His words were as fierce as his resolve. He would have her. She belonged to him. She loved him. "She'll come to understand, James. She knows what happened to me, to us. Once the Triple C is gone, we can start over."

"Oh, Deac," James said sadly. "She already has."

The blood drained from Deacon's face. "What do you mean?"

James stood up, shook his head. "She got a job offer in Colorado, and she's taking it."

As his brother's words barreled hard and fast through him, Deacon struggled to keep himself from exploding. "No," he uttered. "She can't. I won't let her."

"Christ. You just don't get it, Deac," James said in a dark voice.

"Get outta here, James. Now."

But the man didn't move. "Unlike everything else in your life, you don't have control over her."

Deacon shot to his feet. "I fucking love her!"

James stood his ground, undaunted. "Obviously not more than you love taking down the Triple C." He stared hard at Deacon. "You had everything. You had real, brother. Something most people never find. Shit, something I'll never have. And you just let it walk right out of your life. Or was it run?"

"Get out of here, James," Deacon growled through teeth so tightly clenched they made his jaw ache. "I'm not going to tell you again."

"Fine." Shaking his head, James turned and headed for the door. "I got a herd of wild horse-flesh to look after anyway."

His blood rushing hot and fierce inside his veins, Deacon struggled to hold on to his anger, his pain. What the hell had just happened here? His brother cussing him out over the woman he loved and the land he despised. Goddamn, after all these years—the plan in place, the reasons so clear—now everything looked so wrong and felt so precarious.

Mac was leaving?

LEAVING?

He dragged a hand through his hair and kicked his chair away. Gone from River Black, from Texas—from his goddamn life! He hadn't even considered the possibility. In his warped, arrogant, vengeance-hungry mind, she still belonged to him, and someday she was going to let her anger go and forgive him, and . . . what? Live happily ever after?

Fuck. He was a moron. A bastard. And like James had said, stupid.

He scrubbed his hand over his face. He was sweating, tense.

She wasn't going to be foreman at his ranch. Redemption Ranch. She wasn't going to be kissing him good-bye in the dawn light, then going off to drive his Angus or, hell, the cattle she'd once worked on the decimated land she would see every damn time she went to town.

The scar on his shoulder burned suddenly, and he closed his eyes and pulled in a breath.

No. He was worse than stupid. He was pointless in his vengeance and careless with the heart he'd been given and entrusted with. The heart that was packing for Colorado and a life without him this very moment.

Was he actually going to let that happen?

His teeth set, he turned back to his desk and opened his iPad. Stupid he could reverse. Careless he could fix. But mending a heart he himself had wounded? That was going to take every ounce of vulnerability and honesty he possessed, not to mention a willingness to finally leave his pain and his memories in the past.

*   *   *

Deacon's breath was warm and sweet, his lips soft, wet, and impatient. He dragged his mouth over hers, groaning, deepening his kiss, demanding a response. Mackenzie was on fire, hungry—famished—and nothing would satiate her but him. Her hands grazed over his back, her nails digging into his skin as she forced him closer, down on top of her.

His delicious weight—his raw strength—his sex, swollen and expectant against her belly. Restlessly, she moved against him, silently begging him to calm the raging sea inside her. But the delicious torture continued at a frantic pace. His hands raked the insides of her thighs, his thumbs searching for her heat. It was ecstasy. Pure ecstasy. He wanted her. He loved her.

"Mackenzie," he called softly.

"Yes, Deacon," she murmured. "God, yes."

She watched him trailing hot, wet kisses over the rise of her breast. She ached for him so badly—there was nothing she could desire more in a thousand lifetimes. He licked at her nipple, urging it to pucker, to harden.

"Mac."

His call was more insistent now, but she couldn't do anything except whisper his name over and over. His mouth had closed over her taut bud, and he was sucking it into his mouth gently, urgently. Lust was caught in her throat, her breathing ragged—

Sudden and insistent pounding on her front door woke her.

Her eyes jacked open to bright sunlight. Startled, she blinked, trying to focus, trying to reason what that sound had been and why she was asleep in the middle of the day. Oh, right, she hadn't slept all night and had lain down for a quick fifteen-minute shut-eye.

Bam. Bam. Bam. Her front door rattled with the effort, and she sat up, clutched her pillow to her chest. Who was it? She hated that her first thought, her first hope, was Deacon. But that ship had sailed and she needed to just let it go, wish it well and safe passage.

She glanced at the nearly packed bags on the floor near the dresser. Maybe he could do the same for her.

"Foreman!" came a shout from outside. "We got a problem."

Mac's heart plummeted into her belly. Not Deacon's voice. She scrambled off the bed and hurried out into the hall. Another knock sounded just before she opened the door.

"Sam?"

The ancient barn manager stood on the porch, Stetson off, wiping his brow with a blue handkerchief. He took one look at her and frowned. "You sleeping? Sun's been up for hours—"

"What's wrong?" she asked.

"It's Deacon."

Every nerve ending, every hair on her body stood up. "Oh my God, what happened?"

"No, no," he said, brushing off her quick panic. "It's nothing like that. He just needs to see you."

Gripping the door tightly, Mac heaved a gigantic sigh of relief. Nothing wrong with Deacon. Not hurt. Not dead.

"Come on then," Sam said, gesturing for her to follow him.

As her pulse started to return to normal, she shook her head. "No. I can't. Sorry."

The cowboy gave her a wry grin. "I promised I'd bring yah, Mackenzie."

"Bring me where?"

The wry grin widened. "Do this for me? For old times' sake?"

"Sam . . ."

"Please, Mac."

She groaned. She didn't know what the hell was up with Sam. What he'd promised or why. But she didn't want to see Deacon. Well, she *wanted* to see him. He was all she could think about. Every minute of every day. But seeing him was going to make her heart explode with pain. Maybe even regret her choice to move to Colorado. What could he possibly want? To discuss moving cattle? What buildings he should demolish first? Well, he could just forget it. She wasn't going backward, wasn't—

"Mac," Sam interrupted impatiently. "I'm not getting any younger out here."

"Fine," she said gruffly, knowing her acquiescence was probably one of the biggest mistakes of her life. "Let me go put on my boots."

Deacon moved from room to room inside the nearly finished house. The living area, the kitchen, the sunporch. It was going to be a fine place with lots of wide open spaces and tons of light. Lord, he needed light.

When he'd designed the main house on his property, he hadn't been thinking of anyone, not even of himself, but now, as he walked through the framed front door and onto what would be the large wraparound porch, he was thinking of her. Only her. Would she like it? Could she feel at home here?

Would she forgive him?

In answer to his silent query, Deacon heard the crunch of gravel beneath tires and he knew that Sam was coming up the drive. His heart kicked. His gut too. Would she be riding shotgun next to the old cowboy? Or was he heading in solo, after Mackenzie had told him to get lost, that she had no interest in whatever it was Deacon was selling?

With all the dirt Sam's pickup was kicking around, Deacon couldn't see who was inside the cab. Not until the thing pulled in and stopped. It was then that Deacon saw her. Face tight with tension, but beautiful. So beautiful. His Mackenzie. It took every ounce of self-control to not rush the hunk of metal, yank the door open and pull his woman out and into his arms, kiss her senseless. But there would be time for that later. After she forgave. No, he thought with a nervous smile. After she flipped him the bird, refused to hear what he had to say, cussed him out right good, then God willing, forgave him.

He watched as she got out and started up the dirt path toward the house, leaving Sam in the truck. Deacon gave the man a quick wave. He owed him big time. Sam just shook his head as if to say "Don't know what good this'll do, but I did my part," then flipped the Chevy into gear and peeled off back down the drive.

Mackenzie came to stand before him, her eyes connecting with his. She didn't look nervous, just curious. But his damn heart was stalling in his lungs with every breath he took. It felt like he hadn't seen her in days. Her eyes looked bluer, her hair lighter, and her skin seemed tanner next to the pale green tank top she wore.

"What am I doing here, Deacon?" she asked.

"I need your help with something," he said, forcing an even tone to his voice. He didn't want her to see him breaking. Hell, not yet. Not until it really mattered.

She cocked her head. "Why would you think I'd want to help you? Or have anything to do with this place?"

He moved down the steps and reached for her hand. She gave it to him tentatively, but her eyes were wary now.

"C'mere, Mackenzie," he said gently. "I need to show you something."

"I don't have much time, Deacon. I'm leaving for Colorado in a few hours."

Pain seared his gut, but he didn't say anything. Just led her past the house and to the barn. Or what would someday be the barn. For now, it was just a framed-in promise. Trouble was saddled and ready near the hitching post, and when they reached her, Deacon offered her a leg up.

"We're going for a ride?" she asked, even more wary-sounding now.

"Yup."

She sighed. "You going to show me your vast lands, Deac? All the water? Everything you can offer this town when the time comes?"

He didn't answer, just leaped up into the saddle and held a hand out to her.

She stared at it a moment, then cursed and stuck her boot in the stirrup.

When she was safely behind him, Deacon called out a quick, "Just hold on to me, Mac." Then kicked Trouble into a gallop. For a solid five minutes of clean air and blue skies and her hands on him again, no one said a word. Not until Deacon pulled Trouble up short just before an easy drop-off. He waited for Mac to get down first; then he followed.

"What is this?" she asked, walking right up to the edge.

He came to stand beside her, ached to slip his arm around her waist and pull her close. "It's not the Hidey Hole, exactly, but it reminds me of it. Of her. Of you."

"Oh, Deacon," she uttered, her voice breaking.

He took her hand and led her down the slope toward the small lakeshore. Once there, once the breeze was ruffling her hair and sun was shining on her skin, he turned to look at her. "I love you, baby."

Tears pricked her eyes. "Not fair."

"Mac—"

"Goddamn you, Deacon," she said, shaking her head. "I love you, too. You know that. But it doesn't change things."

Deacon's heart felt so full in that moment. So full he almost couldn't get the words out. But he needed to. Really needed to. "See, I thought that, too," he said, looking deep into her eyes. "Until I heard you were leaving. Until my heart and my guts and my brain all came together to under-stand what a complete and total fool I've been."

"James told you?"

He nodded, and his hand tightened around hers. "Honey, you can't leave."

"There's nothing here for me now."

"That's not true," he countered passionately. She had no idea. No clue. But she would. If he could just get the goddamn words out of his mouth.

"I got your offer," she said softly. "I respectfully decline."

"Well, that's good because I brought you here to tell you it's off the table."

Her brows knit together. "What?"

"I don't want you as foreman."

She gave a pained cry. "Deacon, what the hell are you doin' to me?"

He reached up and cupped her face. "Baby, stay at the Triple C if that's what you want."

"I don't understand. You. This." She stared at him, utterly confused, her eyes pricking with tears.

"I'm so sorry, Mac," he said, his voice heady with pain. "For all the shit I put you through, for a cause that was never worth pursuing. I don't know if I'll ever get over what happened or my anger toward Everett, but all I want now is you in my life."

"But Blue and your meeting . . ."

"I'm not going to call the C home, honey—that's for sure. But I'm not taking it away from all of you who do." He smiled at her, leaned in and kissed the tip of her sun-warmed nose. "The only thing I want, the only thing I'm fighting for here, is you."

She stared at him, her eyes moving over his face. Did she believe him? Christ, did she forgive him? Deacon was nearly beside himself with worry, was about to repeat the whole goddamn thing, when she suddenly burst into tears and flung herself at him.

She wrapped her arms around his neck and cried against his hot skin. "I love you so much, Deacon."

Relief, pure and intense and plentiful, washed through him, and he pulled her impossibly closer. His. *Mine. She's mine, and I'm hers.* Forever.

Forever.

"I love you, baby," he said with a passion-filled growl. "I want to be here for you always. In good and bad and crazy. I want you to be my best friend for life, my partner and my wife."

Mac stilled and her sobs receded. She drew back. Her eyes were red and tear-bright as she looked up at him. "Say that again."

Deacon smiled. Damn, he loved this woman something fierce. "Man and wife, Mackenzie. You being a Cavanaugh for real, like you were always meant to be. And I want this to be our home. I want to make new memories in River Black. Good ones, happy ones." His voice broke. "Loving ones."

"Oh my God," she cried, nodding, over and over.

Deacon brought his hands up and cupped her face again. "Marry me, Mac?"

" 'Course, Deac." Tears sprang to her eyes again.

"Honey, don't," Deacon soothed, pulling her back into his arms. "There's no need for tears. Not anymore. We're together. Everything's all right. Just the way it should be. The way it was meant to be."

"I know," she whispered. "And I'm so grateful. I love you so much. I never thought . . . It's just, being here, it makes me think of Cass."

"Sweetheart . . ."

"It's okay," she assured him, sighing as he rubbed her back in slow, gentle strokes. "Really, it's okay. I just wish she were here. I wish she could see this. A new beginning."

"Oh, she's here, Mac," Deacon assured, his voice heavy with emotion, love and a newfound hope. "I know she is."

Twenty

"No wild horses on my land, hear?" Deacon announced, then waited for someone at the table to reply. It was lunchtime the following day, and three of the Cavanaugh brothers, along with the Triple C Ranch's beautiful and way-too-sexy-to-be-out-of-his-bed ranch foreman were gathered around a table at the Bull's Eye.

James grabbed his beer and took a healthy swig. "Don't look at me. I've got enough to handle with all the mustangs I have to take care of at the Triple."

"Well, you don't *have* to take care of them," Cole put in.

"Hell, yes, I do," James said, looking pointedly at Mac. "And that one knew it. I've been manipulated."

A wicked kitty-cat grin touched Mac's mouth, and Deacon wanted to lick at it, then tell her not to be giving it away to anyone besides him from now on.

"We have the land," she said with a shrug. "And those poor horses had nowhere to go."

Deacon found her knee under the table and ran his hand up her denim-clad thigh. "You won, darlin'. No need to keep up the altruistic pretense."

Her grin widened and she turned it on him. "No, darlin'. *You* won."

He laughed and squeezed her thigh. Hell, yes, he had. Mackenzie was his, forever and always. He couldn't wait to marry her, call her his wife.

"What about Blue?" she asked him, her eyes losing about fifty percent of their luster. "Have you talked to him? He won't say but two words to me these days."

"I saw him riding out earlier," James said. "Said he was going to check on a few fences."

"He still wants to be gone," Deacon said. "Away from here, from Elena."

Mac groaned into her beer. "He doesn't know what he's doing."

"Regardless, I'm going to honor our agreement and give him the money I promised."

"Damn," Cole remarked with a whistle through his teeth. "That's a nice 'I'm sorry.'"

"Don't give it to him yet, Deacon," Mac said, her blue eyes thoughtful, worried. "Let me talk to him first."

"Honey, that choice has to be his. I know he's your friend—"

"He's more than that," she insisted.

Deacon growled deep in his chest. "I just asked you to marry me, woman. Don't tell me you're sweet on someone else." His fierce expression broke into a wide grin. "Especially a relative."

She rolled her eyes at him. "I meant to say he's family."

Deacon shrugged. "Okay, that's better."

"Wait—what?" Cole stammered, looking back and forth between the two of them. "You asked Mac to marry you?"

"I did." Deacon looked at her and winked.

Mac melted and her insides purred. God, he was so gorgeous, and so sexy. How was she ever going to get out of bed in the morning if he was still in it?

"Isn't that a little sudden?" Cole asked.

"I'd say it's been in the works for years," Deacon answered, his eyes remaining on Mac. "Wouldn't you agree, darlin'?"

She nodded. "Absolutely."

"So what did you say, Mac?" James asked with a straight face.

Deacon turned and tossed him a mock black stare. "Very funny, pony boy."

"I said a very enthusiastic yes," Mac told them all. "Then I cried and cried. But don't tell any of the cowboys. They'll never let me forget it."

James put a hand up. "Not a word."

"Well," Cole said. "This calls for another round."

"How about some champagne?"

Everyone turned to see Deacon's assistant, Sheridan, coming their way.

"Oooo, champagne!" Mac agreed. "Great idea. I wonder if they have it here." She motioned to Sheridan. "Come sit with us. Celebrate. Your boss is getting hitched." After Sheridan was tucked in next to her, Mac leaned in and whispered loudly, "Which will make him much easier to deal with on a day-to-day basis, I promise you."

"Don't count on it, Sheridan," Deacon said tautly. "But my wife-to-be can certainly try to make that happen." He leaned in and kissed her ear suggestively.

Mac shivered and smiled. Then her eyes caught on something and held. "Hey, that woman's staring at you, Cole," she said as Deacon's hand found her thigh again under the table. "And I'm telling you this because I'm hoping a good woman will get you to stop fighting."

"Problem is," James began, "he can't get a good woman looking like something that a dog threw up."

Turning to check out the woman at the bar, Cole grinned. "Maybe she likes black eyes."

"You mean black-and-blue eyes."

"Shut up, J," Cole said; then he stilled. "Wait a

minute. That's the woman from the other night. The one I saw with James at the diner. The cute, dark-haired filly. And she's coming over here."

James's head came around so fast Mac was pretty sure he'd end up with a sore neck later.

"Excuse me," the woman said, her pale green eyes flickering around the table nervously.

But James didn't let her get any further than that. He was up and out of his chair, his body as tense as the expression on his face. "How about we take this outside?"

The woman looked up at him—like she knew him—and shook her head. "I know you wanted to keep this between us, but things have progressed—"

James took her hand and said through tightly gritted teeth, "Please. Outside."

It was Cole's turn to stand. "What's your problem, J? Let her go. Now." He eyed the woman. "What's wrong, honey?"

"My name is Grace Hunter."

"The new vet," Mac supplied, suddenly realizing where she'd seen the woman.

Grace nodded at her, then looked at Cole. "I've just recently moved back to town." Her eyes flickered to James. "My father was the sheriff in River Black when your sister was taken."

The words settled over the table like a fog, and it was as if everyone stopped breathing at once.

Jaw hard, James gripped the edge of Cole's chair. "Goddammit," he uttered.

"You knew about this?" Deacon asked him.

"She approached me," he admitted. "I didn't want to upset anyone until I knew if there was something to be upset by."

"What's this all about?" Cole asked the woman, his tone as cool as his expression.

Her eyes lifted to his now and remained. "He admitted something to me a few months back. My father. He's ill, and is getting progressively worse."

"What did he admit?" Cole said with deadly caution.

"As I told your brother, my father admitted that the man, the suspect, they'd initially been looking for on Mackenzie here's tip—"

"Sweet," Mac said so softly it was nearly a whisper.

The woman nodded. "The two other officers didn't believe he existed. But my father says he did. And that there was proof."

"Oh, shit," James uttered.

Deacon groaned. "No." His hand left Mac's leg and found her hand instead. She squeezed it tightly.

This was too much. This day . . . And yet she wanted to hear more. Had to. She looked over at Cole. He looked like a man possessed. His eyes were fighting black and he bore down on the woman in front of him. "What proof?"

"Your sister had a diary."

Mac nodded. This time when she spoke, it was clear and impassioned. "We had the same one. She wrote in it all the time. We couldn't find it after she was taken. The police didn't believe it existed, and after a while I just assumed it was lost or—"

"It wasn't lost." The woman looked grim. "My father has it. He's had it for the past twelve years. And according to him, it names Cass Cavanaugh's murderer."

Acknowledgments

A great big thank-you to agent extraordinaire, Maria Carvainis, for all her support and encouragement.

To Danielle Perez: D–LW appreciates everything you do, how hard you work, and how much patience you show her. ☺

To everyone at New American Library: You amaze me! Thank you, thank you, thank you!

And to all of my wonderful and very loyal readers: Thank you, you mean the world to me, and I truly hope you enjoy the Cavanaugh brothers.

Don't miss the next novel in
the Cavanaugh Brothers series
by Laura Wright,

BROKEN

Available in October 2014 from Signet Eclipse.

Diary of Cassandra Cavanaugh

May 2, 2002

Dear Diary,
*I saw Sweet again today. This time, it was
outside the diner and we only got to talk for a
second or two because he had to go somewhere.
But it was enough for him to ask me to meet him
later out by Carl Shurebot's old place. I CAN'T
WAIT! I've never felt so excited about anything in
my whole life. He's just so cute. So DIFFERENT.
He doesn't look like the other boys around here.
With their mud-caked boots and Wrangler jeans.
Sweet looks like one of those surfer guys on TV.
And every time he smiles at me, my cheeks feel
hot.*

I asked him why I hadn't seen him around River Black before. Everybody knows everybody in this town. But he didn't answer me. He had to go. But I'll ask him tonight. That, and what his real name is.

Maybe it's something like Tristan or Brad or Dillon.

Ahhhhh! What if he doesn't want to tell me? He seems to like me calling him Sweet, just like I like him calling me Tarts. I guess I could ask my brothers, see who's new in school. But then they'd start asking me questions, and I REALLY don't want them in my business. They'll ruin everything. They'll say he's too old for me, and they'll tell Mom and Dad.

I don't think he's too old for me. He can't be more than eighteen, and I'm almost fourteen. It's perfect. He's perfect. I know, I know. I said Deac was way too old for Mac, and he was practically a man and that's gross and everything. But it's different somehow. He's my brother and she's my best friend, and Sweet is soooooo amazing.

I still haven't told Mac about him.

Is that bad?

I'll report back later,

Cass

One

"Lemon's the clear winner, right?"

Before Sheridan could answer, Mackenzie Byrd shoved another forkful of cake into her mouth. This time rich, creamy chocolate assaulted her tongue. *Very nice.* But frankly, you couldn't go all that wrong when it came to chocolate. Unless, of course, it was covering up grasshoppers or scorpions or whatever the crazy insect-eating population was pairing their cocoa with these days.

She swallowed, licked her lips, then reached for her napkin—which had been folded into a lovely bird of paradise and set next to her plate as soon as she'd taken a seat.

Mac stared expectantly across the white wicker table at her. "So? What do you think? Raspberry, lemon, or chocolate?"

Sheridan noted the look of panic on the forewoman's face and wondered once again how she'd been roped into cake tasting with her boss's fiancée.

Oh, that's right. She'd been strolling down the street when a hand had suddenly shot out of the Hot Buns Bakery, curled around her arm, and yanked her inside the oh-so-precious pink-and-white establishment.

"Well?" Mac pressed good-naturedly. "Thoughts? I need them. Normally, I have them. But today, for some reason, it's just blank upstairs."

A smile touched Sheridan's lips. She really liked Mackenzie Byrd. The dark-haired, ever-grinning forewoman of the Triple C Ranch was funny and smart and took no shit from anyone—male or female—which was an attribute Sheridan wholeheartedly admired. In fact, in another life, where Sheridan didn't work for the man she worked for, she and Mac could've been great friends. But as it was . . .

"They're all excellent," she offered in a professional tone.

Mac groaned and held her fork above her head, the tines stained with bits of frosting. "I know. But which one is the best?"

"I'm not really much of a cake person, Miss Byrd."

Dropping back in her chair, Mac's blue eyes narrowed. "Sheridan, seriously, you can't call me that. We've talked about this."

The small smile that had touched Sheridan's lips a moment ago expanded into a full-fledged grin. Yes, she really liked this woman. Such a bummer. Especially when you were lacking in friendships of the female variety. "You and Mr. Cavanaugh are engaged. I am his employee. There's no fraternizing with the boss's family."

"Oh, Lord have mercy," Mac said with an eye roll.

"And forgive me for saying so, Miss Byrd," Sheridan continued, "but isn't this something you should be doing with Mr. Cavanaugh?"

"Deacon's in Dallas for the next couple of days, and this needs to get done." A slight wickedness flashed in her blue eyes. "And as his right hand, his most trusted employee—"

"Oh, dear."

Mac laughed. "Come on, you know what he likes."

"As do you, I'm sure."

"He's abandoned me in my time of need, Sheridan," Mac said dramatically. "This wedding is a month away, and things like cake and flowers and food need to be decided on. Am I supposed to make all the decisions alone?"

"I believe some women would find that a blessing, Miss Byrd. Total control of the remote, so to speak."

Mac snorted. "I'm not that kind of woman, Miss O'Neil. Now, if we need beef for the dinner, that I can do."

Sheridan laughed. "What about one of your friends from high school or someone at the Triple C . . . ?"

"My closest friend is Blue." Sobering, she released a heavy sigh. "And he's run away from home."

"Right. I'm sorry about that. I know you two are very close."

Mac's eyes went kitten-wide. "Don't say you're sorry. Say you'll be my wingman."

"Miss Byrd—"

"Mac."

"You're really stubborn—you know that?"

She snorted. "Hell, yes, I know. Part of my charm." She wiggled her eyebrows. "And this 'no fraternizing with the boss's relatives' business ain't gonna work anyway. James won't like you calling him *Mr.* Cavanaugh when he's kissing you." Then she cocked her head to the side and grinned. "Or maybe he will."

Heat slammed into Sheridan's cheeks, and the entire bakery seemed to shrink around her. "Wh-what?"

As she dipped her fork into the raspberry-cream cake, Mac's grin widened. "Oh, come on, Sheri."

Sheri? What the hell was happening here? This town and all its residents were getting to her, making her forget why she was here—question things that should never be questioned. She'd come to River Black to work. Not to get caught up in any local's dramas, imaginings, or, for God's sake, wedding plans!

Sitting up just a little bit straighter, Sheridan said in her most controlled voice, "I'm not dating anyone. Especially not James . . . er"—she cleared her throat—"Mr. Cavanaugh."

If truth be told, she had noticed James Cavanaugh and his many . . . attributes. Frankly, you'd have to be blind not to. The man was something to gawk at. But professionalism demanded that looking was as far as it went.

As she studied Sheridan, Mac popped a chunk of cake in her mouth. "So, he hasn't asked you out?"

"Absolutely not," she said quickly.

"Really? I mean, how is that possible? I swear, whenever you're around, the guy can't keep his eyes off you, or his tongue inside his mouth."

"That's not true," Sheridan said tightly. Although she couldn't help but wonder if it were. Not that she was going to share that thought with the woman across the table. If Deacon got wind of her *admiration* of his brother, she could lose her job. And she'd worked way too hard to get to where she was to drop the ball over a pretty face.

A very, very pretty face.

She mentally rolled her eyes at herself.

Something caught Mac's attention out the window and she sniffed. "Well, well . . . speak of the devil."

Sheridan turned to see what she was talking about.

"Holy cripes," Mac remarked. "He's got one of the mustangs out. Is he nuts? Riding that stallion down Main Street like he was a tame little pony driving to Sunday service."

Sheridan's pulse jumped and her skin tightened around her muscles. A man was riding down the street atop a very rebellious-looking black-and-white horse. No. Not a man. A cowboy. The hottest cowboy she'd ever seen in her life. Dressed in jeans and a black thermal, pieces of his brown hair peeking out from under a black Stetson, James Cavanaugh kept strict command over the snorting, frustrated animal beneath him. Not by being big and loud and cruel. But with that quiet strength he always seemed to possess. It was one of the many things about him that intrigued her— one of the many things that would remain a tightly held secret from the woman across from her, if she wanted to keep her job secure.

"Looks like he's in the process of breaking that stallion," Mac observed, chin lifted, eyes narrowed. "I've heard about his work, but I've never seen him in action. Quite a sight. Eh, Sheri?"

Sheridan was just about to tackle the "Sheri" issue when James Cavanaugh turned to look in the direction of the bakery and caught her staring out the picture window. As heat infused every cell of her body, Sheridan held his gaze. For a heartbeat, or maybe two, she forgot everything else around her. All she saw were his gorgeous blue-green eyes. Then completely without her permission, her hand lifted and gave him a small wave. To her dismay and embarrassment, he didn't wave back. Just nodded once, then turned back to the mustang and continued down the road.

Unnerved, she blinked and the world came back into focus. What was that? she wondered, turning back to face Mackenzie, her cheeks flaming and her breathing uneven. What had just happened?

"That was a beautiful animal," she managed to say, then quickly added, "The mustang."

Mac nodded, amusement in her eyes. "They're his passion—that's for sure."

"Do you think he's going to stay at the Triple C to care for them?"

Mac shrugged. "There's a lot that ain't decided over there. With Everett's will. The wedding. And maybe new information about Cass's passing."

The soft heat in Mac's voice gave Sheridan something solid to focus on. Cass was not only Deacon's and James's sister, but she had been Mac's best friend. Sympathy rolled over the lingering unease James Cavanaugh had ignited within her.

"But I 'spect James'll be here for quite a while. I

hope so anyway." Mac's eyes connected with Sheridan's again, and they were ripe with more questions. "For everyone's sake."

Sheridan eased back in her chair, placed her napkin on the table, and got to her feet. She tried not to think about how unsteady her legs felt, or why that would be. "I need to get back to the office."

"Which one you in today?" Mac asked, taking up her fork again.

"Town. But I'll be heading out to the ranch in the afternoon."

"Well, maybe I'll see you there."

"Sounds good."

Sheridan turned to go, but Mac grabbed her hand. "Hey."

Sheridan turned, brows drifting together.

Mac chewed her lip for a second. "I'm sorry. I know you're here to work. Deacon's your boss and you don't want any problems with that. I'm being an asshole."

Sheridan couldn't help but respond to Mac's forthright ways and gave her a bright smile. "No problem. And, Miss Byrd, I'm here for whatever you need." She slipped her hand away from Mac's grasp and headed for the door. But halfway there, she stopped and glanced back. "I think the chocolate cake would be a wonderful choice. Like Charles Shulz said, 'All you need is love. But a little chocolate now and then doesn't hurt.'"

*   *   *

James slid off the mustang's back and gave the young creature a few strokes down his warm neck. Bringing a nearly wild animal into town wasn't the best idea he'd ever come up with, but Comet—that's what he was calling the stallion for now—needed to be looked at. And after all the mini bombs Dr. Grace Hunter had been dropping lately regarding her father and what the ex-Sheriff of River Black did or didn't know about Cass's killer, James needed to give her another small push.

As he moved his hand down the stallion's withers and back, Comet eyed him suspiciously. *You using me, cowboy?* he seemed to be asking. *Because I'm fine. Nothing but a little scratch. What say we head back through town toward home, see if that pretty redhead with the sexy gray eyes is still in the bakery? Get us a slice of carrot cake or somethin'.*

James frowned. None of what had just come ticker-taping through his mind was from the stallion or his cautious gaze. Hell no. That was all him. And, unfortunately, not the first time he'd been entertaining thoughts like that. Since he'd come upon Sheridan O'Neil in the rain, stranded on the side of the road near Triple C, her eyes, that mouth, hell, that ass had been assaulting his mind fast and furious. They were the kinds of thoughts that normally made him antsy, made him get out the duffel, pack up his duds, and head to one of the many hang-your-hat spots he'd purchased over the past five years or so.

But this time, he didn't have the luxury of a quick and painless departure. There were too many glass balls being tossed into the air here in River Black. Someone needed to stand beneath them. Catch them before they fell and shattered. Did some permanent damage. So the unwise attraction to Sheridan O'Neil? Hell, he'd be ignoring that. Because women, in his experience, were the most fragile of glass balls in the world. And his track record for catching those falling ones was dismal.

"Mr. Cavanaugh?" Dr. Grace Hunter emerged from the small veterinary clinic and came down the path toward him. She was a pretty thing. Cole's type all the way. Probably why his little brother's voice changed when he talked about her. Small, lots of curves, thick, dark hair. She came to stand in front of Comet, her green eyes so wary, James wondered if he'd lost the battle before the war had even begun.

"Morning, Doc," he said.

Her gaze shifted to the stallion. "Something wrong with your horse here?"

"Matter of fact. And since you couldn't come out to the ranch, I thought I'd come to you."

"Right," she said quickly. "Sorry about that. I'm just really swamped at the moment."

He took a gander at the empty parking lot. "I can see that."

"So, a flesh wound on his hindquarters, you say?" She headed around back to check things out.

"I did the best I could to treat it, but it didn't seem to heal, and then it started to look infected."

She gave Comet, who was uneasy at best, a gentle pat on the croup, then ran her hand down his thigh. "Probably something still inside the wound." She took out her bag and rifled through it. "I'm going to clean it up first, and then we'll see what we've got."

James watched her work, watched as she used Comet as a protective barrier between herself and him. Anything to discourage a real conversation between them. When he could get a ten-second glimpse of her, he found himself impressed by her skills. She had a calm and gentle way about her, yet was unwilling to take any bullshit from the animal she was treating. The perfect country doc.

After a minute or two, she held up a pair of silver tweezers, a thin strip of brown pinched between the tips. "Looks like we've got a wood splinter. From a fence, no doubt. I'm going to put some topical on it, but I'm also going to prescribe some antibiotics."

"Sounds good," James said, rubbing Comet's neck. "Then after that, maybe we can talk."

She didn't say anything.

"Dr. Hunter—" James started up.

"Nothing to talk about, Mr. Cavanaugh," she answered abruptly, her focus remaining on the horse's hindquarters. "I told you and your brothers. What I said in the Bull's Eye, what I thought I heard from my daddy, it was a mistake."

It took supreme effort in that moment to lock down James's simmering frustration. This woman didn't understand the magnitude of the situation they were all in. Her father might very well hold the key to a twelve-year mystery. The hell of his sister's murder. All those years of not knowing what had happened to Cass. Of *who* had happened to Cass.

His gut tightened. His sister had lain dead and alone, no comfort and no justice. That would not stand. James and his brothers owed the truth to the sister they all had failed. But he knew that to get that truth, he and Deacon and Cole had to handle this skittish woman with care, and he summoned his calmest voice. "If you'd just let one of us speak with your father—"

"No," she said tightly. She stood up, her bag in hand, her eyes lifting to connect with his. "My father is ill. Not right in his mind. He's medicated. He didn't know what he was saying. He doesn't even remember saying it."

James bit back the urge to snarl, *And my sister is dead.* "You said he had the diary—"

"It was just ramblings," she insisted, her tone as tense as her body language. "From the past. Something he remembered in the past. Something he'd wanted to find, no doubt, and hadn't."

Who was she really trying to convince, him or herself? He ground his molars. Shit. Didn't matter, and he wasn't going to bother with arguing. Not now. The woman in front of him was trying to protect her father and pushing her would just make her dig her heels in and resist more. For now, he'd back off.

But they'd find a way to get the information somehow.

"Thank you for patching him up, Doc," James said in a careful voice.

She looked momentarily startled, as if the last thing she had expected from him was to drop the subject. Then relief and professional distance settled over her features. "I'll get that prescription."

He watched her walk up the path, then disappear inside the clinic. Maybe this was a wild-goose chase. Maybe Sheriff Hunter was just a sick old man with wild ravings about a past he couldn't remember, a past that didn't exist. But, either way, the Cavanaugh brothers were going to find out the truth.

About Cass's disappearance.

And her killer.

Also available from
New York Times bestselling author

LAURA WRIGHT

Eternal Demon
Mark of the Vampire

When Erion's son is kidnapped by the evil vampire Cruen, Erion vows to stop at nothing to find his hideaway—including intercepting the traveling party of Cruen's beautiful bride-to-be. But instead of a vulnerable caravan, Erion is met by a feral band of female demons including Hellen, the bride—a creature of dark magic and even darker passion.

Though the safety of his son is his foremost concern, Erion can't deny his unexpected attraction to Hellen. As their bond intensifies, they move toward an inevitable and terrifying battle. With time running out, Erion realizes he must not only find and rescue his son but protect Hellen from Cruen and the underworld forces waiting to destroy her.

"Dark, delicious, and sinfully good."
—*New York Times* bestselling author Nalini Singh

Available wherever books are sold or at
penguin.com

facebook.com/ProjectParanormalBooks